"How did you get telekinesis?" Ian demanded.

"It's not like they hand it out in stores!" said Sara. "It just happened one day. I didn't know what it was, and I was too scared to tell my parents. I was afraid of it for a long time."

"And now you're not."

His flat, blunt words stabbed at her heart. He might as well have slapped her down into a seat in an interrogation room. They traded stares. "Yeah. Now I'm not."

"When did your father die? How did he die?"

Her thoughts flew to the amulet in Ian's pocket. "What has any of this got to do with my father?"

"Maybe nothing. Could be more. This stuff might be genetic."

Icy dread crawled across her skin. This time, she did hug herself. "I'm done talking to you."

Quick as lightning, he reached forward and snatched the boat keys from the ignition. "This necklace has to be important if you're willing to risk being shot to fix it, Sara. That's not even going there about you risking *me* being shot at. You're not getting it back until you talk."

She felt naked. Worse than she had at the inlet. Then, she'd seen desire in his eyes.

Now, she saw only hatred. "This isn't about me," she said, startled. "It's about you."

"Never mind me," he snapped.

"What is it?" she asked. "What happened to you?"

"How did your father die?"

Pain and betrayal surged anew through every cell in her body, and that little girl from twenty years ago gave a silent wail of outrage. "He. Was. Murdered."

Praise for *THE SERPENT IN THE STONE*

3rd Place, 2006 Barclay Sterling Contest

The Serpent in the Stone

by

Nicki Greenwood

The Gifted Series, Book One

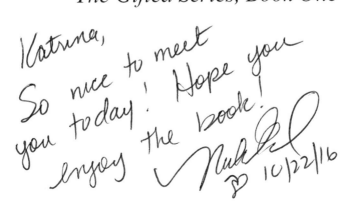

Katrina,
So nice to meet
you today! Hope you
enjoy the book!
Nicki 10/22/16

The Serpent in the Stone

Cover Art by *Kim Mendoza*

The Wild Rose Press, Inc.
PO Box 708
Adams Basin, NY 14410-0708
Visit us at www.thewildrosepress.com

Publishing History
First Faery Rose Edition, 2013
Print ISBN 978-1-61217-816-5
Digital ISBN 978-1-61217-817-2

The Gifted Series: Book One
Published in the United States of America

Dedication

To Heather,
for the phone call

Chapter One

Twenty years later, Sara Markham still struggled to erase the images of her father's blood.

She rubbed at her aching temples. Last night, she'd relived the old nightmare again—Robert Markham, a noted archaeologist, found murdered at his ransacked university office. The papers and networks had a field day with it, splashing photos and speculation around like they were playing at a water park. No one stopped to think about the family whose life had been ripped apart. No one had any answers. Or clues. Or leads.

Until now.

Yesterday, in his safe deposit box, she'd discovered a stone amulet and a beat-up book of fairy tales. What those things had to do with her father's murder, she couldn't have said, but they had been worth hiding in a little steel box for two decades. *God, I want coffee.*

The ocean breeze misted across her face. Gulls wheeled overhead, their cries drowned out by rushing waves and the whine of the speedboat's engine. Sara touched the stone pendant, secreted away under her sweater with the silver locket her father had given her on her tenth birthday. That was the day all hell had broken snarling off its chain and rampaged through her once-normal life. Celebrating it had been unbearable. Forgetting, impossible.

The amulet and her father's work were definitely connected. He had never in his life done anything without purpose. Now, the trail of clues had led her, her sister Faith, and their own team of archaeologists here: Hvitmar, Shetland, a tiny uninhabited island at the archipelago's northernmost tip. She hoped—and feared—she'd find the answer to that lifelong "Why?" hidden under the soil of this lonely scrap of earth in the middle of the ocean. Maybe then, they could put his soul to rest at last.

Faith spoke over the noise of the engine. "Lambertson says the island is normally quiet. Nothing but seals and birds. The earthquake last month opened a fissure wide enough to see the field wall buried a few meters down."

Faith's flaxen hair caught the sunlight as they sped along. As twins went, they were polar opposites: Sara with the chestnut hair and hazel eyes of their mother, Faith as blond and blue-eyed as their late father. Like night and day, particularly in the way they handled the secret they'd shared since that tragic birthday. Sara thought it a curse. Faith embraced it. But they'd always had each other.

After all, they'd never met another gifted person with whom to share the burden—let alone a multi-gifted one. Paranormal power bonded them as surely as blood.

Dustin Sennett looked back over his shoulder from the driver's seat. "There it is. Looks nice and inviting," he said, pointing.

Sure enough, the profile of Hvitmar reared up from the sea ahead. Sheer cliffs on its southern end sloped off gradually to the north.

Sara crossed her fingers. Not superstitious. Just...cautious.

"You don't think Lamb will try to hand this off to Flintrop's firm if we find something, do you?" Faith asked. Her tone snapped with dislike. She and their competitor, Alan Flintrop, had dated briefly, but Flintrop, L.L.C had been scooping projects out from under Gemini, Limited's nose too long for that to last. And this, of all projects, was too important to lose.

"Lamb knows how much we want this," Sara said, though she wasn't so sure herself. Their old mentor and Robert's onetime partner, James Lambertson, had offered them the project and even loaned them two men from his own London-based firm to help. That didn't mean he wouldn't call on Flintrop's larger, better-supplied firm if their find proved major. She seethed just thinking about it.

They neared the dock at the island's southern end. When they reached the pilings, Dustin cut the motor and moored the boat. Thomas Callander began unloading supplies. Sara shouldered her own pack and stepped onto the dock, surprised at the warmth in the air. For late winter, it sure felt like spring. At least they wouldn't freeze on this project.

The fissure lay on the island's north end, a mile or so from the dock. She groaned at the thought of trudging that whole distance loaded down with supplies, but there was no other boat access. Their larger equipment had been flown in a couple days ago. Absorbed in planning, she walked along beside Faith without seeing her surroundings, until her sister paused and nudged her arm. "What?"

Faith jerked her chin ahead of them. Sara looked

up to find a tent staked near the southern cliffs.

Someone had beaten them here.

She marched toward the tent, fully expecting to see Alan Flintrop and his smug, toast-of-New-York's-anthropology-circles smile. Instead, she found a man in a denim jacket and blue jeans, sitting in a camp chair and writing in a small leather book. She dropped her bag. "Who are you?"

The man looked up, and she formed a quick impression of stubble and magazine-worthy good looks. His storm-blue gaze traveled over her figure, sending tiny frissons of awareness—and hazy recognition— through her body. A fringe of chocolate brown forelock couldn't quite hide the thin scar over one of his eyebrows. He didn't seem surprised to see her, which sent her hackles up instantly as he laid aside his book and stood up. "Ian Waverly," he said, and held out his hand.

Suspicion elbowed her interest aside. That name. Why did she know that name? She slid her hand into his.

Slam. She felt her eyes change color from hazel to emerald, the way most people felt rippling gooseflesh across the skin. The influx of power sent a chill up her spine. His grip tightened on her hand, convulsive, and then his thoughts rushed into her mind in a flurry of images.

Her grade school playground. Todd Garrett was picking on her sister again. He'd plucked Faith's locket, a golden one, from around her neck and was taunting her with it. When Sara reached out, her sister's necklace flew unaided across the schoolyard and into her hand. She looked up, scared and shocked

4

at what she'd done, and her gaze locked onto that of a boy with storm-blue eyes.

Sara screwed her eyes shut to cut the images off. She reopened them cautiously, though she knew they would have turned back to their normal color the moment she closed them.

This man knew what she was. If he remembered. If he believed what he'd seen. She'd guarded the secret of her gifts ever since that first instance, that unprepared childhood fumble. Fear sliced through her and she stamped it back.

What in God's name was he doing here? Fighting to control the dread galloping along her nerves, she risked another look at him. The expression on his face spoke volumes.

Hell yes, he remembered.

****

Ian hadn't wanted to believe what he'd seen then, and didn't now. Hating the savage righteousness clawing through his gut, he pulled his hand from hers and fisted it, as if digging his nails into his palm could stop the proof in its tracks.

This was why he'd followed her to Shetland. This was why he'd volunteered to do a birding project on this godforsaken little speck in the ocean. Hell, he'd been torn between watching her and avoiding her for the past twenty years. He'd often wondered—against his will—what happened to her after they graduated high school. Did she still have her power? Had he been mistaken?

No question now. Her eyes had changed color. This woman, this slip of a woman, had power just like—

He stifled the rest of that thought and forced a

smile. "We work at the university together. I teach in the biology department. Wildlife," he added, tilting his head toward the cliffs, where scores of seabirds circled in the salty air.

"Sara Markham. *Doctor* Markham," she said. Her gaze scoured him.

She'd grown. Obviously, she'd grown, what the hell had he expected? But time had been unfairly kind to Sara—Doctor—Markham. He tried to ignore the curves of her body and the way her hair blew loose around her shoulders. The way she held herself rigid in the flight-ready pose of cornered prey. She looked like a wild creature herself, belonging more to wind and water than to his childhood nightmares.

Like a selkie. The ferryman who brought him to Hvitmar had told him stories about the mythical seals-turned-women that haunted the Shetland coastlines and took human mates. Crazy stories.

Not so crazy right now.

They weren't alone. Behind Sara stood another woman, tall and blond, with a knapsack over her shoulder and an interested stare on her face. On her right were two men, carrying bags of their own. "I'm doing a study on the local birds," Ian said at last.

Sara crossed her arms. "On my island? That's quite a coincidence."

Her island? The image of the selkie evaporated in a cloud of territorial insult. He forgot what she was. "This island is big enough for two researchers," he said. "You don't interfere with my birds, and I won't interfere with your dig."

Her voice went frosty. "You know about the dig?"

"Yeah, I know about the dig." And even now, part

of him wished more and more that he'd never learned of it.

The blond woman bent and hoisted up the pack by Sara's feet. "We'll go set up the tents," she said, and she and the men hurried away.

Sara followed their retreat with an open-mouthed look as though she wanted to call the others back. Then she came toward him with slow, deliberate steps. Her eyes were hazel, not the bright green from before. He found himself wanting to step back anyway. She studied his face, her own as pale as porcelain, but her full lips firmed. "Luis Rivero."

"Yeah," Ian said, thinking of his friend back at the university. Luis worked in Sara's department. It was he who had told Ian of her upcoming assignment in Shetland.

"Man can't keep his mouth shut," she muttered. With uncanny insight, she fired, "Are you following me?"

"No," he lied. "I'm here to study birds. Think you can handle that?"

She backed off one step at a time, with a look that seemed to go right through him. Torn between hostility and unbidden curiosity, he watched her turn to walk away.

Well, you got what you wished for, he told himself. What was he supposed to do with the proof, now that he had it?

It was sure as hell too late to give it back.

****

"He's cute," Faith said as she and Sara checked Sara's tent stakes.

Sara shoved a lock of hair behind her ear and tried

to trade fear for focus. No such luck. Her belly was in knots. "Are you nuts? I'm telling you, that man is the same kid who saw me first use telekinesis!"

Faith gave one of the tent ropes an experimental tug and said, "I don't see why you're all wound up about it. If he didn't blow you in when we were ten, what makes you think he'll do it now? He might even think he dreamed it." She grabbed another stake, looking much calmer than Sara felt. Uncharacteristic for Faith, whose temper had legendary changeability.

"You didn't see the look on his face," Sara snapped. "He remembers, Faith."

"Well, since he's here, you should at least have asked him if he wants to come down for dinner," chided her sister. "He's alone up there, or didn't you notice? No army on his heels, waiting to arrest you for being you. You could examine him more closely for nefarious intent." Faith wiggled her outspread fingers with what Sara assumed she meant to be scathing sarcasm.

Sara refused to admit that she hadn't noticed much beyond the pulse-pounding look he'd given her...and her reaction to it. Part terror, and part...well, she wasn't willing to admit what that other part might be. "Sure, I'll just waltz up there and volunteer to become a government guinea pig," she said. "What if he's working for a lab, and waiting to dissect me once he's proven what I did? I'm not about to make myself his best pal."

Faith shot her a look of impatience. "Honestly. Don't you think you're overreacting even a little bit?"

Snatching a mallet, Sara pounded the last corner stake into the ground. "Need I remind you that his presence here endangers you, too? *Mom* doesn't even know what we are, and I trust him a lot less."

Jabbing toward her with a tent stake, Faith said, "If you won't go up there, I will. Come on, Sara, this is just crazy."

Sara flung a hand toward Ian's camp. "You want him? Go get him. Just don't cry to me when he goes mad scientist on you. If we're lucky, we'll finish this dig without having anything to do with him."

Her sister secured a last rope, then stood up. She shook her head. "It's been years. You might consider actually *talking* to him before you decide he's out to lock us up." She stiffened, and her gaze swept the moor. "Did you hear something?"

"No." Sara checked, but Thomas and Dustin had returned to the boat for a second load of supplies. Faith often heard things Sara couldn't, but she knew Faith wasn't using her psychic power at the moment. Worried that Ian might be watching them, she turned in a circle. Nope, nothing. At least, nothing *she* could see. "Birds?"

"Maybe." Faith waved a hand through the air as if testing it for vibrations. "I could have sworn— No." Her mystified tone returned to normal. "If you're so worried about Ian, you should go up there and keep an eye on him. Just saying." With that, she walked away to her own tent.

Feeling chastised—and irritable, because Faith was right—Sara watched her go, then swept aside her door flap and entered her tent.

It smelled of old canvas. At the moment, it looked like a bomb had gone off. Crates, chairs, and her camp table had been scattered on the tent floor. Her cot stood waiting for setup in the corner. In a few hours, the disaster would be transformed into a tidy microcosm of sleep, study, and on-site labwork.

First things first, then. She'd need somewhere to sleep after the long day ahead. She pulled the cot open and locked it in place. She'd forgotten they were so small.

A flash of Ian's eyes barged into her memory. Vivid. Intense. She'd never seen such a blue. Even now, the warmth of his hand seemed to linger on hers.

Damn it! Get out of my head! She tossed her sheets onto the cot to rub her palm on her jeans as if she could wipe away the remembered feel of his skin against hers. "You have no business being in there," she said aloud.

"Are you talking to the cot, or someone invisible?"

She turned around. Thomas stood in the tent doorway, scratching his sandy-blond head.

She gave him a wan smile. "Sorry. A little internal argument. Too many things to do, and not enough caffeine in my system."

"Equipment's set up for survey, and Dustin's working on preliminary photos. Anything else?"

"No, that should do it. I'll be out after I tame the tent mess."

When Thomas left, she went back to spreading the sheets out on her cot. Faith's scolding rang in her ears. If she weren't so cautious, they'd have been lab experiments by now. She hugged the wool blanket to her body, pressing her fingers into the rough fabric.

She'd never been on a dig alone. Teammates kept each other out of trouble, called for help when it was needed, and prevented injuries. What if something happened to Ian, with no one around to know it? She grimaced, not wanting that on her conscience no matter *what* his intentions were.

What the hell was he thinking, coming out here alone in the first place? *Birds. Yeah, right.* She pitched the blanket on her cot, and stalked out of the tent.

Faith met her before she'd gone more than a few steps in the direction of Ian's camp. "Good, you're out. Ready to start surveying?"

"I was going to... Never mind. What needs doing?"

"If you had something to do—" Grinning, Faith tilted her head toward the south end of the island.

Sara raised a hand to cut her off. When Faith wouldn't stop grinning, Sara added a glare that she hoped Faith interpreted as *Shut up and quit looking so smug.* "It can wait."

So could giving that man a piece of her mind. First chance she got tomorrow.

****

What in hell is this? Ian wondered. *He was locked in a room he didn't recognize, barely able to see and without a clue what was happening.*

The small room's murkiness closed in on him, coffinlike. He tried the door again, but the handle still wouldn't budge. The air boiled with hissing voices that made his skin prickle. A sharp metallic scent stung his nose.

Blood.

"Okay, not liking this now." Determined to escape, he crept forward into the space. His questing fingers landed on what felt like a bookshelf, littered with heaps of scattered volumes. As he paced along, he kicked a few more of them and they slid across the floor.

He groped blindly, and winced when he touched something sharp that sliced across his fingers. His hand fell upon a banker's lamp. He switched it on, squinting as the room came into focus.

A scarred cherry desk stood before him, all its drawers ripped out and the contents tossed on the floor. Broken glass. Shredded paper. File drawers thrown open and kicked aside.

The surface of the desk bore a blackish stain. He reached out to touch it.

A hand slapped down on his shoulder in a vise grip. He whirled around.

A man loomed over him, his face stark-white, his blue eyes burning. Blood covered him from head to foot.

Ian swore and wrenched backward over the desk in a futile effort to escape.

The man gripped Ian's shirt in both hands and hauled him closer. Ian's heart thundered in his chest. His attacker's eyes shone like knives in the gloom. "Hhhhelp her."

Ian gasped and sat bolt upright on his cot. The nightmare faded, giving way to the soft pre-dawn gray of his tent interior. His heartbeat crashed in his ears. Panting, he raked a hand through sleep-tousled hair.

He examined his stinging hand, half-expecting to see blood where the glass had sliced it in his dream.

Nothing.

He tried not to admit to relief. He'd never experienced real pain in a dream before, and he hadn't had a nightmare in years. Must be coming to this place, seeing Sara. Everything was messing with his senses.

Your own fault, he scolded himself. He'd been the one to follow her. He'd been the one to ask for Shetland.

What the hell was he thinking?

He grappled for his watch on the table beside his cot. Almost five o'clock. With a sigh, he swung out of bed and onto his feet to start work.

****

Hvitmar had been made with a shapeshifter in mind.

Sara ran as a wolf, with the wind whistling through her fur and reveling in the shape. It brought her speed. Power. Joy in the simple act of being alive. Freedom she'd never known as a human. She galloped along the shoreline, her broad paws eating up the ground. The air was crisp with the scents of earth and ocean. Cries of seabirds rang out in the sky.

Ian's birds, she thought with a snort.

She hadn't even gone in the direction of his camp yet. Skirting the dig site to avoid leaving tracks, she'd explored the northern edges of the island. Gulls scolded her, and she spied a seal dozing among the rocks offshore.

She decided to head up to Ian's camp before the fog burned off and left her visible to any observers. She'd start by asking him down to breakfast, a safe enough opening. Then she'd follow it up with *Get off my island* and see how he took that.

But first, she owed her sister an apology for their spat yesterday. She set off toward Faith's tent.

Sara approached it with caution. A long yawn came from within. Tongue lolling, she padded to a halt outside and snuffed aloud.

She heard a rustle. The door flap opened and her sister ducked out, struggling into a heavy wool sweater. "What are you doing outside like that?" Faith whispered.

Sara didn't bother to shapeshift back to her human body. She twitched an ear and glanced around the foggy moor, then back to her sister.

Faith crossed her arms. "All right, so no one's up. I hope you didn't leave tracks everywhere for me to scuff out."

Sara shook her shaggy lupine head.

Faith looked southward toward Ian's camp, then smiled at her. "You're planning to go see him, aren't you? Told you, you should."

Sara flattened her ears. God, she loved having ears that flattened. Very eloquent.

"Get out of here before the guys get up. Say hi to him for me."

Sara sent her a last, annoyed glare before loping away.

****

Ian tossed a fleece vest on over his thermal shirt, then hooked an extra set of carabiners to his climbing harness. He glanced around his tent before realizing he must have left his rope bag hanging outside last night. In his hurry to record data on yesterday's climb, he'd dropped most of his gear and gone straight into the tent to write as soon as he got back.

Outside, he threw the coil of rope over his shoulder and headed for the sea cliffs. He'd spotted a nest sheltered in a crag about halfway down, and itched to get a closer look.

When he reached the cliff edge, he looked out over the ocean. The view took his breath away. The sunrise had just begun, burning off the fog and painting the few clouds with a champagne-pink blaze. Unst made a faint, misty shadow on the horizon. This, he could handle. To hell with people and supernatural powers and all that head-case stuff that made living day to day such a pain in the ass. A view like this made it all go away.

He'd learned from a young age to spot good holds, and which surfaces were secure enough for a chock or cam that would support him. The southern cliffs of Hvitmar were high and challenging, but not impossible. He hitched up his anchor points and auto-belayer, then secured a mat at the cliff edge to prevent rubbing on the rope. "All right, lady," he said, "let's see what else you're hiding." He hooked the rope to his belt, then started over the edge.

Once he found his seat in the harness, he touched the toes of his shoes against the cliffside and pushed off, feeding the rope along and rappelling downward. The sun went from pink to brilliant red and began to turn golden. Birds squabbled far below on the beach at the cliff base.

He had almost reached the site of the nest when the rope gave a *twang*, followed by a sickening lurch. Ian jerked his head up. More than a body length above on the rope was a telltale frayed strand hanging loose. "Shit, shit, shit," he whispered. How the hell had this happened? The rope had been perfectly sound on inspection last night. Jamming his fingers into the nearest crevice, he twisted his hand sideways just as the rest of the rope snapped.

His body plunged downward, until his handhold yanked it to a halt. Fire seared up his left arm from shoulder to wrist. He snarled in agony. His shoes scraped madly against the cliff, seeking a purchase as the remainder of the rope slithered past him on its descent. *Don't look down, Christ, don't look.* He swallowed back his fear and thought fast. Stones crumbled under his feet and plummeted away. He dangled against the side of the cliff, trying to lie flat against the stone. Winds battered dangerously against his body.

No one would hear him in this wind, even if he screamed.

"Son of a bitch." He had to look.

No footholds, no handholds, nothing at all. Smooth as glass for far too much space underneath him. More than a hundred feet below lay the rocky cliff base. His arm throbbed and threatened to pry his handhold from the rock. Panting, he closed his eyes against stinging sweat and pressed his forehead against the stone.

When he checked, upward didn't look any better. The next closest handhold was half a body length up. Even if he swung, he didn't think he could reach it, but he had to try. His hands were sweating, and he couldn't reach his belt bucket to rechalk.

Face it, Waverly, you're screwed. His handhold began to loosen, sending shards of pain down his arm. He took a breath and used what leverage he had to push sideways.

His fingers slid out of the crevice.

He went backward, slipping away from the cliff in a free fall. He didn't even have time or breath to scream.

Wind whistled past him. The cliffside went by in a speeding blur.

Ian knew he was going to die, and there was nothing he could do about it.

Chapter Two

Oh, my God. Still in her wolf shape, Sara summoned her telekinesis and stopped Ian's plummeting body in midair. Even from this distance, standing far above at the cliff's edge, she heard his grunt of shock. Her heartbeat slammed. Every hair of her pelt stood on end. Her horrified moan came out as a low-pitched whine.

There would be no way out of this.

She watched him look around and notice that he dangled by nothing. The ocean crashed against the rocks some seventy feet below him. "*Jesus!*" he shouted. He pulled his arms and legs closer to his body, and she almost lost her hold on him. Breathless, she struggled to steady his weight with her gift.

He looked up and found her standing at the cliff edge. She trembled under his stare, but dared not look away. Gently, she lifted him with her power. His body rose upward.

His gaze never left her through each foot of his ascent. At last, he reached the top of the cliff, floating over the lip to solid ground. She sidestepped as she lowered him down. He kept right on staring until she wanted to cower before him.

His hand came up to his left shoulder. Sweat trickled down his forehead. She smelled the distress of his pain and heard his breath shuddering in and out. The thought repeating in his head barged into her senses, even without her seeking it.

Wolf eyes aren't green.

Terror seized her. She bolted straight for the cliff edge.

He lunged forward. "No!"

She catapulted over the precipice into space and dropped out of his sight. Her stomach swooped as she fell. Quickly, she called on the shape of the gulls squawking in alarm around her. In a flash, she changed into one of the birds, then circled high into the air.

Ian staggered toward the cliff edge, clutching his arm. He leaned over and looked, down, down, down to the water. After a few moments, he turned away from the cliff and stumbled to where she—the wolf—had been standing. He dropped to one knee, pressing his injured arm close to his body, and scanned the ground.

Shaking so hard she could barely maintain the gull form, she soared northward down the island, craving escape. Only when she was sure he wasn't looking did she let go of the gull shape and return to her human one. For a few seconds, she could only stand there and tremble with shock. *What have I done?*

Minutes passed. She had to force herself to walk toward him. Every step felt like a move toward a noose with her name on it. She approached him from behind, light-footed, prepared to run again. Her voice shook a little as she spoke. "What are you doing?"

He looked up and blinked as if he thought she were a hallucination. With a grunt, he lurched to his feet and swayed.

She hurried to his side. "What's wrong?"

"My shoulder. I think it's dislocated."

Flushed and fearful, she examined him from head to foot. There was no choice. "Come on. I'll help you into your tent." She touched his uninjured arm.

He radiated heat through the jacket. She almost let go, but he slumped against her and she willed herself to stay put. He bit off a gasp and stumbled along with her. As soon as they got into the tent, he fell onto his cot and blacked out.

The sudden silence was alarming. Sara shifted her weight from foot to foot, uncertain what to do. Every impulse screamed at her to run. She could have slipped out at any moment...but she didn't.

Dislocated. No matter how much she wanted to, she couldn't leave him like that. She knelt and pawed underneath a small table, looking for his first-aid kit. If he even had one. *What kind of a fool...*

He moaned behind her. Sara whirled around, tried to rise, and banged her head on the underside of the table. She winced and crawled out from under it to rub her throbbing scalp. That would be her penance for deciding to come see him.

But if she hadn't...

His eyes opened and he tried to sit up. When he put weight on his left elbow, his face contorted in pain. He dropped back with a groan.

Without thinking, she shot across the tent to the cot, then slid a hand underneath his back. "We need to get you to Mainland and have your shoulder X-rayed."

He groaned again as she helped him sit upright. "No."

"What do you mean, 'no'? Your shoulder's dislocated. You might have a frac—"

"I said no. Can you put it back in place?"

"Ian—"

"Can you, or can't you?"

She hissed outward through her teeth and sprang to her feet. "Yes. I can. Right now, I'm likely to leave you this way. Go ahead and give me an excuse."

He closed his eyes, panting, and relief washed through her at the respite from that intense stare. Sweat trickled down his forehead.

Her own concerns forgotten, she moved toward him again. "For God's sake, Ian," she said, softening her tone as she knelt before the cot. She reached for his arm.

His eyes opened again as she touched him. She made herself look away. "H-How did it happen?"

"My rope broke."

She caught her breath. If she'd been just a few seconds later... She might not have had to worry about someone knowing about her powers. Her stomach somersaulted. Rattled, she placed one hand on his left bicep and cupped his elbow with the other. *I can't believe how warm he is*, she thought, feeling the muscular curve and sinew of his arm under her hands. "Hold still. This will hurt." She gave his arm a firm shift in the right direction.

With a *pop*, the joint slid back into place. Ian grunted and his breath whooshed out. "Thank you," he said at last.

Without answering, she reached for the buckles of his climbing harness and undid them one by one. She felt his gaze raking her face as she worked. Heat crept into her cheeks. Commanding her hands not to shake— and not getting the results she wanted—she reached for the last buckle on his waistbelt. Just as she laid her hand on the strap to undo it, he seized her wrist in an iron grip.

She yelped and tried to jerk away...but he wasn't looking at her. He dropped her hand, then picked up the length of cord still hanging from his belt. He thumbed the broken end. "I'm not leaving the island."

"You don't think you're going to go back to climbing down cliffs, do you? You need a hospital."

He held up the broken rope, so close that she had no choice but to look at it. "This was cut."

She focused on the end of the rope and saw the neatly sheared fibers. "Who would want to c-cut it?"

He dropped the cord again, this time gripping both her wrists in spite of his injured arm. "My question exactly."

She recoiled, but he kept his hold. It took all her resolve not to hit him with telekinesis. "Let go of me," she whispered.

He didn't. His stare went icy, and she found herself wishing for the blazing look from moments before. She tried to pull away again. He held on, gritting his teeth through what must have been an excruciating jerk of his shoulder. "Let go," she repeated with as much indignation as possible.

He released her wrists and sat back. Pain crept into his features, but he masked it so fast she knew he hadn't meant her to see.

"Here." She reached for his waistbelt again, but hesitated. "Do you want help, or not?"

His expression lost some of that hard edge. She unbuckled the waistbelt with forced calm. Her gaze drifted lower. Ears burning, she followed the seam of his pants to the juncture of his thighs. Her heart pounded so hard, she dreaded he'd hear it.

Ian shifted and sat ramrod-straight. Her fingers flew to the buckles of the leg loops. His thigh muscles were rigid as marble. She loosened the buckles and slid the harness off his body, then reached for his fleece vest. "You're going to need some help...unless you can do this one-handed..." She trailed off with her fingers on the zipper, feeling heat flush her face.

When he didn't respond, she dared a look upward. The barest suggestion of humor had crept into his pain-glazed eyes. "I can figure it out," he said. She lowered her hand and he undid the zipper, then shrugged his good shoulder. The vest came off one side. He reached across his chest and eased it down the other arm.

Watching him undress—even one innocent piece of clothing—brought on a fresh wave of jitters. Her stare fixed on the broad planes of his torso, visible under the snug thermal shirt. Well-defined shoulder muscles sloped into the curves of arm and chest. Mesmerized, she let her gaze fall lower. *He's built more like a marathon swimmer than a teacher. How does this man spend time in a classroom and look like that?* "D-Do you have a sling? Painkillers?"

"Under the bed. The first-aid kit."

She bent and fished around under his cot for it. Sweat glistened on his face. She shook herself out of her daze and opened the kit to find a prescription bottle. "You came prepared."

"Not the first time I've had a shoulder problem," he ground out.

She handed him the water canteen from his bedside table, then helped him put on a sling. Tension rippled through his body under her fingers. She longed to ask him about his memory of Faith's necklace, but the thought of saying it aloud terrified her.

Her gaze traveled downward over the sling to his left hand. Dried blood crusted his bruised knuckles and torn fingertips. She reached into the first-aid kit for a packet of antiseptic wipes, then tore it open and dabbed gingerly at his wounds.

His body shivered and she looked up. The corner of his mouth had twisted into a wry smile. He shook with silent laughter, then winced and held his arm closer to his body. "What?" she whispered.

When he spoke, his voice rasped with mingled discomfort and mirth. "I have a dislocated shoulder, and you think a little peroxide is going to hurt me?"

She scowled to cover her nerves and finished wiping the blood off his hand. Fearing the answer, she plunged ahead with her next question. "How did you get back up the cliff?"

"I don't remember."

Of course he did. She'd caught the rise of his voice, the clipped edges of his words. She looked up, and her pulse quickened. He sat so close she saw tiny flecks of green in his eyes. His mouth quirked, bringing out a dimple in his stubbled cheek.

She snatched up the contents of the first-aid kit. "You have to keep your arm in a neutral position. Put something under the elbow to keep it a little away from your body. It could take a month to heal. You should do some exercises, ice it. And you shouldn't raise it over your head for a while—"

Ian took her hand in his good one. His warm fingers coasted over her palm. "Sara."

The contact, and the sound of her name on his lips,

froze her in place where she knelt. She sucked in a lungful of air and held it.

"Look at me."

She quivered with the force of her powers begging to be released. Her heartbeat slammed so hard she couldn't catch her breath. *Not now, not now—* Swallowing, she looked up.

His expression had gone dead serious, and his gaze skimmed her body. Something stirred, heated, in those stormy depths. He searched her face—looking for the change?—and leaned closer. Closer. If she raised her chin, and shifted just...a little...bit...

"Hello?" came a voice from outside the tent. A moment later, Faith ducked in. "Well, this is interesting."

Sara yanked her hand out of Ian's and sat back so quickly, she almost pitched over.

Faith smiled. "Where've you been? I thought you'd be back by now." She turned to Ian. Her gaze fell on his sling. "What happened?"

"I dislocated my shoulder," he answered, standing up. He tested the joint with his opposite hand.

Sara watched her sister's entire attitude change at the admittedly pleasant timbre of Ian's voice. Faith burst into a brilliant smile. "I don't think we've properly met. I'm Faith Markham, Sara's sister."

"Ian Waverly." He shook her outstretched hand, then stepped back to allow her room. "Sara was helping me put my shoulder back into joint. Come in."

"Really? You all right?" When he nodded, she added, "I started to worry when you didn't come back down, Sara. Breakfast has been over for half an hour." Faith sidled into the tent, crouched down, and helped her gather the spilled contents of the first-aid kit. *Wo-o-o-ow!* she mouthed, eyes bright.

Sara flushed and glanced up through her lashes at Ian. His gaze took on an intensity that made her heart start thumping again, equal parts foreboding and something much more disturbing. She took a box of bandages from her sister and put it away. "We'd better go," she said, shoving the kit back under the bed. "I've probably already missed breaking ground."

"Not really," Faith interrupted with a cheerful shrug. "We've been busy setting markers. I'll just go back down and let the guys know you're okay." She stood again.

Sara shot to her feet. "I'm coming with you. Just give me a second."

Faith gave her a last, knowing look. "Nice to meet you, Ian. Come down for dinner, if you get the chance." She left the tent.

Before Sara could follow, Ian stopped her at the tent doorway with a hand on her arm. She stiffened, struggled for something to say. "You should put some ice on that shoulder."

"Yeah. Thanks."

She eased out of his grasp and hurried away.

She caught up with her sister partway down the slope. As she drew alongside, Faith said, "You can lose it, now. He's out of earshot."

"You are the biggest thorn in my side I've ever known," Sara said, "but your timing is impeccable, so thank you."

"Yeah, you looked like you were dying for an interruption back there." Her sister shrugged. "I used to hate that term 'bedroom eyes,' but I have to admit, he's got 'em. If I were you, I'd have told me to piss off and come back later."

"You're not funny."

"Come on. You're going to die an old maid at this rate. I only wanted to meet him and see what my sister's all flustered about."

"Flustered! He was climbing down the cliff, and his rope broke! I had to use telekinesis on him!"

At that, Faith stopped dead, blood draining from her face. "What?"

"As the wolf, he only saw the wolf." Sara's breath escaped her. Now that she was free to panic, the weight on her chest doubled.

"Oh, God," Faith murmured. "He knows, then?"

"Well, I didn't take out an advertisement, but I'm sure he's bright enough to figure out that something's not quite right. Would you just happen to volunteer to work on the same island as me, if you were him?"

"All right, all right. Don't bite my head off. I'm as freaked out as you are."

"I somehow doubt that. For all he knows, you're normal," Sara said.

"I'm worried about *you*, half-wit. What did he say?"

"Nothing. Absolutely nothing. Which, if you're wondering, is a hundred times worse than questions might have been."

By the time they reached their camp, the digging had begun. Dustin and Thomas had laid out the parameters of their site with Eurocon's usual efficiency. Not for the first time, Sara wondered if it wouldn't have been smarter to join Lamb at his firm in London than to strike out on their own, but she was damn proud of the way they'd clawed their way up from the bottom. No matter what else she and Faith were, no one could take that away from them.

She entered her tent to the chirping of her satellite phone. Stacks of books covered her camp table. She pushed them aside to reach the handset. "Hello?"

Static fizzed in her ear. "Sara? Is that you?"

Sara recognized their secretary from the office at home. Agitation laced the woman's voice. "Holly, what's wrong?"

"Th-There's been a burglary."

Her heart skipped. "Are you all right? Is everyone all right?"

"Yes. Everyone's fine. It wasn't at the office." She paused, and Sara sensed her reluctance to continue. "It was your house."

Sara's throat constricted. She dropped shaking into a chair. "Did someone see what happened?"

"Mrs. Shoemaker next door said she saw a man walking around the building yesterday. He told her he was from the power company. Did you have them scheduled to read the meter?"

"No. Did the police come?"

"He left before they got there. She gave them a description and a report," Holly explained, sounding calmer now that the bad news was out.

Sara fidgeted with her books. Mrs. Shoemaker was a nice, elderly woman with a penchant for being into her neighbors' business. For once, Sara was glad of it. "What did they take?" she asked.

"Some jewelry..."

Sara's fingers flew at once to the amulet hidden under her sweater. She eyed the cooler in the corner, longing for a large bottle of cold water to ease the sudden, desert dryness of her mouth. "What else?"

"Your stereos and televisions. A lot of your things got opened, dressers and boxes and stuff. I don't think anything else was stolen. What do you want me to do?"

"We can't leave the dig. Give me the number to the police station, and I'll call them. I don't think we'll be able to do anything until we're home. Is the office all right?"

"Yes. Should I call your mother? She's in the Keys this week, isn't she?"

"Yes, please," she replied, thankful for Holly's composure. Right now, she couldn't claim the same attribute.

When she hung up, she hurried to the dig site, feeling cold to the marrow of her bones. "Faith."

Her sister stood ankle-deep in loose earth, sweating with the effort of digging in spite of the cool morning. She jammed the end of her shovel in the peat, then climbed out of the trench. "What I wouldn't give just to be able to pull this all out with a backhoe," she muttered once she reached Sara's side. She gave a groan, stretching the muscles of her back, then lifted her golden-blond mane to air the nape of her neck.

In the middle of a catlike arch, Faith stopped, listening. "All right, that's it. Something's here, and—" She scanned the dig site, but neither Thomas nor Dustin were around. "I'm not even using my power," she added in a harsh whisper, "and something keeps trying to get my attention."

"Our house was robbed," Sara blurted.

Her sister blanched.

Sara hadn't meant to let it out so quickly. "No

one's hurt," she added. She explained what Holly had told her. Her hand went toward her throat, then dropped again. "I don't think this was a random event."

Faith pursed her lips. Her gaze went to Sara's sweater. When she spoke, her voice was low. "I think we'd better find out what that necklace is, and quick."

"We're out of stakes," Dustin announced behind them. "Do either of you have more in your tents?"

Sara flinched at his appearance, but Dustin didn't notice. "I'll go get them." She shot a meaningful look at her sister.

Faith nodded understanding. They would hit the books tonight, and find out more about the amulet.

Before someone else found them in possession of it.

****

The day's digging progressed faster than Sara had hoped. The sun rode its arc overhead, and by the time it dipped into the western horizon, they had managed to remove the first layer of earth from around the wall. She was bone-tired at the end of the day, and only too happy to flop down beside the cooking fire. Comforted by its glow, she rubbed her sore neck muscles. "This is a well-earned meal."

"That's for sure," Thomas agreed, tossing hamburgers on the grill.

While they waited for the food to cook, she recounted the facts of the day's work and went over their goals for tomorrow. Dustin sat nearby, sketching in a notebook, his face glowing in the firelight. Across the fire, Faith watched him work with a drowsy abstraction and began to nod off.

A moment later, her sister's head snapped up. "Hi,

Ian," Faith called into the darkness.

Sara's belly flopped. She looked past Faith. As he neared the campfire, Ian's form grew more distinct. If knowing he was present sent her stomach into a frenzy, *seeing* him sent her into such a state of disorder that she could barely think.

Ian lowered himself to the ground beside Faith. "How'd you know?"

"You're the only other human being on the island," said Faith. "That, and I'm smart."

"I came down to see how everything went today." He cast a glance around the fire, visibly assessing the company at hand. His gaze landed on Sara.

She shifted where she sat, glad for the flickering light that hid the blush warming her cheeks. She didn't want to admit it, but she'd been thinking of him all day, no matter how much his knowledge of her gifts worried her. Every time her thoughts went to the way he'd looked at her before Faith showed up, she caught her breath. "How's your arm?" she managed.

"It feels like a truck ran it over, but I'll live."

The way he held her gaze, as if there was no one else on the island, unnerved her. Needing to get his attention off her, she cleared her throat. "I don't think you've met our crew. This is Thomas Callander, and that's Dustin Sennett. Guys, this is Ian Waverly."

Dustin waved and went back to sketching. That was Dustin: all work and no conversation.

Thomas shook Ian's hand. "Pleasure. What brings you to Hvitmar?"

"Just lucky, I guess," Ian answered. His glance drifted toward her before going back to Thomas. "I study wildlife."

Thomas began dishing out the hamburgers. "You hungry?"

"Thought you'd never ask." Ian accepted a plate with a grin that transformed his features and set off an entire Fourth of July of sparks throughout Sara's body. She ripped her gaze away to the fire.

The group ate in silence for a while. The quiet began to get almost as uncomfortable as words. Ian's stare had *weight*. "Were you able to get anything done today, with your arm like that?" she asked at last.

"I can't get down the cliffs, but I did get a pretty accurate population count using binoculars and my camera. Tomorrow I want to take a quick look around the north end, if that won't interfere with your dig."

"There are seals," she said. "I saw one this morning."

He looked up from his plate with a speed that she didn't think had much to do with seals. "Want to show me where?"

A distant boom of thunder interrupted the conversation. The wind began picking up, and the fire guttered in its wake. "I think the fun is over for the night," Faith announced, getting to her feet.

The group collected the remains of their meal. Dustin headed to his tent to continue working on his sketches, and Thomas made off with the grill and dishes.

Faith started toward her tent, then hesitated. "Sara?"

"I'm fine," she assured her sister. *No, I'm not.* "Go on." *Stay, stay, for God's sake, stay.*

Her sister nodded and walked away.

Sara watched her go. If Faith sensed her agitation,

31

she ignored it skillfully...and willfully. With a grimace of resignation, Sara picked up a last few maps scattered about the ground, then put the fire out. The wind whistled around the tents, and she smelled rain on the air. She had mountains of research waiting, including whatever she could find on the amulet, but frowned at the thought of Ian walking back up to his camp in the rain. She hesitated, hardly believing what she was about to say. "The storm may not last long, if you want to stick around."

He looked up. The gathering clouds had obliterated all traces of the stars. Thunder rumbled again, louder this time. "Yeah, I guess I'll wait it out."

They headed toward Sara's tent as the first drops splattered down. From there, the rain increased tenfold, drenching them both and rushing them along. They made it to shelter just as the first flash of lighting arced across the sky. The wind surged. She wondered if her tent wouldn't be blown flat by morning.

Inside, she lit the lantern on her bedside table. She grabbed a towel to dry her sopping ponytail. "I'm sure I could have used a bath, but not like this." Her sweater stuck like a wet sponge to her skin. She peeled it away with a disgusted sneer.

Ian turned his back to her. "Go ahead and get changed."

She caught her breath at the view of him thus presented. His rain-soaked jeans and jacket were plastered to his body. She followed the lines of his broad shoulders down to a narrow waist and stopped on a very nice ass. *Oh, my God... Quit looking!*

So not a teacher's body. She did an about-face and snatched a T-shirt from her trunk, shucking out of her sweater as fast as possible. She threw the T-shirt on, only to discover it was inside out and backward. She cursed under her breath, and ripped it off to turn it right side out.

****

Ian knew he shouldn't, but he looked over his shoulder. His mouth went dry as he fixed on her near-naked back. Lantern light glistened on her damp skin. As she wrestled with the shirt, her shoulder blades arched above a bra gone transparent with water.

Heat blazed up his spine. From where he stood, he could have reached her in three steps. Pained, he closed his eyes. *Don't. Fucking. Move.* Already, his body had formed other ideas.

All of which sounded way too good.

For whatever she was.

For a minute, all he heard was the sound of shuffling cloth. Then she asked, "Are you okay?"

He chanced another glimpse back over his shoulder. Dressed now, she frowned at him in an expression of concern. He frowned, too. He couldn't call it relief, but it was sure as hell easier to say something when she had her shirt on. "Yeah."

She picked up the towel and offered it to him. He took it to dry his own dripping hair. It smelled like her: earthy, with an undertone of something spicy that made him want to act on his earlier impulses. He tried not to breathe it in, feeling suddenly trapped in her tent while the storm howled outside.

"Do you want something dry to wear? I could ask one of the guys for a set of clothes."

"I'm fine."

"At least something for a dry sling. Do you need

any ice? We have an icebox hooked up to a generator."

"No. Sara, the sling is fine. My arm is fine. Don't worry about it." He dropped the towel on her trunk, took a few steps away, then sat in an empty camp chair. She stayed where she was, crossing her arms over her body as if she were cold. He warred with the confusion etched like a neon sign into her posture. "I'm sorry. It just hurts, so I'm punchy. I didn't take any painkillers tonight."

"Oh."

"You gonna sit?"

Prodded into motion, she fished in the cooler by her table. "Normally after breaking ground on a dig, I finish up the day with a beer. Sort of an opening ceremony."

"Don't let me stop you."

She offered him a drink. He took a water, even though he would rather have downed a six pack in one shot. She got a beer for herself, then sat with a long sigh in the table's opposite chair. "I hope it doesn't rain tomorrow. I'd like to get further than we did today."

He recognized the nervous chatter for what it was. He knew what she was. *She* knew he knew it. His good manners prodded him just enough to push out some conversation, while they were stuck here. "What got you into all this, anyway?"

The rumble and hiss of the storm filled the silence for a minute. "My father." She smiled, and Ian found his gaze locked on it. "Dad was an archaeologist. He taught at the university, and they sent him all over the world on assignments. I used to love it when he came home with stories about where he'd been and what he saw. Archaeology seemed like such an adventure. He was brilliant."

"Was?"

She took the cap off her beer. The bright look in her eyes faded, taking something indefinable with it, and Ian wished it hadn't right up until she added, "He's dead."

He went rigid. "So's mine."

"Oh." She fidgeted with her beer bottle. "How?"

"I don't want to get into it. What happened to yours?"

Her expression cooled. For the first time, he saw why people back at the college called her Shark Markham. "I don't want to get into it." She took a long drink of beer. "I don't suppose you want to tell me how you just happened to choose Hvitmar for your birding project."

He opened his water bottle. "I had to come to Shetland, anyway." When she gave him a *get-real* look, he raised his hands. "I swear to God. My assignment was to study the coastal birds of Shetland. You want to see my proposal?"

"Lucky for you, Hvitmar's in Shetland."

"Yeah, lucky me."

She took another drink. The silence stretched out some more, and he tried not to fidget. He wanted to leave. To hell with the storm. But then he caught another whiff of her earthy-spicy scent, and his body refused to move from the seat.

A crash of thunder made them both flinch. "God, the weather's in rare form tonight," she murmured.

"This is nothing compared to Maine during a good summer storm."

"Oh?"

"My first internship was at a wildlife preserve in Maine. Stormed practically the entire time I was there. We had to bail out our tent with a coffee can the last night."

Thunder boomed again. "I think we might be in for a repeat performance," she said over the rain beating on the tent canvas. He thought he saw her cheeks flush. "I hope you don't mind being here for a while."

He stared at her across the table. Did he?

She got up and pulled a blanket from the foot of her cot, then draped it over her shoulders. "Are you sure you don't want me to find a dry shirt for you? If we don't get you out of that stuff—"

Whatever she was, she had a way with words. He broke into a grin. "What's it gonna take to get you to quit asking me to take my clothes off?"

She jerked the blanket tighter around her shoulders, iron-faced. He marshaled his expression into order, but it was too late to stop the visuals playing in his head of *both* of them shedding their clothes. It was a bitch, and it was unfair as hell, but Sara Markham had a body that could start a four-alarm fire. He cleared his throat and shifted in the seat. "I'm all right. Sit down."

A few seconds passed, then she dropped back into her chair and snatched up her beer bottle.

He watched her for a while. Her body—all woman, all distracting—started sucking up more and more of his attention. It had been too damn long.

He leaned forward and propped his uninjured elbow on the table. "So now that you know something personal about me, what about you? What are those necklaces all about?"

She went white. Her hand flew to her throat as if

she hadn't realized she was wearing any jewelry, then fell away again. "They, er— They're from my father."

"What's that stone thing?"

"I don't—"

"You don't want to get into it, I got you." He pushed his water bottle away. Already frustrated with the argument between his mind and body, he angled his head toward the door. "Should I leave? Because everything I say seems to set you off."

"What's that supposed to mean?"

He couldn't make himself ask what he really wanted to know. Instead, he said, "Since yesterday, you've been looking at me like I'm going to attack you. What is it with you? It's like you completely detest human contact."

"I'm not the one who came out here by himself. What in the name of all that's holy made you decide to go on a dangerous research project alone?"

"Dangerous? They're birds, not man-eating lions."

She shot out of her chair and the blanket fell away. "Rock climbing, you idiot! What possessed you to do that alone?"

He surged up, boiling with hostility fueled by his suspicion of her. "What are you, my mother?"

"You are totally out of your mind!" She took a step toward him, face flushed, her gaze snapping sparks. "You could have been killed up there, and no one would have known a thing about it. Do you realize what would have happened if I hadn't—" She stopped short and clamped her mouth shut.

This is it, Waverly. He stalked toward her until they stood nose to nose. His pulse hammered. He wanted like hell for her to admit what she was, even as his body begged her not to. "What? Hadn't what? Tell me!"

She trembled. Wayward strands of rain-damp hair fell across her rose-red cheeks. A pulse pounded rapid-fire in the hollow of her throat.

His self-control snapped. He lunged forward, thrust the fingers of his good hand into her hair, and kissed her.

She whimpered once, terror in the sound, and then the selkie came to life. The wild thing. Whatever she was, oh, God, he didn't care. His blood crashed through his veins like whitewater as she kissed him back. Her arms came around him, and when she brushed his bad shoulder, shoots of agony lanced through him. *I don't care, I don't care.* He growled at the pain, at everything in his screwed-up past.

She tasted like heaven. The spicy scent of her washed over him and his body went into mutiny. With a need bordering on madness, he teased at her lips. She shuddered and opened for him. He slanted his lips over hers and swept her mouth with his tongue. *Mine.* He reached around her back and fisted his hand in a fold of her shirt. *Mine.*

She shook under his touch. Her hands came up and threaded into his hair. He stepped into her, urging her backward with his body. She bumped a chair, and it fell against the table with a crash. Bottles clinked to the floor as he steered her toward the cot. He buried his face in her neck, kissing satin skin. Her breath came fast in his ear. "Ian—Ian..."

She stumbled to a halt as the cot hit her in the back of the legs. His teeth grazed her neck. She gave a soft moan that almost undid him. Desperate to breathe past the pounding of his heartbeat, he raised his head.

She looked up, dazed with passion, and reached for him again. Ian froze.

Her eyes.

Blazing green.

He lurched backward. "What the hell are you?"

"Wh-What?" Her lashes fluttered. Her eyes faded to hazel.

He spun on his heel, went to the door, and swept out into the storm.

Chapter Three

Ian fumed during the entire slog back up to his camp. Fat raindrops pummeled his body like handfuls of dropped pebbles. He wiped a hand across his face, slicking away the rainwater, but it didn't erase the taste of her. "Fuck!" The gusting wind whipped his curse away. "I'm out of here. I should have gone to Mainland in the first place, instead of asking for this middle-of-nowhere post with some insane—"

Thunder crashed overhead. "Whatever!" he shouted—at the storm, at Sara, it didn't matter which. "I've had enough of this stupid circus. Keep your goddamn nightmares, keep your flying necklaces, keep me out of it. Should have forgotten all this shit a long time ago."

He reached his tent and ripped open the flap. The storm followed him inside. Wind and rain swirled around, blowing papers off his table and into the corner. With cold-numbed fingers, he fought the tent zipper and managed to pull it closed. He wrestled out of his wet sling, furious that he couldn't just rip it off without hurting his shoulder.

More furious still, that part of him wanted to march all the way back down there and finish kissing her. He gave an incoherent roar and flung his jacket and sodden shirt on the back of a chair.

Shirtless and soaked, he stood in the middle of his

tent. He thrust his good hand through his hair, sending a shower of droplets onto the floor. For a satisfying minute, he thought about nothing at all.

Then he remembered her moan when he'd nipped at her neck. The smell of her. The taste, too. Cinnamon, that was it. Whatever she'd had between dinner and that beer, he wanted to drown in it.

He cursed again and snatched a towel from the foot of his bed, then scrubbed it through his hair. His injured shoulder throbbed. He swallowed a couple of painkillers without water. Lightning flashed, illuminating the interior for an instant. He lit a lantern, then flopped onto his cot.

Instead of seeing the roof of his tent, he saw her face, her parted lips, the way her eyes begged him to touch her.

He snatched his journal off the bedside table and opened it to write something, anything. A blank page stared him in the face. He let the pencil hover over the paper for a few minutes. When that didn't work, he flipped the switch of the small radio sitting on the table. Most of the channels brought static. The one clear station played some weird thing with bagpipes. He sighed, turned it off, then set the tip of the pencil to the page. What the hell had she done to him? Was this part of what she was?

Or was it just that he'd wanted so badly to bury himself inside her that he'd forgotten everything he knew about her?

I can't deal with this, the pencil scribbled out. *Not now, not her.*

Another minute passed.

She saved my life. I know it was her. How the hell

else did I end up back on solid ground? That wolf, somehow it was Sara. Green eyes, for God's sake.

And telekinesis.

He hissed and hurled the pencil across the tent. It clattered into an open crate. Coming to Shetland had been the worst idea of his life.

The past should damn well stay buried.

****

Sara woke with a start to the rising morning light. Ian's kiss had resonated through her dreams, bringing restless flashes of rasping stubble against her heated skin. She shivered in the bitter air and sat up, pressing her fingers to her lips as if she could still feel him.

So. He knew. What would he do about it?

Nothing good, judging from the way he'd flown out of her tent. It had taken her a few moments to realize her eyes must have changed again. Caught up in the kiss, she hadn't even felt it happen. When she tried to go after him, confront him, Dustin had stopped her with some maddening, trivial thing about soil compositions. She'd been forced to stay at the camp and deal with it, all the while casting furtive looks up the slope of the island.

The night storm had blown over. The roar of wind had faded to a periodic whooshing around the edges of the tent. She swung her legs over the edge of the cot—

—and froze.

The tent door hung partly open, its corner flapping in the breeze. She knew she'd shut that last night. She went to it and peered out. A glance down revealed no tracks on the ground. That proved nothing; they might have been washed away by the rain. She zipped the door shut, then hurried into a warm change of clothes.

The amulet. Ian knew about that, too. She touched a hand to her throat; the stone disk was tucked safely under her shirt. She pulled it out and examined it, a thin, discus-like object less than five centimeters across. Each side bore the same worn carving: a serpent winding in and out of a Celtic knot, then circling back to swallow its own tail. A small oval depression lay in the center of the discus on either side.

She traced a finger along the center depressions, as she'd done maybe a hundred times since finding it among her father's possessions. "Something's missing, Dad," she murmured, noting the sharp edges where the centerpieces had been pried loose. "But what?"

One hour and five reference books later, she had gained no insight into the amulet's origins. She couldn't bring herself to draw or catalogue it, as she would any other artifact. With her books exhausted, she turned to the Internet. She opened the browser on her laptop and began the arduous task of sifting through innumerable Web sites on Celtic lore. "Come on. One mention, that's all I want. Give me something to work with," she pleaded.

Footsteps sounded outside her tent. "Sara?"

Ian.

A chill rushed through her. She wondered if she could bluff her way out of what had happened between them last night.

Confidence, she reminded herself. One slip, and he'd pounce. Closing her laptop with a snap, she said, "I'm here. Come in."

He unzipped the tent door and stepped inside, lowering a knapsack from his good shoulder. His gaze roved about the tent with an expression of deadpan calm, then landed at last on her. "I just wanted to tell you—"

She sat up straight and matched his deadpan look.

"—I'm leaving."

Dismay warred with relief. "What?"

"I'm leaving," he added. "Changing my post. I'm going to Mainland first thing tomorrow."

She stood up. "Why?" she asked before she could stop herself.

He shifted and skimmed her tent with a look before bringing his attention back to her, as if he had to make himself do so. "You've got things you don't want to tell me. Things I don't want to know, and probably shouldn't."

She opened her mouth to reply, but couldn't. The words hovered on the tip of her tongue. *Do you know what I am?*

He crossed the tent to stand in front of her, looking caught between reluctance and determination. "I'm sorry for last night. For the kiss."

Her heart began thumping faster. "Oh." *I don't think I am,* she wanted to say. Even now, she had to work to keep from moving toward him.

He shouldered the knapsack again. "Anyway, I've got a favor to ask you. Will you show me where those seals are before I go? I want something from here to take back with me, for the college." When she didn't respond, he added, "Is now a bad time?"

"No one's going to be up for another half hour, at least. I can take you."

By the time they reached the rocky northwestern shore, the sun had just begun its ascent, painting the sky in stained-glass hues. They walked down to the beach.

Safe topics, she thought. *Stick to the animals.* "I'm not sure any will be here," she said. "I only saw the one yesterday."

"There's probably more. They tend to have favorite spots where the fishing's good."

That piqued her interest. "Will there be pups?"

"Not likely, this time of year."

"I minored in zoology in college. Never studied seals," she said.

Why was she sharing anything about herself with him? He didn't care. She didn't want him to know. He was leaving, and she should thank God for it. She pointed to a large cluster of rocks jutting from the surf offshore. "That's it."

Ian crouched low and pressed a hand to her shoulder, urging her down beside him. The touch resounded through her body. She knelt, watching him, but his gaze had fixed on the rocks while he listened.

"I hear them," he murmured. He crept away, beckoning her with a silent wave.

They moved stealthily around the edge of the beach, until at last the seals came into view. Five of them lazed about on the rocks, barking in irritation when one tried to usurp the best spot from another. "I didn't realize they were so big," she said. "That one in front is *huge.*"

He leaned toward her to whisper, "That's a bull. These are gray seals. The bulls can reach about five hundred pounds." He set his knapsack down, then pulled out a camera.

She watched him take several photos, one-handed, with a long lens. He set the camera down to pull out a small leather journal. Balancing it on his knee, he made neat, quick notes. He worked with the same efficiency and self-confidence she felt when studying a new artifact. Recognizing a professional in his comfort zone, she couldn't help smiling.

He caught her looking and frowned. "What?"

She sobered at once. "Nothing." Being around him was beginning to unravel her. She almost wished last night had never happened.

No. She *did* wish last night had never happened. Did. Firmly.

Almost, she thought, looking at his mouth.

He put his journal and camera back in the knapsack. "I think I'm all set here. Thanks for showing me where they were. We can stand up now." He rose to his feet, then shouldered the pack and began to move back the way they had come.

She stood and dusted off her pants. Her heartbeat stumbled. How much did he know? She couldn't stand it anymore. She took a long, full breath. "Ian?"

He stopped, but didn't turn. "Don't. Please? Just don't."

The pain in those few syllables pulled at her. *What is it?* she wanted to ask, but she bit her lip and followed him back to the camp without another word.

When they reached her tent again, she hesitated outside. "So...tomorrow morning?"

"Yeah."

"Do you need help getting any of your stuff together?"

"No. I have a guy coming from Unst."

She stared at his boots for a second. "Well, why don't we make you dinner tonight? That way, you can pack your mess kit."

He stiffened, but his gaze remained cool and unaffected, light years from that look last night. "Sure."

"Okay. See you then."

He nodded and turned to leave. She watched him go with a knot in her throat, wondering why she wasn't happier.

When he had left, she ducked into her tent. Her research waited at her camp table. She sighed and sat down, but her body yearned to get back up and rush out of the tent after him.

How could he leave now, after a kiss like that? Kisses like that didn't exist.

She seized the first book and flung it open, thrusting her thoughts as far from him as possible. Words swam on the page, impossible to shepherd into sense. What did he know? What would he say? Who would he tell?

She managed after a while, and only due to years of practice, to shut off her internal chatter and get to work. After a morning of fruitless searching for information about the amulet, she joined the rest of the crew at the dig. The work engrossed her so fully that she barely noticed the shadows lengthening across the ground. By then, she couldn't stand herself. "If I don't get a real bath before dinner, I'm going to go out of my mind," she grumbled to her sister. "A camp shower just isn't going to cut it today."

"I feel like I ought to soak in bleach, or I'll never get this grime out," agreed Faith.

Sara glanced around the site. Dustin and Thomas were still working. She moved close to her sister's ear. "When I went exploring yesterday morning, I ran across an inlet on the western side of the island. I'm going to go for a swim. I'll show you where it is."

"I'll settle for the camp shower tonight, but that might come in handy tomorrow. Be back by dinner. Is Ian still coming?"

She tried to sound casual. "As far as I know."

"Sara." Faith gave her an unnerving *Don't-bullshit-me* look.

"I'm fine. I told you, he's leaving anyway. I'll see you in a bit." She headed to her tent.

She gathered a towel and change of clothes, then set off toward the inlet. By the time she reached it, there were only a couple of hours left before dusk. Time enough for a quick bath.

Setting her change of clothes on the high rocks near the water's edge, she stripped naked, leaving only the necklaces hanging around her neck. The breeze was balmy on her skin; thank God it had warmed up over the course of the day.

Looking at gold-washed ripples, she debated shapeshifting into a seal or some other seagoing creature. The water at this time of year would still be chilly, and a human body wasn't insulated for cold ocean swimming. She didn't know much about seals, except what she'd learned that morning from Ian. What little she knew wouldn't be enough to sustain a shapeshift for more than a few seconds. *Shark Markham, indeed.* She scanned the water again. "It's either this, or the camp shower."

That decided matters. She went down to the water. Gravel gave way to fine granite that shifted under her stride, sandpapery and pleasant on the soles of her feet. The cold as she splashed into the inlet drove the air from her lungs. How much insulation did those seals, have, exactly? She hunched down into the water.

After a while, her body seemed to adapt, and the water felt warmer than she'd first thought. She swam a couple of laps, then dove under the waves. Grabbing a handful of granite sand from the bottom of the inlet, she scrubbed it over her skin until it glowed. The cool water glided along her skin as she swam, a welcome change from the heat and sweat of her workday. Not only that, but it had begun to wash away all the *other* things on her mind. Letting herself relax for the first time since finding the amulet, she stretched out to meet the sensual wash of current flowing over her body.

She came up in the middle of the inlet and swept her hair back. The distant calls of seabirds mingled with the lessening shush of waves against rock. The tide had begun calming for the night. She supposed she'd better rinse out her grubby clothing as well, before the sunset caught her still out in the water.

When she looked back toward shore, she felt a chill that had nothing to do with temperature.

Her clothes and towel had been moved.

She remembered leaving them on the first rock, a rounded boulder sitting where the shoreline dropped away. They now sat on the ground beside the rock in a jumbled heap. Sara ducked lower into the water, scanning the beach. "Faith?"

No one answered. "Stop kidding around," she called, expecting her sister to jump out from behind one of the high rocks. Again, nothing happened.

As she realized what her unseen stalker had been searching for, her breath came faster. She checked; the amulet still hung safely around her neck beside her locket. She swam to shore, got out, then began walking toward her pile of clothes.

She'd only made it partway up the beach when she caught the crunch of footsteps on gravel behind her. She spun around, only to halt where she stood.

Ian rounded a clutch of boulders at the opposite end of the beach, carrying a towel. He glanced up from the ground and stopped dead, looking poleaxed. His breath came out in a long, loud *whoosh*.

Her heartbeat charged through her chest like a steam train. She couldn't breathe, couldn't think, couldn't speak. Words bottlenecked in her throat.

He closed his mouth. His stare heated and traveled over her naked body.

Fire coursed through her veins, eclipsing the cool water running in rivulets down her back. The primal instinct to answer that look in his eyes sent a wave of chills rippling across her skin.

He took a step, then halted. She saw his hand clench on the towel, and then he tossed it into the air toward her.

She caught it and flung it around herself. Shaking, she spun away, then bent to scrape up her clothes.

Gravel crunched again. Closer, and closer yet. "Sara," he said, sounding strangled.

She shot to her feet and gripped the towel tighter, panting around the fierce thudding of her heart. She didn't turn to face him.

"Get out of here, and do it quick."

She ran.

****

Sara stopped only when she knew she'd put enough distance between them. Even then, she paused just long enough to jerk her pants on and thrust her head and arms through her sweater. She arrived out of breath at the campsite. Dustin called her to dinner. He and Thomas had started a fire and begun laying out everyone's dishes. "I'll be there in a few minutes," she puffed, going straight to her tent.

Inside, she felt a little safer. She only wished her mind would tell her body to calm down, as well.

"Sara?" Faith ducked her head into the tent.

"I'm here."

Faith entered. "Have you seen my journal? I can't find it anywhere."

"No." Distracted, Sara swept a glance around her tent, then shuffled a couple of books on her table. "Did you leave it with me for some reason?"

Faith shook her head. "It was in my trunk this morning. I checked my whole tent. Sara...it had stuff about the necklace in it."

Her blood iced over. "*You wrote it down?*"

"Shhh!" Faith held up her hands.

Fresh waves of trembling flooded Sara's body. Her worst nightmares rushed back with terrifying clarity. "We should never have taken it from the safe box. Someone went through my clothes while I was swimming. I'll give you one guess what they might have been looking for." She lowered herself into a chair, then ran a hand through her damp hair.

Faith mimicked the motion and sat in the table's other seat. She cast a quick, suspicious glance at the tent doorway. "Did you see anyone?"

"Ian showed up. A little too conveniently timed." She braced her elbows on the table and put her face in her hands, masking both her agitation and the blush she felt burning in her cheeks.

"Maybe you shouldn't be wearing the amulet."

"The hell I shouldn't. I'm afraid to let it out of my sight. We don't even know what it is, yet. I've looked. I can't find anything."

Faith reached out a hand. "Give me it. I'll just read the damned thing with my gift."

"I don't think that's such a good idea, Faith. What if—"

"What if, while we're trying to figure the stupid thing out, someone comes and murders you in your sleep? Let me worry about what I see or don't see. If someone is after this thing, I'd just as soon know what we're protecting. I've looked too, and we're not getting anywhere the easy way."

Sara pursed her lips and removed the amulet from her neck. "Do you think Ian might be the one—"

"Ian wasn't even there to break into our house."

"Well, there are only five of us on this island!" Sara lowered her voice to a harsh whisper. "He knows what I am, or at least he knows enough to make me worry."

Her sister reached for the necklace. "Just give it here," she said, "and let's get this over with."

Sara handed it over with reluctance.

Taking a deep breath, Faith called on her psychic sense. Her eyes melted into silver, and fixed on the amulet. She grew still and silent.

Sara waited. Five minutes passed, and Faith did not rouse from her trance.

Ten.

Fifteen.

Anxious now, Sara leaned forward and touched her sister's arm. "Faith, wake up."

Faith shook and blinked awake, looking confused. "A man," she said. "Not Dad. Not a Celt, either. I'm not sure *what* he was. Everything was indistinct."

"What did he do? Did he say anything?"

"He had a sword. I saw him kill another man in white robes and take the amulet. He held it up and said something, I don't even know what. The necklace started spinning, and these lines of light shot out from it along the ground, and then he screamed..." Faith shuddered and looked down at the amulet in her hand. "This thing has blood on it, Sara. Lots of it, I feel it. I think we should destroy it."

Sara's body hummed with agitation. *"What happened?"*

"It killed him. He fell, and the necklace fell, and I saw his spirit rise from his body and just vanish into the lines of light. We need to smash the thing." She rose from her seat.

Sara jerked to her feet as well. "Dad gave it to us on purpose, or he would have destroyed it himself!"

Faith hesitated. "Maybe he didn't have time, once he found out what it was. Before he was—"

"*We* still don't know what it is," interrupted Sara. She paced the length of her tent. "Did you see anything else?"

Muscles worked in her sister's jaw. She sighed and rubbed her forehead. "I saw what's missing. The pieces on either side in the center of the necklace. Oval inlays." She touched her locket. "One gold." She gestured at Sara's throat. "The other silver."

Open-mouthed, Sara touched her locket. She unfastened it with shaking fingers. "We have to melt these down. They belong in the amulet."

"Are you nuts?" Faith strode forward until she was toe to toe with Sara. "Dad took them out for a reason. He wanted to disable the amulet. It's dangerous. You know it is."

Sara shook her head. "He would have smashed it himself. I'm sure of it, Faith. I think he wanted us to do something with it."

"Like what, get killed?" Faith slapped the amulet on the table and snatched an empty glass bottle. She raised it to strike.

"No!" Sara shouted, jumping toward her.

Faith brought the bottle down on the amulet with a crash. The bottle shattered, and a deafening chime reverberated off the tent walls. Both of them cringed and covered their ears until the sound faded away.

Faith clutched her now-bleeding hand and looked at the amulet, resting intact on Sara's table. She bit off a moan and held her hand against her body. "Smashing it is out," she snarled.

Sara snatched the amulet up, then looped it over her head and tucked it quickly into her sweater. The stone pulsed with heat against her skin.

Thomas ducked into the tent. "Everything okay in here?"

"Yeah, we're fine," Sara answered. "We'll be out in a few minutes."

Thomas passed her an unconvinced look, but left again.

When she was certain of their privacy, Sara reached her hand out to her sister. "Give me your locket."

"You're out of your mind."

Sara stepped toward the tent door. "Do you want to

figure this out, or not? Give me the locket. We'll go to Mainland and get them put back in the amulet tomorrow morning."

Faith grabbed Sara's first-aid kit and dropped it on the table. She flung it open to rummage for bandages and antiseptic. "Sure. We're just going to walk in there with this knick-knack, which no one is going to get curious about and ask questions about, and *come looking for*. Not to mention, I don't think we should leave the dig site."

"Fine. You stay with the dig. I'll go to Mainland myself. Just give me the locket."

Faith frowned and finished wrapping her hand with disgruntled motions. She grasped her locket and jerked. The chain snapped. She dropped the locket into Sara's palm. "Take Ian with you."

"What about Dustin or Thomas?"

"Ian," Faith repeated flatly.

"You don't trust them, do you?"

Faith closed up the kit and put it back in its place. She went to the tent door and paused, pursing her lips. "At this point, I don't trust much of anyone. Ian's the least of my worries, especially if he's leaving." She stepped out of the tent.

Most of the time, Sara trusted her sister's intuition with her life.

This time, she feared she might regret it.

Chapter Four

The nightmare again.

Ian waded through the mess on the office floor. He groped for the desk lamp, then flipped it on with a sense of dread.

He knew the precise moment when the wraith appeared behind him. A flush of frigid air chilled his back. Ian steeled himself and turned around. His blood ran like ice water at the sight of the man.

Saying nothing, the gory man staggered forward and reached for Ian's left arm. Ian jumped backward, but the man seized his shoulder in a crushing grip. Fire shot from Ian's shoulder throughout his body. He screamed in agony and struggled, but the man stepped forward and pinned him to the desk.

Ian's entire being shrank into that stone-faced stare and the torture of the man's hold. He fought against the man's bearlike grip. Tendons in his shoulder shifted and popped. Muscles contracted. His shoulder burned as if shards of glass were being driven into the joint. The shapes in the room blurred. Everything went scorching white.

He woke in the next instant blowing like a winded horse, and reached for his left shoulder. Pain throbbed along the length of his arm. Ian half expected it to be dislocated again, but the joint felt sound. He groaned and closed his eyes. The ache faded into numbness.

This dream was getting old real fast.

He lay silent a while, drifting in and out of a restless doze, until he heard footsteps outside his tent. He snapped awake at once. After the incident with his climbing rope, every sound that wasn't wind or birds put him on alert. He rolled smoothly out of bed and onto his feet.

The sun had risen. A shadow fell across his tent. "Ian?"

Sara.

A mental picture of her naked body, washed in gold by the reflection of the sunset, charged into his thoughts and obliterated everything else. Wrestling to push the image out of his head—and the reaction out of his body—he reached for a clean T-shirt. "Give me a minute." Or maybe a few minutes, because all he wanted was to keep playing that image and see where it led.

He shrugged his bad shoulder purposely, letting the discomfort force his attention elsewhere. The joint tingled with the same pins-and-needles sensation he'd experienced when he woke from his nightmare. He put the shirt on, careless about his injury, then grabbed his sling and went barefoot to the tent door.

When he opened it, Sara stood there with her hands jammed into her coat pockets, looking like she wanted to be anywhere else. Her cheeks were pink, too pink to be from the exertion of her walk alone, and he wondered if she were thinking of that encounter at the inlet. *Shut up about it,* he ordered his body.

A backpack hung from her shoulder. She canted her head, seeming to weigh her words. "You didn't come down last night."

"I had to finish packing," he lied.

She frowned. "I need your help."

The image of the gory man flashed in his memory. *Hhhhelp her.* Ian jerked in surprise. He'd never ignored his gut responses before.

Something told him not to start now. He wanted to tell her to forget it, but the throbbing of his shoulder reminded him he owed her his life, whether he liked it or not. He hated being indebted to her, being forced to have anything to do with her.

But parts of him really, really liked it.

He sighed. *Help her, it is. This once...then I'm out.*

Her cheeks went pinker, and he saw her try to push herself past the awkwardness of their last meeting. The look on her face tugged at his sense of humor. If it weren't for...everything...he might have laughed. "Let me get my stuff together."

"What about your post?" she asked.

"It can wait a while."

They walked to the eastern shoreline, where he knew it dipped close enough to sea level to admit a small dock. Sara remained silent. She didn't seem to know any better than he what to say in the wake of yesterday.

God. Please stop thinking about that. His pulse quickened. He took a deep breath at the thought of her naked, dripping body, burned indelible in his memory by instant and painful need. He'd almost given in. A couple more steps, and he'd have torn that towel away, and damn all the reasons he didn't want to want her.

He dropped behind her as they walked, trying to put some space between them, but it served only to give him a too-compelling view of her swinging hips.

A motorboat rested at the dock. "This is our ride," she said.

"Where are we going?"

"Mainland. I have to find a jeweler, and quickly. I don't want to leave the dig site too long." She unsnapped the boat cover, then pulled it back as fast as possible.

"A jeweler?" What the hell was so important about a jeweler that it couldn't wait? He moved to help her with the boat cover. "Why take me?"

"Faith doesn't want to leave the dig."

"There's always your crew."

She didn't answer right away. She folded the boat cover, stowed it in the stern of the boat, then unwound the first of the mooring lines. "We need them working. My sister seems to think enough of you to suggest you come with me."

He didn't miss that she left her own opinion unspoken. What had he done to garner Faith's confidence when he'd hardly talked to her, while Sara remained evasive? He started on the other mooring line. "What do you want a jeweler for, anyway?"

"My necklace, the stone one. I'm fixing it."

"Was it broken?"

"There are two pieces missing. I'm having them put back in it."

An unaccountable chill passed through his body. She could have seen a jeweler by herself, at any time. One-handed, he worked the mooring line free, then coiled it onto a cleat. "Why can't it wait?"

She gestured to the dock and moved to the steering wheel. "Give us a push, will you?"

Ian reached over the edge of the boat and gave the

piling a shove. The boat drifted away from the dock.

Sara keyed the engine. It rumbled to life, idling in the water. She waited until Ian sat down to ease away from shore, then took her own seat. "My father gave me the necklace. It's important to me."

True, he was sure, but not the whole truth. Sara stared forward along their course, spine rigid, mute as a statue. He rubbed his shoulder. It still prickled, more a discomfort now than actual pain. "I'll bet. That's why we're rushing off to Mainland."

She answered only by opening the throttle. The boat shot forward. Ian sighed and held on for the ride.

****

The Mainland telephone directory listed four jewelers in their vicinity. The first was closed. The next two refused to do the work in less than a week. The fourth shop didn't look promising, either.

Ian mistrusted the appearance of the people passing back and forth along the street in front of the shop. Most of them streamed out of a sad-looking pub two doors down. He didn't want to speculate on the nature of the other buildings mashed together cheek by jowl on either side of the jeweler. "I'm guessing this part of town isn't in the tour books."

The grimy shop window bore a sign that read *Buy, Sell, Repair* in faded red script. Its door hung open as if waiting for them. Sara headed across the street with a decisive gait. He shook his head and followed.

Inside, the shop didn't improve upon first impressions. They rounded a short counter just inside the doorway. Clutter of every sort swarmed along the shelves and cases. A radio stuffed between stacks of old books droned out a staticky racing broadcast.

The weedy, grizzled man behind the counter glanced up when they entered, then went back to puffing on his cigarette over the newspaper. Ian saw a few gruesome knives in the cases and speculated at their previous use. He bent close to Sara's ear and whispered, "If this is a jeweler's, I'm the king of England."

Sara turned her back on the shopkeeper and murmured, "Just follow my lead, okay?"

She turned around again, and Ian wondered why she didn't move forward. She stood still a moment, just looking at the shop's proprietor. He was about to ask why she waited, but she walked to the counter, withdrew a leather billfold from her pocket, then slapped it down.

The man snapped to attention and dropped the stub of his cigarette on the paper. It began to singe a hole in the sports page. He patted at it with frantic motions, gave up, then doused it with the half pint of beer sitting beside the cash register. "Whassis?" he blustered, sopping up the mess with a dirty handkerchief plucked from his belt.

"This should be sufficient to pay off your substantial gambling debts, plus a little more to renew your good standing at the pub, Mister MacRae."

The man's bloodshot eyes narrowed at her. "Why?" he shot back, which Ian took to mean *Why would you want to help me?*

Ian would have liked to know that and more, himself. How the hell did she know the shopkeeper had gambling debts?

"Let's just say I know your creditors, and I'd hate to see them ruin your good looks. Do you want it, or not?" she asked.

Ian watched the man's gaze shift from the billfold to the gap in the counter, and then to the shop door. He slid into the gap and blocked it with a casual air. When the man gave him a dirty look, Ian answered it with a philosophical tilt of his head.

MacRae turned his sneer back on Sara. "What do you want out o' me?"

Sara set her locket on the counter, followed by another, golden one. She reached into her pocket once more, then set the last item down. Her hair swung forward so that Ian couldn't see her eyes. She took her hand away. The stone necklace rested on the stained wood. "I want you to fix this."

MacRae peered at the amulet as if he expected it to jump up and bite him. "What kind o' trinket you got there?"

She showed her teeth. "A birthday present."

The man grunted and scooped up the lockets.

"I want you to melt those down into oval beads," she said. "One goes in one side of this necklace, and one in the other. You give me my present back in one piece, and"—she picked up the billfold and stuffed it back in her pocket—"I give you your pretty face."

She spoke pleasantly enough, but the underlying menace in her tone made Ian's skin crawl. He hadn't thought her capable. He hadn't wanted to think so.

Of course she was capable. He itched with the desire to be anywhere else. Away from this insanity.

Away from her.

The shop owner divided a guarded look between Sara and Ian. "Who are you people?"

She held out her hand for the lockets. "If you're not

interested—"

"I didn't say that."

"Good." She beamed. "We'll wait in the pub, then, shall we?"

They entered the Rampant Lion to the roaring din of arm-wrestling customers at one end of the bar. Smoke lay thick on the air, mingling with the pungent odor of unwashed bodies. Ian bought two cups of coffee and set them on the table at the back of the pub, well away from the impromptu test of manhood. He sat down across from Sara. "What did you do to that guy in the pawn shop?"

"What makes you think I did something to him?"

"I've never seen a guy cave under pressure that fast, is what."

She studied him. "I thought you didn't want to know anything about me."

He took a swallow of his coffee. The stuff stung his tongue like battery acid. Watching Sara, he set the cup carefully down. He already knew more about her than he should have. Some things, more than others. He closed his eyes, and her naked figure haunted him once more.

They passed an uncomfortable hour looking over everything in the pub but each other. They ordered another pair of drinks and a small meal. The arm-wrestlers declared a champion, a brawny mountain of a man who ordered a pitcher of beer to celebrate his own victory.

At last, Sara gave a soft sigh that he probably wasn't meant to hear. "I'm sorry if I—"

He banged his mug down on the table harder than he intended. "Don't do that."

Lines appeared between her brows. "You aren't even going to let me apologize?"

"What for?" He hunched his good shoulder.

"For making you change your post."

"You didn't make me change anything," he said. "That was my doing."

"Well, then, for delaying your departure," she snapped.

Something in her tone made him look closer at her. She touched a finger to an old beer stain on the table's grainy surface, avoiding his gaze. Sitting in the middle of a rowdy pub, with shouting people on her left and right, she looked desperately lonely.

He spoke without meaning to. "I like you, Sara."

Her gaze flashed up in obvious surprise.

He glanced away. The admission surprised him, too. And did a few other things he didn't want to think about. "I can't be whatever it is you're looking for," he added gruffly. "I'm not that guy."

"What makes you think I'm looking for something in you? I'm here for an excavation. That's it. If you want to leave— No, wait. You *are* leaving."

He backed away from the remark the same way he would from an unpredictable creature. "Why don't we go see if that necklace is ready? I'll pay our tab."

"I've got it. Just go check on the necklace."

He opened his mouth to snap a response, but thought better of it. Glad for the excuse to get away from her for a moment, he left the pub and went back to the pawn shop. He wished it didn't feel so much like a retreat.

The radio had been turned off. The shopkeeper wasn't at the counter, but Ian heard shuffling noises from the now-open doorway behind it. "Hello?"

MacRae swaggered out with a dirty handkerchief in one hand and a set of keys in the other. When he saw Ian, his eyes went wide. He covered it fast and looked around, presumably for Sara.

Ian didn't like the relief on MacRae's face one bit. Even from this distance, he could smell beer, and he wondered just how many the man had tossed back. "Is the necklace ready?"

"Oh, it's ready. Not for you, though."

"I know. She's coming with your money."

The man tossed the handkerchief down. He reached into his back pocket and produced a gun.

Ian froze.

MacRae gave him an unpleasant leer. "Not for her, either. I'm sure that trinket's worth a bit more'n she's paying me. So you'll be leavin' without it, I think. I know antiques when I see them." He twitched the barrel of his pistol toward the doorway and advanced around the shop counter. "You snobby rich kids think you're gonna come in here and threaten me, you got a nasty surprise coming."

"Whoa. Jesus. Hold on a second here, mister." Ian held up his good hand and backed up a step.

"Out with you. This gun's loaded, 'case you were wondering, and I've got no problem usin' it."

Ian heard a low growl. He looked behind him with a quickening pulse.

A wolf rounded the corner of the counter near the door, ears flattened and teeth bared in the shop owner's direction.

MacRae's eyes bulged. The gun faltered in his hand. "What the hell you doing, bringin' animals in my shop? Get that thing out o' here!" He raised his gun again.

The wolf vaulted forward with a snarl and plowed the man over. They barreled into a table, spewing books and stereo equipment that crashed to the floor. Ian heard the shopkeeper scream, but didn't stop to think. He raced through the gap in the counter into the back room.

Another door stood at the rear of the tiny room. Through its small, filmy window, he saw an alley stretching away. The stone pendant lay on a messy workbench. Ian snatched it up and jammed it into his pocket. He jumped back into the shop doorway, hearing growls and human cries. "Come on! There's a way out!"

The wolf sprang through the gap in the counter, and they ran for the back door. Ian shoved it open and bolted outside. The wolf's breath churned behind him as it followed.

Just before they reached the corner of the alley, a gunshot blasted behind him. He ducked instinctively and heard a yip. Ian looked back, but the wolf kept coming. They raced around the corner together and flew down another long series of alleys until he thought they'd escaped their assailant.

He skidded to a stop behind a run-down hotel, clammy with sweat. *Fuck! What the hell just happened?* He glanced down at himself, shaking with shock. No blood, no bullet holes, holy *crap* what had he gotten into?

The wolf galloped into the alley, then its forelegs buckled. It somersaulted head over tail and lay still in the dirt.

For a second, Ian bent double, gasping, unable to trust his senses. When the wolf didn't move, he stumbled toward it.

And then he stopped, because the creature's outline began to glow. Its shape blurred, changed somehow. He couldn't be sure what he was seeing. The animal shape stretched, distorted, resolved itself into a prone woman, and then solidified.

Sara. Without a shadow of a doubt this time. His world flipped over, and he felt sick.

She clutched her upper arm with the opposite hand, her eyes shut. "Did we lose him?" she panted.

Ian staggered backward, heaving for breath that wouldn't come.

She opened her eyes. They faded to hazel, glassy with pain. Even though he'd seen it happen, he wanted to disbelieve it. His skin prickled. The hairs on his arms stood on end.

She labored into a sitting position, then withdrew her bloodstained fingers from her arm. He heard footsteps shuffling down the alley behind them.

Whatever had just happened, an explanation would have to wait. "Come on, you've got to get up," he said. "How bad are you hurt?"

"It's a scratch. He missed...mostly." When Ian reached reluctantly for her hand, she pulled it away. "I can get up by myself."

He hated to admit it, but relief washed through him at her refusal.

She lumbered onto her feet, and they started running again. They emerged from the alley into the street out front, still breathless. She slipped into the crowd and he jogged alongside her.

Sara took off her jacket to examine the bullet wound. She threw the coat under her arm, then clapped her hand over the wound again to staunch the bleeding. "Tell me you got the necklace back."

"Yeah. Want to tell me why we're getting shot at for your birthday present?"

"You ask a lot of questions for someone who wants nothing to do with this."

Fury exploded through him. "I think I have a right to know, Sara!" He scanned the crowd to be sure they weren't being followed, then stopped walking.

She went a few steps farther, hesitated, and then came back.

Pedestrians and cars alike rushed up and down the street, minding their own business. Ian reached into his pocket and held up the necklace, lowering his voice to a hostile whisper. "If I'm going to be shot at, I should damn well know what *you* are, and what *this* is. I'm not playing games with my life, and *you* aren't, either." When she reached for the necklace, he jerked it out of her reach, and stuffed it back in his pocket with a stony look.

She sighed, and the fight went out of her eyes. "Not here, and not now. I'll tell you"—she winced and gripped her upper arm once more—"anything you want to know. Later."

"You had better," he said, and marched away without waiting for her.

****

Sara threw her coat over her shoulder to hide the blood while they took a taxi back to the pier. Ian sat rigid in the back seat, as far from her as he could get without wedging himself against the door. They didn't speak to one another at all.

Once they boarded the motorboat, she dropped her bloodstained coat and started the engine. Ian sat in the other seat—still looking like he'd have preferred a few extra miles between them—and they sped away from Mainland.

A good way past Unst, he said something she didn't catch over the noise of wind and motor. She lowered the throttle just enough to shout, "What?"

"Cut the motor!"

She glanced around. They were still in open water. "Why?"

"Do it!"

Gritting her teeth, she did so, then lobbed the anchor over the edge of the boat. The craft bobbed in the waves. Her ears rang with the sudden absence of noise.

Then she spied the streaks of blood oozing from the gash in her shoulder. She put a hand to the wound and hissed. "I thought I stopped it."

"Yeah, well... No, you didn't. Don't you have a first-aid kit on this boat?"

"The guys must have taken it with them down to the dig," she said.

Ian muttered something she was grateful not to hear, then removed his sling and shucked off his T-shirt. Using his teeth and good hand, he tore a couple of strips off the bottom.

She noticed him using the hand of his injured arm also. Not well, but using it. He was healing really fast. Strange.

"Come here," he said.

She didn't. His naked torso was every bit as broad

and well-defined as it had looked under the thermal shirt when she reset his shoulder. Fine hair dusted his chest. She struggled not to stare and lost.

He held up the pieces of torn shirt. "Do you want to keep bleeding?"

Gull cries drifted overhead in the cool air. She shook out of her daze and leaned toward him, presenting her arm.

He knelt on the floor of the boat beside her chair. He laid a strip of cloth over the wound and wrapped it with fast, economical motions, as though he didn't want to touch her any more than necessary. She couldn't blame him. This morning when he woke, she doubted gunfire had been on his agenda.

She started to apologize, but he had finished and sat back in his seat. "That should hold it for a while." His gaze found hers. "I want some answers."

It was work to hold that stare. She tried glancing away, but the only alternative was his body. She snapped her attention back to his face. "Aren't you going to freeze out here like that?"

He reached behind the seats for her coat and held it up with a question in his eyes. She shrugged, and he draped it over his shoulders. "I'm all ears."

Ah. Therein lay the reason for this mid-ocean pause. "Out here where you think I can't get away from you."

"Can you?"

"Yes."

Ian reached into his pocket and withdrew the amulet. With a hard look at her, he dangled it from his fist over the edge of the boat. "Can you now?"

She twitched, wanting to lunge for the necklace,

but stayed seated by sheer force of will. "What makes you think I wouldn't throw *you* overboard?" she said in a rush.

His eyes burned with a look that infuriated her even as it made her heart beat faster. "Why would you have caught me at the cliff instead of letting me fall, if you wanted to get rid of me?"

She sucked in a long breath. Hearing him speak of her abilities aloud brought it home:

Someone knew. There could be no more hiding. As much as that realization terrified her, a sense of relief flooded her body, so strong that it made her want to cry.

Someone knew.

He studied her, hard-eyed, suspicion traced in every line of his posture as if he were watching a venomous snake for the moment of attack. She bit her lip, just managing to stop a flood of tears. She'd be damned if she let him see her crumble.

"What—*exactly*—are you?" he demanded.

Alarm bells clanged at the hostility in his voice. She had to force her voice past them. "You've seen me shapeshift. I can read minds sometimes."

"I've got time for the long version." He put the necklace back into his pocket. The shuttered look on his face raised panicky flutters in her belly.

She drew a long breath. "Telekinesis. I caught you with telekinesis."

"How did you get telekinesis?"

"It's not like they hand it out in stores! It just happened one day. I didn't know what it was, and I was too scared to tell my parents. I was afraid of it for a long time."

"And now you're not."

His flat, blunt words stabbed at her heart. He might as well have slapped her down into a seat in an interrogation room. They traded stares. "Yeah. Now I'm not."

"When did your father die? How did he die?"

Her thoughts flew to the amulet in Ian's pocket. "What has any of this got to do with my father?"

"Maybe nothing. Could be more. This stuff might be genetic."

Icy dread crawled across her skin. This time, she did hug herself. "I'm done talking to you."

Quick as lightning, he reached forward and snatched the boat keys from the ignition. "This necklace has to be important if you're willing to risk being shot to fix it, Sara. That's not even going there about you risking *me* being shot at. You're not getting it back until you talk."

She felt naked. Worse than she had at the inlet. Then, she'd seen desire in his eyes.

Now, she saw only hatred. "This isn't about me," she said, startled. "It's about you."

"Never mind me," he snapped.

"What is it?" she asked. "What happened to you?"

"How did your father die?"

Pain and betrayal surged anew through every cell in her body, and that little girl from twenty years ago gave a silent wail of outrage. "He. Was. Murdered."

Chapter Five

Murder.

He didn't want to draw parallels. Not with her. *Especially* not with her.

Memories rushed him. He held his breath and tried like hell to stop them, but they came anyway, clear as the day they'd happened.

He saw his childhood home in his mind. The stranger in their kitchen raised a hand toward the knife block on the counter. Ian watched, stunned, as a knife flew through the air without help and sank into his father's chest. He screamed and shot toward the stranger with all the rage his ten-year-old body could muster. His mother shouted behind him. *Don't hurt my boy, please don't hurt my boy...*

His eyes snapped open. Sara sat straight up in her seat, hands fisted in her lap. She shuddered when their gazes met. "Can I have my keys back now?" she asked. Her voice trembled.

Ian searched for something to say, fought for a calm voice as he said it. "How was he murdered?"

Her gaze didn't budge from his even as she flinched. "I don't know. He was staying late at the college when it happened. I was only a kid."

He frowned. He'd suspected, for one tense minute, that his father's murderer had been *her* father. Lots of things were genetic. Why not telekinesis? The rage drained out of him as fast as it had boiled up, leaving confusion in its wake.

The killer hadn't been Sara's father. That man had been shot by the police soon after killing Daniel Waverly. A better death than he deserved. "What about your sister?"

Sara's eyes went green so fast it gave him chills. Her voice was rock-steady when she spoke. "Faith's different. And she's none of your business."

"And your mother? Is she 'different,' too?"

"No. And I better not hear you ask about my family again."

Somewhere underneath his distaste, he felt oddly moved by her swift and ferocious defense of her family. It only made him angrier to have any kinship with her in that way. He shrugged, trying to ease the knots in his shoulders. "What about the wolf? How do you do the wolf?"

She fidgeted. "It's a shapeshift. I just think about it, and it happens. It's harder than telekinesis."

He paused for a long minute, struggling with conflicting emotions. "You saved my life. Thank you."

She gave a stiff nod.

"How did you get away from me at the cliff?"

"I changed into a bird," she said.

Excitement flashed along every nerve in his body, betraying him. He had to force himself to remain still, when all he wanted was to jump up and grab her in his surprise. "Can you talk to them? Other animals, when you change?"

"I—I've never tried."

His mouth dropped open. "Do you realize the advances we could make in animal behavior if we could communicate with them?'"

"What do you expect me to do, start a road show?"

"Sara, this could change science as we know it."

"I can't tell anyone!" she protested. "If people find out I can do these things, what do you think is going to happen to me?"

He watched her a few seconds more. Her shoulders arched as if she expected an attack. Her fingers, clasped on her knees until the knuckles were white, shifted once, twice, three times. He realized then that her fear lay not in his knowledge of her abilities, but that he would expose her to others.

Would I?

For a frightening second, he thought he might. Her very existence made her dangerous. And valuable, to the right people.

She looked away, rubbing her arms. When she met his stare again, her eyes had changed back to hazel, wide and intent. He knew she was wondering what he'd do, now that he'd heard her secret. And he knew he couldn't betray her, no matter what she was.

But he could learn about her. "I'll make you a deal."

She jerked in her seat and pursed her lips as if she were trying to bite back words. For a moment, there was only the sound of water lapping against the boat.

Hardly able to believe his own mouth was forming the statement, he added, "You help me with my birds, and I say nothing about any of this."

"Are you serious?"

He tossed her the boat keys and cursed his own madness. "Let's just get off the water."

****

They arrived back at Ian's camp by midday. He entered the tent ahead of her. Dropping her coat, he grabbed a flannel shirt lying rumpled at the foot of his bed.

Sara caught sight of several long, faint scars criss-crossing his back. Lean muscle rippled under the damaged skin. She drew in a breath, but couldn't stop staring.

He pulled the shirt over his shoulders and turned around. He stiffened as their gazes met. She felt the blood drain from her face.

Hostility flickered in his expression, then vanished into resignation. "Don't ask."

"How do you expect me to trust you if you get to ask all the questions?"

He shoved his hand into his pocket, then came out with the amulet and demanded, "What is this thing?"

"I don't know."

"You don't know. You're getting shot for it, and you don't know what it is."

"That's right. Can I have it back now?"

He came forward and handed it to her. She took it and looped it over her head, then tucked it into her shirt.

"If you have no idea what it is, why do you hide it?" he asked.

"You tell me about those scars on your back, and I'll tell you what I know about this necklace."

He opened the first-aid kit on his table. "Sit down."

Stalking to his cot, she flopped on the edge and began pulling at the strips of cloth over her wound.

"I'll get it," he said, sitting beside her and putting the open kit at his feet. He slid the point of a pair of scissors under the makeshift bandages and cut them away.

She gave a nervous chuckle. "Next injury's your turn." When he didn't respond, she fell silent and watched him work. At last she added, "Tell me about your back."

"Tell me about your necklace."

"I asked you first."

"Are we doing the grade-school thing now?" He gave her a brief look of amusement that washed away the serious look on his face and set her belly fluttering, at complete odds with her apprehension. When he applied antiseptic to her wound, she cringed at the sting.

He jerked his hand away, but she couldn't tell whether he was still leery of her, or sorry he'd hurt her. "Fine," she said irritably. "We think Dad was murdered for this necklace. We don't—"

"'We,' meaning you and Faith."

"Yes. Can I finish, since you want to know so badly?"

He went back to applying the antiseptic. "Go on."

She suspected it was easier for him to look at her injury than meet her gaze. That stung more than the wound. "We don't know what it is, and we don't know what it does. It's old. It's important enough to kill someone over. It's a stupid piece of rock, and I want my father back."

Ian picked up the first-aid kit and set it on his knees. He looked at her at last. Something dark and heart-rending flashed in his eyes and was gone before she could interpret it. He shrugged his good shoulder. "Why fix the thing, if you don't know what to do with it?"

"My sister..." She trailed off, wary of speaking about Faith. Talking with Ian was a swampy, trackless journey with no indication of where to step next. She swallowed. "Our father would have destroyed it if he hadn't intended to do something with it. What about your back?"

He looked down at the kit and concentrated on tearing open a package of tape stitches. His jaw muscles twitched. This close, she smelled a chalky scent on his clothes, and under that, a warm, undeniably male scent that unsettled her to her very bones.

But then he spoke. "Knife scars. I was ten. It's what you get when you try to protect your parents from a telekinetic."

He said it so fast, it took her a few seconds to absorb the meaning of his words. The world shifted sideways. "Th-There's another one?"

"There *was*. The cops shot him." Ian pressed the tape stitches over her wound and closed up the kit. He sprang up from the cot and dropped the kit on his camp table. "I don't think I need to explain any more of what happened. We're done here."

In shock, she bent to scoop up her coat from the tent floor. Her hand trembled so hard it took a second try. Her gaze found his broad back as if she could see the scars under his flannel shirt. "I d-don't know what to say—"

"You can't undo what happened."

She ached and shook and stared at him, frantic for answers, afraid to ask the questions. Who was the man? What had he wanted? Why had he hurt Ian's family? She couldn't imagine using her power to hurt another human being.

Ian turned on his heel. By the look of censure on his face, he could imagine such a thing well enough.

Sara's hurt gave way to a stab of righteous indignation. She stood up. "Thank you for going with me to Mainland. I won't ask you for any more favors."

"You still owe me."

She jerked to a stop. "Owe you? You just forced me to blow any protection I have against people who might want to exploit—"

"The birds. That's all I'm asking."

She shuddered. "You're willing to hate what I am, but not so much that you won't use it to your own advantage?"

He had the grace to look ashamed—for a moment, at least. That dogged expression returned to his features, as though he were compelling himself to face her.

As though she might shapeshift into a monster and bite him.

She rushed out of the tent without waiting for him to speak further.

All the way back to the dig, she tried not to think of him. The memory of his vicious glare pierced her over and over. She had never told anyone but Faith about her gifts. Now she knew why.

The sun threw long late-afternoon shadows by the time she got to the camp. She found her sister taking samples of earth to be shipped back to Eurocon. When Faith spotted her, she climbed out of the dig trench. "How'd it go?"

Sara struggled to find enough anger to push aside the hurt. "Next time you ask me to take Ian somewhere, you'd better recheck your gut feelings."

Faith glanced toward the dig, where Dustin and Thomas still labored in the afternoon sun. When she looked back, her gaze fell on the bloody tear in Sara's coat sleeve. Her sun-bronzed skin paled. "What happened?"

"We had some trouble, but the amulet's fixed. I'm tired. I'm going to lie down for a while. We'll talk later." Ignoring her sister's concerned frown, she turned and hurried away to her tent.

The minute she entered it and closed the tent door, hot tears spilled down her cheeks. The scars on his back flashed in her memory again. So many of them, and he was just a boy when they'd happened. Her stomach turned.

He knew everything and he hated her for it. Just because of what she was.

She almost hated herself.

****

Digging advanced rapidly over the next few days. The find began to show signs of being more than just a field wall. Sara allowed the flurry of activity to consume her thoughts, trying to forget Ian. He'd be leaving, anyway, if he hadn't already. She'd told her sister only that he knew of her abilities and wouldn't speak of them to anyone else. Since that day, his name hadn't crossed her lips. She couldn't bring herself to speak it. Every time his image flashed in her memory, it was coupled with that look of distaste and distrust.

She spent her waking hours with pick and shovel, laboring in spite of her injury. When it became too dark to see outside, she worked on her laptop, entering measurements, logging soil compositions, and keeping a precise record of their progress. Anxious for hard data, she logged onto her computer twice a day to check for lab results from Eurocon.

The e-mail response came at last on the morning of the spring equinox. Without reading it, she rushed from her tent in search of her sister. She found Faith surveying the perimeter of the site. "Hey. It came. Lamb responded."

Faith shot upright, all attention. "Well? What'd he say?"

"I didn't read it yet. Come on."

They hurried back to Sara's tent. She dropped into her chair, clicked on the e-mail, then read it aloud. "'Sara—The lab results from your dig samples suggest the find to be of Norse origin—'" She let out a wild whoop. Everything their father had worked for might be right under their noses. At last.

"Come on, finish!" Faith danced in place and waved her hand at the screen.

Sara made herself sit still. "'Carbon dating placed the samples within the period of Viking occupation of Shetland. Should you find artifacts, please photograph them immediately and send them here to the lab. I will be coming to the site within the week with more crew to oversee—'"

"Here it comes," Faith snapped. "He's going to send for Flintrop, I just know it."

"He can't. Shetland was Dad's baby. I'll kill him if he tries it!" Jittery, she started tapping her heel.

"Hello?" came a male voice from outside the tent.

Ian. Still here? Sara clapped a hand over her bouncing knee, but it did nothing to stop her jitters. She found Faith's gaze. "Why don't you go tell Thomas and Dustin? I'll catch up with you."

Faith responded with a doubtful expression and crossed her arms. "Why don't you just tell me what's going on between you two?"

"Nothing I can't deal with."

With a last, unconvinced smirk, Faith ducked outside. Sara glanced around her tent as if it might provide some excuse for remaining within. Nothing. She'd have to face him. Resigned, she emerged in her sister's wake.

Ian strode toward the camp wearing a T-shirt, fleece jacket, and jeans.

And no sling.

Faith stood outside with her hands on her hips. She cast a brief, apprehensive look at Sara before she called to Ian. "Hey. Didn't realize you had stayed. Your sling's off. Better already?"

He came to a stop before them. "Yeah, it feels pretty good. Two days ago, I was photographing some gannets, and the tripod tipped over. I caught it without thinking, but it didn't hurt. It's just about back to normal." He flexed the fingers of his left hand and waved his arm.

"That's great." Faith met Sara's gaze with an expression that made it clear she sensed an undercurrent of tension.

"I'll catch up with you," Sara said reluctantly.

Faith gave her a long look that echoed the reluctance. "All right. If you hear anything else from Lamb, let me know. See you around, Ian."

Ian jerked his chin in the direction of Faith's retreating figure. "How's the dig coming?"

She struggled with nerves. Why was he still here? *Why, why, why?* "You didn't walk all the way down here for small talk."

"Well, yes and no. I came to say I'm sorry."

"Sorry for which part? Forcing me to confess my laundry list of unsavory traits, or being willing to make use of them?"

He sighed and angled his head toward her tent. "Inside?"

She allowed him into the tent ahead of her. She caught herself watching the way he angled his broad shoulders through the narrow doorway and cursed under her breath.

He didn't sit. "I don't have a right to accuse you of anything just because you're...what you are."

Okay. Unexpected, but not unwelcome. She crossed her arms and waited for the other shoe to drop.

"And you don't have a right to involve me in whatever you're doing with that necklace—"

Her temper flared. "Listen here, you—"

"—*without* telling me the whole story. What your sister is, what your father was. Why you had to drag me into it when you could have brought one of your own people with you to Mainland."

She glowered at him, afraid that if she didn't, he'd see how much his contempt had hurt. "I think I told you not to ask about my family."

Advancing, he said, "I'm asking anyway. You owe me an explanation."

"I seem to be owing you a whole lot of things, while I get nothing in return."

He laid his hands on her elbows. "Sara—"

"Get your hands off me."

He snatched them away and raised them into the air. The quick, defensive gesture pained her. Did he think she'd use her power against him? "Why aren't you gone?" she snapped.

He looked her up and down, then scraped a hand through his hair. "I don't want to fight with you."

"At least we're in agreement on something. Only in my case, it's because I can't afford to."

"I told you, I'm not going to squeal on you," he said. "If I was going to do so, I'd have done it by now, wouldn't I?" He dropped into a chair.

She remained standing, wrapping herself in offended dignity.

After a few minutes of charged silence, he sat forward just enough to pull a leather journal from his back pocket. He laid it on his knee and studied it as though it were a precious artifact, staring at it instead of her. "The man who attacked my family wanted something from my dad. I don't know what. My dad wouldn't cooperate, so the guy killed him. When I tried to fight back, the sick son of a bitch spent the next half-hour using telekinesis to draw little knife marks all over my back while my mother cried. Is that enough information for you?"

Bile rose in her throat. She swallowed back the burn and sank onto her cot, rubbing her arms against the sudden chill in the tent. She longed to say something, but words lodged in her throat. They stared at one another for a long, uncomfortable stretch.

At last, Ian spoke. "Anyway, there's a reason I'm still here." He opened the book on his knee and flipped through it. He stood and carried it to her, holding it out.

She saw a beautiful pencil sketch of a falcon in flight. *"Falco p. peregrinus,"* she murmured, reading the words scribbled below the sketch.

"A Eurasian peregrine falcon. An endangered species."

She searched her memory. "I thought they delisted the peregrine."

"The American peregrine was delisted. This is a different subspecies. I need your help with him."

"Him?"

"I'm pretty sure it's a male. He's been roosting on the cliff. I saw him the day before I dislocated my shoulder." He closed the book, then put it back in his pocket.

"You want me to help you—what? Take pictures?"

"That, and get some information on his habits. You said you were a zoo minor. This is a big deal for my work, finding this bird out here."

"I have a full-time project going on, Ian. I can't just leave it to help you with this." Not to mention, the idea of working shoulder-to-shoulder with him sounded far too appealing, in spite of their mutual misgivings. She stole a sidelong glance at him. His attention was on the page. Expressive eyes. She remembered the way he'd looked at her the instant before kissing her. Hungry. Possessive. She wrapped her arms around herself to quell a giddy shiver and said nothing further.

His gaze came up. "I left my work to help you with your necklace."

She hugged herself harder.

He mistook her silence for reluctance. "If I help you dig, will you come climbing with me?" When she still remained wordless, he added, "What, I can't manage a shovel?"

Words. Say something. "What about your shoulder?"

"I already said it's healing. Besides, if the rope breaks this time, I've got you right there to back me up."

"Don't joke about that." She shuddered, not wanting to think of what might have happened to him if she hadn't gotten there in time.

He crouched in front of her. The motion washed his chalky scent and body heat around her. He stilled, seeming to realize how close they now were. She held her breath and jammed her hands between her knees to keep herself still.

Those eyes. Those eyes traveled all over her. Curious. Cautious. Something more that was too dangerous to name. She shivered and wondered how it would feel if his hands followed where his gaze led. Shivered more, because as scared as she was, she wanted it.

He snapped out of it first. "I'm calling a truce. Or trying to. Give me a day, two at most. I'll help you for today, and you try rock climbing with me. If you don't like it, we don't do it." He extended his hand.

There was no way out of this but to touch him. She took his hand. The sensation of his warm skin on hers set off a shivery chain reaction that started from the tips of her fingers and traveled all the way down to her feet. She couldn't let go. She wanted to stay angry with him for the way he'd cornered her. Outraged. Something. Anything that didn't feel quite so much like the need to kiss him again. Flustered, she dropped his hand and jumped to her feet to move away.

Ian stood, too. "*Please* help me with the falcon?"

Absorbed in the movement of his mouth, she hardly registered his words. Her pulse raced. She managed a nod.

He reached for her hand again and shook it, smiling a little. The contact surged through her body. His gaze dropped to her mouth and the smile faded. Her every nerve screamed "Kiss me," and to hell with their baggage. *Do it, just do it.*

As if he'd heard her thoughts, he bent his head closer. His gaze caught hers and sizzled.

A wild shriek from outside brought them reeling apart. *Faith.* In an instant, her fog of desire washed away in a flood of fear. Sara bolted from the tent to see what had happened.

Dustin stood at the edge of the dig, chuckling. Faith sprawled on the ground several feet away, shaking with laughter.

"What's wrong?" Sara called. God, she was getting jumpy.

Her sister clambered to her feet and windmilled her finger in the air. "We were doing the victory dance over the good news, and I slipped."

Thomas ambled toward them with a bucket of tools. "Don't get victorious just yet. We've got a long way to go, and that's not counting the uncertainty of finding any artifacts."

"Spoilsport," Faith groused.

Sara felt Ian come up behind her. Her skin tingled in response. "We'll have help," she blurted. "Lambertson's coming in a few days with more people. And until then, Ian's offered to pitch in."

Faith, Dustin, and Thomas swiveled as one to stare at her. Sara took a quick step away from Ian. "In exchange for my helping him with his wildlife project. I'll need a couple hours the next few afternoons. I'll make up the time after dinner...uh, doing charts or something."

Okay, now she was babbling. And why did she feel like she had to explain this to them? She wanted to go back to her tent and crawl under the cot in mortification.

"Lambertson," Ian said. "He's a big-time archaeologist, right?"

"Yeah. How'd you know?"

"Luis Rivero talks about him all the time. Lambertson's kind of like his god."

Sara gave a small, edgy laugh. "Yeah, he has that effect on people. I guess we should start by giving you a tour of our project, then?"

"Sure." He cast a meaningful glance back at her tent, but then he grinned and started toward the ruin.

She offered up a silent prayer for strength, and jogged after him.

As she showed Ian around the dig, the team fell back into the rhythm of their work. The men appeared delighted to have another strong back to add to their crew, if only for a little while. Faith didn't seem so easily persuaded. Her sister labored over a plot of earth with her shovel, not speaking. Sara picked up another pair of shovels for herself and Ian, then descended into the pit.

Faith glared at her. *Not now,* Sara mouthed, glaring back.

For most of the day, she worked side-by-side with Ian on one end of the excavation site. He asked intelligent questions, and listened to her answers with a scientist's ear. His interest in her work surprised and pleased her.

She found it hard not to stare when he hefted shovelfuls of earth as if they weighed nothing. *Thunk.* The shovel bit into the peat. *Shoosh.* Soil and stone hissed off the metal blade and sailed into the wheelbarrow outside the pit. Almost before that scoop had *thump*ed to a rest in the wheelbarrow, he'd started on the next. The sheer physical demand of digging often left her body aching by the end of the day.

Ian seemed to have enough stamina for both of them.

Heated flames poured into her cheeks and she looked away...but not for long. Her gaze returned to him as if drawn by a magnet. He'd thrown aside the fleece jacket as the day's warmth increased, and the back of his T-shirt was dark with a vee of sweat. His hair lay plastered to his scalp. A bead of perspiration ran down his unshaven cheek. Did men have any idea how sexy they looked while doing manual labor?

He caught her eye and smiled. The work seemed to have loosened his knots where she was concerned...or at least he was willing to put them aside for now. "Tired already?"

"Already? We've been at it for hours." The remark didn't sound right the minute it left her mouth. He grinned, and she knew he'd caught the unintended double meaning.

She bent over her shovel and thrust it into the peat. "How's your shoulder?" she flung at him.

"Fine. How's your ego?"

"What?"

He laughed, full and throaty. The sound rang out across the moor and vibrated in her spine. "I think I've done most of the work here. Not bad for a rookie, wouldn't you say, Doc?"

She scanned the pit and saw that he'd cleared over half their plot while she'd been lost in her thoughts. With a look of chagrin, she said, "You'd have made a decent archaeologist."

He leaned an elbow on the handle of his shovel. His dimples resurfaced. "I can find more interesting ways to get dirty."

Was he flirting with her? Why was he flirting with *her*?

Did she dare flirt back?

Should she?

Oh, God, how she wanted to.

Dustin's light-brown head was bent over the sieve box. Thomas had taken away another wheelbarrow of peat. Faith swung a pick into the earth a few plots away.

Ian cast an eye at the lowering angle of the sun. "Ready to get out of here?"

"Yeah." She wiped sweat from her brow and came away with grimy fingers. "Ugh."

"We could go for a swim first." He leaned closer and his smile vanished. "I promise not to sneak up on you this time."

His nearness almost overwhelmed her. Every molecule of her body seemed to fizz with awareness of him. The very air between them heated. "I don't—"

"For crying out loud, you two. Go swim!"

Sara jumped and spun around.

Faith laid her pick over one shoulder and wound her way through the markers. She grabbed Sara's elbow and pulled her a few steps away. "I can feel the sparks shooting off you two way over there," she hissed in

Sara's ear. "You are *scrambling me*. Get out of here so I can hear myself think, for God's sake."

Horrified, Sara said, "I am *not* sparking."

"In about five minutes, I'm going to radio the fire brigade from Unst to come put you out. *Go.*" She gave Sara a little shove in Ian's direction, then stomped back to her plot.

"What was that all about?" Ian asked, pushing sweaty bangs off his forehead.

"Nothing. Let's get out of here." She walked ahead of him toward the edge of the pit, as fast as she could without making it look like running.

Chapter Six

Ian stared as Sara waded into the inlet without looking back. She shivered as the water inched up her slender legs. His gaze traveled up the back of a sensible red bathing suit that had driven the sense right *out* of him the instant he saw her in it. There was nothing wrong with looking at her, he told himself. But oh, God, she had curves in all the right places.

Then she ducked under and came up with water sluicing down her back, and he wanted to do a whole lot more than look. *Get in there, you idiot.*

Dustin had offered him a pair of swimming trunks—quite possibly the ugliest Ian had ever seen. He'd refused. His jeans were good enough. He hoped they would also do a better job of keeping his growing interest in her dripping, hourglass figure in check.

Before he could embarrass himself, he stripped off his T-shirt and tossed it on the sand beside his jacket. He strode down the beach and splashed into the water.

Cold water jolted his exertion-heated body, and he huffed in surprise. His arousal fled before an onslaught of chills. Thank God for that.

Watching him shivering with the sudden cold, she laughed. His pulse jumped at the soft sound as though she'd touched him.

He'd thought that by forcing her to admit to her abilities, he could drive away the blazing desire to kiss her the way he had the night of the storm. Even now, he battled the urge to feel her satiny skin under his hands again.

She was everywhere, damn her. At his camp, she haunted his waking hours. A chill would fly up his back as he worked. He'd get the feeling that if he just turned his head, she'd be there waiting. Hair whipping in the wind, arms reaching for him...

He'd have taken a hundred such days over the nights. At night, his dreams boiled with images of a blood-covered man who ordered Ian to help her.

What he wanted right now didn't qualify as help.

"Ian. What's on your mind?"

"I thought you could read minds."

"I can. I choose not to. It's invasion of privacy." She waded closer and sank neck-deep.

Good thing she felt that way, because the direction of his thoughts might have earned him jail time. Below the water's surface, he saw the glint of gold in her repaired necklace. The stone pendant rested just above the curve of her breasts, onyx-black against her opaline skin. He warred with himself, aching to kiss her, longing to retreat.

She backed away and dipped to her chin. Her hair swirled on the water, dark and slick as sealskin. "What's so important about this falcon of yours?"

Good, a safe topic. "Aside from being an endangered species? I'm hoping for a breeding pair."

"Was there another?"

"Just the one. If he has a mate, I haven't seen her yet."

Breeding? Mate? Okay, maybe not so safe a topic. His body agreed in the most painful way possible.

Should have gone with the ugly shorts, he thought, wishing he could loosen the fit of his jeans without being obvious.

"So the falcon is why you haven't left for Mainland?"

Yes. No. "Partly." Frustrated, he dove underwater for some distance. He waded back up the inlet until the water level dropped to his waist, and began stretching out his shoulder.

"Does it hurt much? I can't see how digging all day has helped it," she said.

"It's all right. Better than it's been. I'm off the painkillers, at least."

He heard water slosh. He looked around and confirmed that she'd submerged.

She surfaced right in front of him. "Will you tell me something?" she asked.

"Hmm?"

"When that man attacked your family..."

He angled a look at her. She wouldn't meet it. "Say whatever you're not saying," he prompted.

She took a breath. "Did his eyes change color the way mine do?"

He stopped working his shoulder and frowned. "I don't remember."

She knew he was lying; he saw it on her face. He remembered like it had just happened. One moment, the man's eyes had been nondescript brown, and the next...

Then came the knife. Then his father's grunt of shock, and the *thud* as he crumpled to the floor.

Days earlier, Ian had seen someone else call an object across thin air. A tiny waif of a girl, and her eyes had changed, too. After his father's death, he'd gone out of his way to avoid her.

Until now.

Sara's lips parted. "Did he...? How did he...?"

Her gaze flicked away and back like an indecisive dragonfly. Ian saw how much she yearned to ask the questions he didn't want to answer. He steeled himself. "You want to know how much like you he was."

"Never mind," she said, too fast. She turned and started to wade off.

He caught her by the hand. "Gold." He let go, and wished he hadn't. "Just before it happened. They were gold."

She crouched in the water. Ian, still standing, tried not to think about how close she was to his groin. He flew through a mental recital of the Latin name for every bird he could think of. When that didn't work, he sat down in the shallows beside her, shifting furtively to ease the tightness in his pants, and the conflicting tension in his neck.

"He did the same thing you did," Ian said at last. "With your necklace, as a kid. Raised his hand and—" He reached into the air and waved his fingers.

"It's not the same," she said at once. "*I'm* not the same."

He dunked his head backward, washing off the rest of the sweat. Saltwater trickled stinging into his eyes, and he wiped it away. For a time, they both fell silent.

"My sister has pyrokinesis, among other things," she said at last. "Fires, she can light fires. She could be dangerous, but she's not. We've never hurt another person in our lives."

"And your father?"

"I never saw him do anything like what Faith and I

can do," she said. "But he was a good man. A good father."

"So was mine."

Bird cries sounded in the air over the surging of ocean on rock. Ian looked up. A flock of gulls passed overhead. Reminded of his work, he got to his feet once more. "We should go." He offered his hand to help her up.

She took it, but released it again as soon as she'd gained her feet. Wet tendrils of her hair settled in the hollow between her breasts. Ian gritted his teeth. *Elanoides forficatus, Buteo jamaicensis, Pandion haliaetus.* He spun away, then stalked out of the water after his shirt and jacket.

She'd brought a sweatshirt and jeans. He found it easier to breathe once she'd put them on over her bathing suit.

But not by much.

****

During the walk back to Ian's camp, he explained the basics of rock climbing. Sara tried to listen, but couldn't concentrate. She told herself she only lagged behind because she was thinking about his climbing instructions, but then she looked up.

He'd tucked his shirt and jacket under his arm, and she had an uninterrupted view of his naked back. She followed the line of his broad shoulders, down through a mesmerizing vee to his narrow hips. As he walked, she stared at the play of muscle. He had such a beautiful back. She hated to linger on the scars.

Seeming to notice she'd fallen behind, he paused. "Something wrong?"

She shook her head and hurried to catch up.

They said nothing more until they arrived at his tent. He showed her how to buckle his spare belt and ropes and adjust them to fit her body, then donned his own gear. "Ready?" he asked.

"You know you're crazy to do this kind of thing voluntarily?"

He grinned and led the way to the cliff.

When they reached it, Sara craned over the precipice with apprehension. "So you *want* me to jump off a cliff?"

He laughed. "It's easier than it seems," he told her. "The ropes do a lot of the work. I'll show you. Grab the other helmet."

"Are we rock climbing or doing high-rise construction?"

He buckled his own helmet. "The falcon likes to dive-bomb if he thinks you're too close to his roost. Ever been around a pissed-off bird with sharp talons?"

Shrugging, she picked up the other helmet and buckled it on. "Aren't we going to scare him off?" she asked.

"We've worked out a mutual safe distance. The helmets are just insurance against him redrawing his lines." He gave his anchor points an experimental tug, then started over the edge of the cliff. Feeding out the rope, he lowered himself down, placing his feet in the sturdiest crevices. When he was a short way below, he looked back up. "Come on."

"I think I'd rather fly," she said, hanging back.

He cocked his head. "You could do that, couldn't you?"

Was he teasing her? No, not about her powers. He couldn't be. "Yes, if I shapeshifted. I can't levitate myself, or I'd be floating down there instead of attempting suicide with this contraption." Setting her jaw, she knelt and climbed down. The ends of her hair, still damp, billowed in the updraft.

Placing her feet where he instructed her, she made it to his level before her foot slipped on a ledge. She yelped and started to slide. Gravel spilled away under her.

He grabbed her by the harness and steadied her as the ropes caught. "I've got you. You're doing fine."

"You're loving this, aren't you?"

"A little," he admitted, flashing a dimple at her. "It's nice to be back on the other end of the professional know-how."

"So this time, I get to be the rookie."

He chuckled and continued down the cliff. "Keep it coming, rookie."

He showed her how to rappel downward until they got within sight of the roost. He swung near enough to put a hand on her arm and stop her descent, then pointed.

The roost huddled in a crag out of the wind, no more than a shallow ledge of granite. Crouched on its edge, watching them with suspicion, was the falcon.

Excitement surged through Sara. She bent close to Ian's ear and spoke in an exuberant whisper. "He's beautiful. This is amazing!"

Ian lifted the camera hanging around his neck and leaned back in his harness to photograph the bird. "And you thought this wasn't going to be any fun. Check out the view. This is prime real estate."

At his gesture, she turned around in her harness. The lowering sun glittered on the waves. Birds keened below, and the ocean pounded in her ears. Unst lay just visible on the horizon. "Wow. It feels like we're the only two people on earth out here." And that, she thought privately, had far too much appeal right now.

"This is why I'd hate being tied to a desk all the time," he told her.

The falcon took flight and soared away over the water. She watched it go, captivated by its grace. When she looked back, she saw Ian smiling at her. "Thank you."

"What for?"

"For the cliffside with a view," she said, then smiled. "What do you need my help with?"

He sobered at once. "I was hoping you'd try an experiment with me. If you don't mind..."

She frowned when he didn't continue. "Shapeshifting."

"If you can," he added. "Just to see if you can understand him. I wouldn't ask you to get too close or do anything dangerous. And I'd really like to know what it's like to fly."

Underneath his guarded exterior, she saw a flash of wonder that made her heartbeat skip. She felt the same thing every time she shapeshifted. "It's scary. Incredible." She cast her gaze up at the top of the cliff. "Did you ever just stand up there with your arms spread and let the wind rush through your fingers?"

He shook his head.

"That's what it's like. Stepping off the edge of the world."

Something flickered in his eyes then, the subtle but unmistakable connection of understanding. "That's the way it is when I climb."

They stayed on the cliffside, talking and birdwatching until the sun began to descend. By the time they reached the top again, she couldn't contain her enthusiasm. "I can't believe you do that for a living. What a rush!"

They removed their gear and sat on the cliff edge, dangling their legs over the side. "Well, it isn't always this much fun," he told her. "The tradeoff is that I have to spend most of the year in a classroom or in board meetings, justifying the fun part of my career."

"Board meetings, ugh." She swung her legs back and forth, heady with the sensation of sitting on the edge of a cliff. With him. And for once, having a conversation that lacked suspicion on both sides.

What a nice change.

Warm with sunshine and good humor, she asked, "What information do you have about peregrine falcons?"

"A few photos, some of my sketches. Nothing else that's specific to the Eurasian subspecies. Why?"

"The more I know about an animal, the easier it is to shapeshift into it." At his look of interest, she hurried to add, "I'm not promising much. I can try it, but I might not be able to keep the shapeshift for long. And as for talking to it, I can't promise anything at all."

He nodded soberly, but she could tell he was bursting with questions. She folded her hands in her lap and wondered why she'd agreed to this insane endeavor. "I'll come tomorrow afternoon. Can I see your sketches?"

"Yeah, they're in my tent." He got to his feet and picked up the rest of their climbing gear.

She took a last look at the copper-gold water and

followed him back to his camp.

Inside, he combed through a stack of books on a table. He handed her a thick volume on North American wildlife. "That one has a good color plate and a writeup on the American peregrine. The Eurasian is similar, so it might be what you're looking for. I've got a couple days' worth of notes on our friend Horus down there—"

"Horus?" she interrupted, then smiled. "The Egyptian falcon god?"

"Seemed appropriate." He flashed that dimple again.

She clasped the book to her chest. "Well, all we have to do next is find him a mate, and you'll have your Hathor."

"Who's Hathor?"

"She was the wife of Horus. Goddess of music, dance, motherhood, and"—she cleared her throat and opened the book, staring hard at a picture of a grizzly bear—"sexuality." She hugged the book to her body like a shield while her cheeks flamed.

He crossed the tent. When she looked up, he was holding his journal, flipping through the pages. Their gazes met.

Ian lowered his journal. He glanced down at her lips, and ages passed in silence. Sara wanted to run away, run toward him, escape, ignore it, and savor it, all at once. She swallowed, not knowing what to do. Not knowing what *he* wanted to do.

He took a hesitant step closer and then stopped, rigid with tension. "Oh, for Christ's sake." He pitched his journal on the cot, strode forward, and kissed her.

The contact exploded through her. Her every nerve fired like a Roman candle. She breathed him in, smelling saltwater and fresh air as he plunged his hands through her hair and pulled her closer. His stubble scraped her chin. With a muffled moan, she parted her lips.

He slanted his mouth over hers, deepening the kiss. Oh, God, everything she remembered about their last kiss was wrong, so wrong, only a shadow of what he really felt like pressed against her. Invading her mouth, invading her space, tearing her senses asunder and putting them back together in totally the wrong order. Careless of anything but the need to touch him, she dropped the book.

It fell on his foot. "Ow!" He lurched backward.

"Sorry!"

He gave her a rueful, sidelong look and sat down on his cot. "Was that a hint?"

She blushed, still feeling the tingle of his mouth on hers. "No."

"Good." He grabbed her by the hand and pulled her down onto his lap for another scorching kiss. His mouth left hers to skim along her jawline. She gasped, feeling him nip at the tender skin just under her ear, and splayed her hands across his back to trace the ridges of his shoulder blades under the taut muscle.

In one fluid motion, he raised her arms and pulled her sweatshirt off over her head, then tossed it to the floor. His hands settled on her waist, burning hot through the thin fabric of her bathing suit. He bent his head to her throat and rained feather kisses there. It felt so good...

Too good. The last time she'd been like this with anyone... Had it really been so long?

Oh, God, how embarrassing.

She felt the weight of the amulet lift from her chest as he pushed it aside. Realizing where his trail of kisses was leading, she stiffened.

He stopped at once and raised his head. "What?"

Words stuck in her throat and she closed her eyes, trying to blot out humiliating memories. She hugged herself in dismay. Why was it still so hard?

His hands came to rest on her arms, urging them out of their protective embrace. "Don't you want this?"

Oh, how she wanted it. There was no measurement for how she wanted it. She hesitated, trying to put the awkwardness into words, but he was so close, still touching her, confusing her. Had she spent the last couple decades buried in work just to avoid this? "You wouldn't..."

"Understand?" His hands slid down to grasp hers. "Try me."

Her cheeks burned even as she forced the embarrassment down. "I haven't... Not since I was sixteen."

When she stole a look at him, his expression hadn't changed. He waited for her to continue.

"He was popular, good-looking, all of that. I thought he really liked me. We... Things didn't go well the next day. I feel like such an idiot." She tugged one of her hands out of Ian's to rub at the back of her neck. "He spread it all over school. A couple of his swim team friends followed me around for the rest of the year, asking if I'd help them with *their* workouts. I never faced him about it, because I was afraid to get any closer to him, because then he'd find out about my powers, and make everything worse—"

Ian stopped her with a finger over her lips. "Kyle

Wagner?"

"Oh, God." She shot up. Bad enough that she'd spent the rest of her school years trying to live down the undeserved reputation Kyle had put on her...the attention from which had made it all the harder to hide her gifts.

Worse, that the man now kissing her and doing such mind-exploding things to her—and she *still* wanted it—had heard the gossip.

Ian stood, too. "Don't even think about him. He doesn't have a right to be in there," he said, touching her temple.

The gesture was so close to a caress that she arched backward in surprise. "What do you know about him?"

"I know he was a punk, and he ought to have been castrated. He and his little cronies had a bet going on girls. One of them did the same thing to a friend of mine." He touched a finger to the scar over his eyebrow. "That's how I got this. And as for your..." He sighed. "As for what you are, he never found out, did he?"

She shook her head, studying him. "I could have used a friend like you."

As soon as the words were out, she pulled away. She picked up the wildlife book from the floor. "Can I borrow this?"

"Sure."

She moved toward the door.

Ian bent and scooped her sweatshirt off the floor. "Sara...why don't you stick around for dinner?"

She smiled. "Okay."

****

Ian enjoyed Sara's company, which wasn't very

surprising in itself. The surprise was how *much* he enjoyed it. They had talked about their jobs with companionable enthusiasm, and now the sun dipped lower and lower in the sky. "Pass the coffee, would you?" he asked as they finished dinner.

She handed over the pot, and he poured himself a fresh cup. He sniffed it and took a sip, rolled it critically around his tongue, then swallowed.

She wrinkled her nose at him. "Why do you do that? You did the same thing at the pub. It's just coffee, and you look like you're at a wine tasting."

He gave a lopsided smile. "Old habits die hard. My mom owns Waverly's Deli back home. When she opened the shop five years ago, she was looking for the perfect blend of coffee. I got to be the test subject."

"Well, I've tasted the end result, and I think she hit the nail on the head. I go there on my way to work. What's her secret?"

"I could tell you, but then I'd have to kill you."

She shot him a playful scowl, and he chuckled. When she flung a cloth napkin at his head, he caught it and threw it back at her.

Joking with her. Who knew?

She'd be returning to her camp soon. He found himself looking for ways to stall her. Even though he knew what she was, now. Even though he'd spent twenty years believing that anyone with such abilities ought to go straight to hell.

But damn it, she made him laugh—especially when he said something that caught her off guard, and she gave him that cute smirk. Not to mention the way his body reacted when the wind shifted, and her hair lashed around her shoulders. Why, oh, why had he given her that sweatshirt back? He liked the bathing suit a lot better, even though it was getting cold out and he knew if that was all she had on, her nip—

Hot coffee sloshed out of his cup and onto his hand. "Son of a..."

"What's wrong?"

"Nothing. Just me being—damn it—never mind." He lowered the coffee cup to the ground, and sucked on a burned knuckle. His gaze zeroed in on her lips, and he pictured them closing over his fingertips one at a time...

He shut his eyes.

More Latin.

"Cinnamon drop?" she said.

He risked a look. She dug into her pocket for a fistful of something and reached toward him, opening her palm.

Candy. He remembered the maddening, spicy taste of her the first time he'd kissed her. *You're really pushing my good behavior, God.* He took a piece and shucked it out of its wrapper into his mouth. "Thanks."

She did the same with another piece. "I should go. Do you need help with the dishes?"

"No, I've got them," he said, getting up. He offered his hand.

She took it and he pulled her onto her feet. She smiled.

A tiny, sharp pain lanced through him.

He couldn't hate her.

He couldn't even dislike her.

They said their goodbyes, and she walked away down the island.

A slice of sun remained visible on the ocean's horizon, staining the sky with its red-orange glow.

Leaving the dishes, he strolled toward the cliff edge to watch it finish setting.

Just before the last glimmer faded, he spread his arms and let the wind rush through his fingers.

Chapter Seven

Faith sprang awake and sat bolt upright in her cot. A pair of books slid off her chest and plopped on the floor of the tent. She shook her head, trying to clear the fog and decipher what had disturbed her.

The air fizzed with a prickling charge that danced along her skin. Fine hairs along her arms stood on end.

A ghost. She felt it clear as day, urgent, almost frantic. She threw aside the covers and stood up. "You," she whispered, realizing it was the same ghost who'd been trying to contact her since her arrival at Hvitmar. "What is it? Show me."

Barefoot, she followed the current toward the tent door. The moment she stepped outside, it felt as if someone had jammed an ice pick into her gut. She gasped and doubled over in agony.

The island was breathing.

Faith sank to her knees with a moan, holding her belly, fighting against the currents of energy in the air. The ghost hovered near, now on one side, then on the other. She sensed it moving, but couldn't concentrate.

An icy chill settled on her shoulder. She gasped again and jerked away from the contact, her skin crawling. She'd communicated with dozens of ghosts in her thirty years, but never had one touched her. Her shoulder stung with the sensation of frostbite. She sucked in a breath and struggled to her feet.

Vibrating with impatience, the spirit drove her to the dig site. She approached the markers at the edge of the ruin, terrified to go on, but dreading the ghost's touch. The very air trembled around her. She stopped, heaving for breath. "I don't want to do this."

The spirit impelled her forward. The air heated behind her with its urgency. Shrinking away from it, Faith stepped toward the first marker.

Buzzing roared in her ears. A lighting bolt of pain ripped through her body. Her breath whooshed out and she crumpled to the ground. Disjointed voices screamed around her. Nausea twisted in her gut.

The ghost touched her shoulder again. Its chill anchored her senses. For a moment, the touch became a single point of stillness in the maelstrom around her. *It wants...help.*

The other voices screeched again, and the storm of energy swallowed her connection with the ghost. Faith cried out, but could not move. The world spun and went black.

****

A shout tore Sara from her sleep.

Faith.

Sara sprang out of bed and bolted from her tent, ready to annihilate someone with telekinesis. Seeing her sister sprawled on the ground, she rushed forward. "Faith!"

"Sara, no!"

She had a split second to register Ian's shout before he tackled her. His arm snaked around her midsection, and he hauled her back from the dig.

"What are you doing? Let go!" she shrieked, thrashing in his grip. She tried to shapeshift, but he

109

threw his other arm around her and crushed her against him. She wheezed, distracted, unable to force the change.

Ian's heartbeat pounded against her back, and his breath churned in her ear. He reached up to her throat, clawing at the neckline of her tank top. She squirmed, but couldn't break his hold. Grasping the leather lace of her amulet, he jerked, and it broke loose. He released her and staggered back.

Freed, Sara charged toward her sister, then dropped to the ground beside her. "Faith. Faith!"

Dustin and Thomas skidded to a halt before her tent. Dustin drew a rifle on Ian. "Get back!"

Ian stood his ground, clutching his ribs and panting. The amulet swung from his fingers. He eyed the rifle, then looked back toward Sara, his posture rigid.

Dustin cocked the rifle, then trained it again on Ian's figure. "God damn it, I'll shoot!"

Sara turned back to Faith, shaking her shoulder with no effect. Near panic, she tried again with the same result. "Faith. Come on, please, wake up!"

Thomas moved toward her. "Sara."

She spun to her feet and lunged without thinking, reactive, just able to stop her power from surfacing. Thomas caught her. "Get off me!" She struggled, but he grabbed her and held on until she gave up fighting him. Ian's expression remained unreadable in the near-darkness. Sara wrestled away from Thomas to crouch beside Faith's body again, stricken.

Clearly calmer than any of them, Thomas bent over Faith, checking her for wounds. He glanced back over his shoulder. "Dustin, put the gun down."

"The hell I will! What did you do to Faith, you son of a bitch?"

Sara divided a desperate look among Faith's body, Dustin, and Ian. There was no time, no time for this!

Still catching his breath, Ian crossed his arms and hid the amulet in the crook of his elbow. "I didn't touch her."

Thomas gathered Faith into his arms and stood up. "Dustin, I said put the gun down."

Dustin watched Ian as if daring him to move, then lowered the rifle.

Thomas carried Faith to Sara's tent. Sara hurried after him, shaking, then burst into the tent right on his heels. Her patience snapped. "Put her on my cot and get out."

"Excuse me?"

"Out," she demanded. "Put her down and go." Squirming with anxiety, she kept her gaze on her sister, looking for injuries, illness, anything, and found nothing. Sara's entire body screamed for privacy. Whatever had done this to her sister wasn't physical. *I can't lose you.*

Thomas lowered Faith's body to the cot. "She needs help."

"I've got this. She'll be all right. Take Dustin with you."

Thomas gave her a skeptical stare, then backed out of the tent. Outside, she heard him tell Dustin to leave with him.

"What about him?" Dustin asked.

"Go home, Waverly," came Thomas's frosty voice. She heard footsteps moving away.

As soon as they faded out of earshot, Sara sat

beside her sister. "Come on, you fool," she murmured, laying a hand on her sister's forehead. "Did you try to astral project? I swear to God, if I lose you, I'll get you back, and then kill you." She lifted one of her sister's closed eyelids. Faith's eyes were blue, but unfocused and glassy.

The longer Faith remained in a trance or a state of astral projection, the harder it would be to awaken her. Precious seconds ticked by as Sara tried everything she knew. Applying ice, shaking Faith, holding her hand...none of it worked. After endless minutes, Sara dropped into a chair beside the cot and put her face in her hands. Her mind raced in a million different directions. *What now?* Panic twisted through her.

"Sara."

She bristled and blinked away tears. Ian stood in the tent doorway. She shot to her feet, irate. "What do you want?"

Entering the tent, he uncrossed his arms. The amulet dangled, spinning, from his grip.

She took it, examining the broken leather lace. "Why did you do that?"

"Don't go out tonight. Not wearing that."

"Why not?" She pressed a hand to Faith's shoulder again, but her sister didn't respond. Sara stomped her fears back. She needed a clear head. Faith *needed* her to have a clear head.

Ian flung a hand up. "Just don't leave your tent. I don't know." He sat in the other chair at the table and frowned. "I've been having these nightmares. You had that thing around your neck, and you walked into this light, this—"

"Ley line," came a hoarse whisper.

Relief washed through Sara, and she spun around to the cot. "Oh, thank God."

Faith wedged an elbow underneath herself and propped upright. Her features tightened with pain. She clapped a hand over her belly.

Sara helped her to a sitting position. "What happened to you? Are you all right?"

"Minus a few years of my life, maybe. There's a ley line at the dig...running from the dig site, straight down the island. Ian's tent is sitting right on it." Faith reached toward the cooler in the corner of Sara's tent. "Water."

Sara stood up, pawed in her cooler for a bottle of mineral water, then handed it over. She moved to her tent door. From the corner of her eye, she saw Ian shift to the edge of his chair as if to stop her. Nothing disturbed the stillness outside. "I don't see or feel a thing out there."

Faith drank down half the bottle of water before she spoke again. "You can't. Take my word for it, it's there." She took her hand away from her belly and sucked in a breath as if to regain her focus.

Sara turned around. "I thought ley lines didn't exist."

Faith laughed without humor and took another drink. "So did I, until just now."

"What in God's name is a ley line?" Ian broke in.

"A band of energy," Faith explained. "They connect ancient sites all over the earth, like an invisible spiderweb."

A wary disbelief crossed his face. "If you can't see or feel it, how did you know it was there?"

"She just knows," said Sara. Faith gave her a quick,

surprised look, and Sara stared back, agitation crawling like ants along her spine. Did Faith really mean to confess her abilities to Ian? She gave a minute sigh, leaving the decision to her sister.

Faith turned back to Ian. "I'm psychic. I can sense things other people can't." She finished off the water, then set the empty bottle on Sara's nightstand.

Ian fixed her with a mutinous look. Sara wondered if this new development would send him packing to Unst after all, and a curious ache settled in her belly. At last, he crossed his arms and asked, "What's this line for?"

Faith leaned forward and cradled her stomach. "I'm not sure, exactly. All I know is what I've read and heard. No one seems to be able to agree whether the lines were there first, or if they popped up when all the old sites were built. Churches, stone circles, castles. The lines seem to connect them. I've heard that ghosts use them as some kind of metaphysical highway." To Sara, she added, "There are dozens of them on this thing. One touched me."

Sara gaped. Her skin crawled with an imagined chill.

"I don't know how it happened," Faith added. "It's the same one who's been trying to reach me since we got here. It was angry, upset, something. It pushed me into the ley line. My skin—God, it was like a swarm of wasps. I had the ghost for a second, but then all these voices started roaring in my head—and then I passed out." She hugged herself as though warding off the remembered sensations.

Sara toyed with the amulet in her hands, thinking of Ian's earlier warning about wearing it and crossing into the ley line. "We've been here all this time, walking back and forth over this whole island, and there was nothing there. Why now?"

Faith pushed a lock of hair out of her eyes. "Beltane? The equinox was today. Who knows? Maybe they only open at certain times, or when you do certain things."

Ian seemed to absorb that for a moment. "What about my tent?"

Sara stared at him in surprise. No demand for explanations about ghosts? No protest that the possibility was insane?

"You might want to move it," said Faith. "Supposedly, being on a ley line can make you see things. You can have nightmares. The ghosts can mess with you. Did you *see* my sister walk a ley line?"

Ian rubbed his forehead. "I don't know what I saw. It was enough to send me flying down here in the middle of the night, thinking it was real."

"Well, what happened?" Sara demanded.

His look arrowed through her.

"It killed her, didn't it?" Faith murmured. "The amulet. Like the vision, Sara."

Ian remained silent, but his face spoke volumes. Sara swallowed the knot in her throat. As familiar as she was with paranormal gifts, even she found herself doubtful about Faith's discovery. Why did Ian accept it so readily? She fingered the ridges of the amulet.

Faith labored to her feet. "The ley lines, then. The amulet has something to do with them. Sara, where's your copy of *Beardsley's Compendium*?"

"H-Home, I think." Sara faltered, trying to sort out her conflicting emotions.

"Never mind. Mine's in my trunk." Faith strode to the tent doorway.

Alarmed, Sara moved to stop her. "Where are you going?"

"I'll be all right." Faith ducked out the tent door. "The line is fading. I can get through it now. What time is it?"

"After one, I think," replied Sara.

Faith sighed. "Beltane is officially past. My new least favorite pagan holiday. Happy Spring, guys. I'm going to try to get some rest before sunup." With that, she left.

Sara hovered at the doorway watching her sister go, trembling when Faith approached the dig. She heard Ian come up behind her, but her gaze remained on the tall blond form marching away across the moor. Not until Faith had almost reached her own tent did Sara turn away. She heaved a shuddering breath. Now that the immediate danger was past, she felt as weak as if she'd drained her gifts.

Ian's hand came to rest on her shoulder. "Are you going to be okay?"

She strained to compose herself and stared at the amulet in her hand. "She was right. I should have found a way to destroy this thing." Mechanically, she tied the broken lace back together, then looped the amulet over her head. "Now, I can't let it out of my sight. Maybe my father was right to have it dismantled. Thank you...for saving my life."

He cast a doubtful glance out the door, then his features softened. "I'm not sure I did, but you're welcome. I don't know how much of this to believe, even when I've got proof, Sara. I just didn't want anything to happen to you."

She tucked the amulet under her shirt, uncertain what to do with that look in his eyes, less certain where they stood now. "You should probably move your tent."

"Probably."

"But you're not going to."

Ian shook his head.

"Why not? You heard what Faith said."

He touched her cheek. "You sure you're all right?"

The unexpected contact of his skin against hers drove any further questioning out of her head. She closed her eyes, willing the touch to mean more than a simple expression of concern. A lick of flame raced across her skin, so strong she knew he must feel it. "I'm fine."

He turned to go.

She took a quick step toward him. "Ian?"

He stopped and looked back over his shoulder.

Sara's heartbeat slammed against her ribs. The word *stay* caught in her throat. She opened her mouth and hesitated. "Be careful."

He smiled and left the tent. Her breath rushed out.

****

The next afternoon, Ian sat near the cliff edge with a pair of binoculars and his journal. The falcon circled in the air overhead. Its presence had scared off some of the other birds. Ian couldn't bring himself to care that day.

He knew he should have been working, but the salt air and sunshine lulled him away from his assignment. He set his journal down. Lying back in the short, windswept grass, he tucked his arms under his head. Cottony clouds rolled across the sky in stately procession. He closed his eyes and let his thoughts drift.

They went right to Sara. Since he'd come upon her naked at the inlet, not a day had gone by that he hadn't conjured that image in his mind. He almost regretted tossing her the towel so she could cover that beautiful body. If he hadn't... Well, it was a good thing he had. Whatever she was, whatever she did or could do, he wanted her too much.

He'd held on so long to the conviction that any telekinetic deserved his hatred. One of her kind had murdered his father, and his attraction to her should have been a betrayal of the worst order. *Her kind.* Like he'd been willing to lump her in with murderers, just because of something she was, something she couldn't change.

That made him the monster.

He felt like the falcon, whirling first one way and then the other. Wanting her, not wanting her. One minute, he'd almost made up his mind to put her at arm's length. In the next, he thought of her soft skin, her sigh of surrender when he'd touched his lips to her throat, her laugh, her smile...

"Hi."

His eyes flew open. Sara stood over him, dimpling. The look sent him into a delirious tailspin.

"Is this a rest break?" She sat down beside him.

He found his tongue. "I'm sick of working today. The terns aren't busy, I've written seven pages on plant life, and Horus is doing cartwheels for my amusement. Sit and watch."

She lay down with a soft groan, then pillowed her head on her arms. "Let me just tell you how good a lukewarm camp shower feels after a day of dirt and grime. By the end of a project, I usually feel like I've been petrified in mud."

The moment she stretched out beside him, Ian ceased to think rationally. If he rolled over, he would have been on top of her, feeling that incredible body underneath him. His hands itched to touch her and banish his inadequate memories of her skin with the feel of the real thing. He inhaled, almost disappointed when he couldn't smell cinnamon on the air.

"I came to help you with the falcon project," she said.

His heated thoughts shattered into pieces. He sat up.

She unfolded her arms and sat up, too. "What? Do you not want the help now?"

"No. Yes, I want the help. I just didn't—"

"You thought I'd back out."

He took her hand, surprising both of them. "I don't want you to do it."

"Why not?"

How could he tell her what she did to him? Where would he even start? "You don't have to prove anything to me. And you don't owe me anything. Besides, I don't want you getting hurt doing this on my account." He realized he still held her hand, and released it.

She stared at him for a moment. He couldn't read anything in that whiskey-colored gaze. At last, she got to her feet. "Do you have a pair of heavy leather gloves?"

"On my trunk in the tent. Why?"

She started toward his tent. He stood up and jogged after her, catching up just as she went inside.

She picked up the right-handed glove and put it

into his hand. "I know I don't have to prove anything to you, but I think we need to do this. I am not dangerous to you. I might even be able to help you."

He glanced down at the glove. When he looked up again, she'd already left the tent.

Outside, she waited beside one of his tarp-covered shipping crates. "What are you going to do?" he asked.

"How close can I get to Horus before he'll attack me?"

He didn't answer.

"Come on, how close? You'd better put that glove on. You're going to need it."

Uneasy with doubt, he shoved his hand into the glove. "Forty, fifty feet. But that's as a human. Are you sure about this?"

"Sure, I'm sure." She walked toward the cliff edge.

He followed. "Be careful about him. I don't know what he'll do if..."

She paused to look over her shoulder at him.

Ian cleared his throat and rubbed his gloved hand through his hair. "...if he thinks you're just another female falcon."

"Are you worried he's going to flirt with me?"

Exactly how did a man get jealous of a bird? "Just be careful, all right?" he shot back.

She paced to the very threshold of the cliff and looked down. Wind swept her hair off her shoulders. He tensed, wanting to pull her back.

"Trust me," she said, and stepped off the edge.

"Sara!" He lunged for her, but the hem of her shirt slipped out of his reach. His heart wedged in his throat. He dropped to his knees at the cliff edge. Strangling, he dug his fingers into the precipice and watched her fall in a graceful swan dive.

Light burst along the contours of her body. She blurred, and—*Flash!*—a falcon rolled in midair where Sara had been. The bird soared outward over the water.

Ian sat back with his mouth hanging open. "Sweet mother of Jesus." The echo of his racing heartbeat pounded through his body.

A long, sharp cry rang out overhead. He looked up. Horus folded his wings and plummeted through the air. *Oh, God, he's attacking her.* Unable to look away, he watched as the other falcon—Sara—wheeled to fend off the assault. She gave a cry of her own and spun sideways.

Horus flashed by and climbed higher, only to round on her again. Ian closed his eyes, expecting Horus to knock her from the air the same way he hunted his food. *Two hundred miles an hour,* he thought, picturing the male's next attack. She'd never stand the strike.

He heard another series of calls from both of them, and opened his eyes. The birds reeled around one another, soaring past and circling back to do it again. It looked like...

Dancing.

Stunned, he watched them spin and plunge in an aerial ballet. He almost lost track of Sara in their dizzying whirl.

Then they separated. Horus rose into the air and went back to circling. Sara, the larger falcon, swept across the sky toward the cliff.

She sailed closer, dropping her tail and tilting her wings when she reached him. He stood up, remembering at the last minute to raise his gloved hand. She landed on it with a drawn-out chirrup that sounded suspiciously like laughter. Air from her flapping wings gusted against his face. He stared into her large, vivid-green eyes in wonder.

She was beautiful.

Awestruck, he held out his left hand. She gave the chirping sound again and swept her wing against his hand. The springy-soft primaries brushed through his fingers.

She leapt from his hand and fluttered to the ground. The light flashed again, and the next thing he knew, Sara stood beaming in the bird's place. She launched herself at him and threw her arms around his neck. "I did it! He talked to me! Why did I never try that before?" She giggled and kissed him on the cheek.

Ian's heart squeezed, and something inside him snapped. Unable to stop himself, he swung her in a circle. He set her down, but couldn't make himself let go of her.

Still laughing, she pushed her hair back. "It was only in the most basic sense, but we communicated. At first, he was angry that I was in his territory. Then he must have thought I was just a female falcon, like you said—"

Ian felt his smile falter.

"—but I think he realized I was different, so he backed away." Her face fell. "He's lonely."

"Lonely?" Ian echoed, still racing to absorb the weight of what was going on inside him. He ached.

A frown crossed her features. "Before I came back, he called out. It wasn't so much that I understood the sound, but I had this feeling—isolation. I've known that feeling since I was ten years old."

The sorrow shadowing her expression pulled at

him in a way he'd never felt before. He couldn't stand to see it. Cupping her face in his hands, he kissed her, very gently. "You're not alone, Sara."

She smiled at him with a brilliance that squeezed his heart all over again. "Thanks."

Chapter Eight

A day later, James Lambertson arrived with more crew. Sara and her sister had been working three hours already when Alan Flintrop appeared at the site. Sara, standing at the edge of the dig trench, saw him first. With everything else going on at the site, she'd forgotten about Flintrop and his history of project-stealing.

Well, if he thought he'd be stealing this one, he had a rude awakening coming to him. "What are you doing here?" she demanded, not bothering to keep the venom out of her voice.

Faith's head popped up over the edge of the trench. "I knew it," she hissed.

Flintrop came to a halt when he reached them, looking regal and golden-haired like a lion holding court over his pride. He peered at them over the top of his sunglasses. "Good morning to you, too, ladies."

Sara vibrated with resentment. *Don't call me "lady," you pompous jerk.* At thirty-five, Flintrop wasn't much more of a veteran than she or Faith, but he had the advantage of learning archaeology at the knees of his father and grandfather. The Flintrop family profession had earned him worldwide respect and admiration. She hated him for it.

"It's 'Doctor' to you, bucko," Faith muttered from the trench. Her sister jammed her shovel into the earth and heaved a chunk into the wheelbarrow standing nearby.

Sara struggled to stifle a smile and lost.

Flintrop removed his sunglasses to reveal cobalt-blue eyes that had charmed many a female student in the field. "Hello, Faith," he said in a tone far too intimate for a muddy dig site.

Faith pitched her next shovel of earth out of the trench and onto Flintrop's designer hiking boot. "Sorry about that. Guess I better brush up on my dig skills."

Flintrop shook the dirt off his boot with an unruffled air and turned his attention on Sara. "Lambertson said you'd need money on this project. I'm the money."

Sara couldn't resist asking about his latest stolen project. "What happened to your South America dig?"

He had enough grace to look abashed. "That wasn't my decision. I gave you a good word with the board. Several, actually. You were very thorough."

Praise from Flintrop? That was new. "Thank you," she said, working to keep it from sounding like a question.

He smiled again. "I'll be setting up. Lambertson's brought some computer data for you when you're ready to look at it." He walked away.

"Jackass," grumbled Faith.

Sara jumped down into the trench with a chuckle. "*You* dated him."

"A momentary lapse of reason on my part," spat her sister. "Now we're going to have to deal with him all summer. Does Lamb hate us?"

Sara sighed. "Well, he's right. We need money, if this is going to be as big as we think it is. As far as I'm concerned, he's welcome to be the wallet, as long as he stays out of my way."

Faith shrugged and continued digging.

A few moments later, Lambertson came to the trench. "I have to say, I'm impressed, girls."

At the sound of his voice, Sara surged out of the trench with her sister close behind. Lambertson was handsome in middle age, with steel-gray hair and pale blue eyes behind a pair of wire-rimmed glasses. He had the aristocratic air of the consummate British gentleman, even when grinning broadly as he did now.

She broke into an answering smile. She'd been too well-trained to throw her arms around his neck and hug him as she'd done in childhood, but the impulse had never waned. She settled for a handshake. "How was your trip, Lamb?"

"Beastly," he answered.

Faith embraced him. "It's good to see *you*. Not so much, who you brought *with* you."

Lambertson chuckled and patted her back, then turned and surveyed the dig. His gaze swept over the surveying level on its tripod, the markers punched into the ground at each plot, and the deepening trench of the excavation. "Excellent," he said at last, giving them each a satisfied look. "You're doing your father proud."

"This is more than a summer's work," Sara said. "There's a lot left to do."

"Which is why I made the decision to bring in Flintrop," he said on a sigh. "I know you'd have liked to handle it yourselves, but this is going to involve more work and better financing than Gemini alone can provide."

"You don't need to explain," replied Sara, waving a

hand.

The corner of Lambertson's mouth turned up. "I know you're angry, Sara. Rest assured, you and Faith will receive top billing when the project is finished. This isn't going to be like South America."

Relief poured into her. Lamb knew her too well.

"By the by," he added, "I noticed another tent when we landed. Which belongs to...?"

"Ian Waverly. He's a wildlifer for the university, working with the birds on the island. It has nothing to do with the dig."

Lamb eyed her, but didn't comment. She felt the full force of his pale blue stare, and worried that he saw more than she'd let on. "Better get back to work," she said brightly, and jumped back into the trench.

Phew.

Within half an hour, Lamb's reinforcements had blended smoothly into the rhythm of the project. With so much help, Sara had to admit that work progressed at a blinding pace. The air hummed with their collective energy. She'd almost forgotten how much fun fieldwork could be.

Lamb and Flintrop had brought four assistants between them. Sara knew almost all of them. Cameron Leone, an undergraduate and the crew's youngest member, hailed her from the trench with a bright smile. She waved back. "Nice to see you again, Cam. How are classes?"

"Good," he said. "Thanks a ton for that book on the Incas. Got an A on the report. I officially love you forever."

"Anytime." She grinned and went on to meet the other arrivals, putting aside her professional differences with Flintrop in the face of teamwork. Easier when she wasn't talking *to* Flintrop.

She stopped when she came to a petite woman with a mane of fiery red curls. "I don't think we've met."

The young woman's hands slipped on her shovel. It dropped against a nearby wheelbarrow with a clang. "Oh! Sorry." She snatched the shovel up again, then smiled and shook Sara's hand. "Becky Palmeter. I've heard a lot about you. I did my senior thesis on one of your digs."

"Are you postgrad?"

"Is it that obvious?"

With a chuckle, Sara answered, "You still have that deer-in-the-headlights look. I had it, too. Are you with Lamb or Flintrop?"

"Lambertson would be a relief. I'm with Flintrop," Becky said. "He's always scowling at me. I feel like whatever I do is wrong."

"I'm sure your work is fine," Sara said, feeling sympathy for the woman. "Half the battle is not letting him intimidate you."

"Who ordered the swarm?" came a male voice.

Ian stood at the edge of the dig. Flutters rushed through Sara's insides, up, down, and back again. "Hi."

He gestured down into the trench with a question in his eyes.

"Lamb's cavalry. Come down. Becky, this is Ian Waverly. He's a wildlife biologist who's here to work with the birds. Ian, Becky Palmeter. She's one of our new recruits," Sara added, then smiled at the redhead.

He shook Becky's hand when he reached them. "Nice to meet you."

"You, too."

Ian turned his attention to Sara. "I need to make a run to Unst for some supplies. Can I borrow your boat?"

"Sure. The keys are on the table in my tent."

"Want me to bring something back for you?"

Warmth filled her body. Not so long ago, she wouldn't have dreamed he'd be so thoughtful to her. Now...

Well, now she ought to be keeping her mind off dreaming about him and on her job.

As hard as that was.

"Coffee," she said briskly. "If I don't get more coffee, this project is going to come to a screeching halt."

He grinned at her, and she knew he was thinking of their mutual love of Waverly's secret blend. "One large bag of caffeinated goodness. Check."

Lambertson approached them. "Sara, where did you—" He stopped when he saw Ian. "You must be Mister Waverly."

"Yes, sir," Ian replied, shaking his hand. "I've heard a lot about you."

Lambertson's gaze swept Ian's figure from head to foot in what Sara thought was a look of scrutiny. "You're here for wildlife?"

Ian didn't seem bothered by Lambertson's evaluation. "Yes. I'm studying coastal birds on the north end of the island."

"Waverly, you lucky son of a bitch!" chortled another voice.

Ian peered over Lamb's shoulder at the man jogging toward them. "Lu! How'd you land a gig like this?"

Luis Rivero clapped Ian on the back. "I was about to ask you the same thing."

Sara raised her brows. How, indeed.

"I pulled some strings at the university," explained Ian. To Lambertson he added, "Luis is the reason I've heard so much about you. He talks about your work nonstop." He turned again to Sara. "Thanks for the boat. I'll catch up with you later." He went to the edge of the trench and climbed out.

"Coffee!" Sara called after him. "Lots of it!"

Walking away, Ian waved a hand in the air to indicate that he'd heard.

When Sara spotted Lambertson, the smile vanished from her face. "What?"

Her mentor surveyed Ian's retreating figure. "How long is he going to be here?"

"I don't know, another month. Lamb, he isn't going to interfere. He's not interested in what's going on down here."

Lamb made a doubtful noise and walked away. Luis went with him.

Becky stared after Ian. "Wow. Maybe I should have gone into wildlife."

Prickles danced across Sara's shoulders. She picked up a stray shovel and tried to sound amiable. "I'll see you around the dig. It was nice meeting you," she murmured, then strode off.

At sunset, the entire crew gathered around a fire. Sara sat cross-legged beside it with her sister, discussing the project. She was in the middle of a lament about not finding any artifacts yet when she noticed Faith wasn't paying attention. Sara prodded her. "What's the matter?"

Faith snapped out of it and leaned toward her. "I've spent the past two days reading the books Dad had in with the Shetland research. In *Beardsley*, I came across something about—"

"Good day's work," interrupted Flintrop, sitting down on Sara's other side.

Faith sank into reticence. Her mouth pinched like someone had just force-fed her minced leeches.

Sara hunched her shoulders. "Yeah. You, too."

When Faith touched her arm, Sara turned away from Flintrop. Her sister made an urgent face.

Sara gave an imperceptible nod and called on her power. From where they sat, the others would not be able to tell her eyes had changed. She released her hold on mind reading.

A serpent ceremony, Faith told her silently, *performed by a religious order that manipulated the ley lines for some kind of ritual. If I'm right, and the amulet is part of it, the man in the white robes may have been a druid.*

Faith's explanation was overlaid with the disturbing image of her vision from the amulet. Sara saw a large blond man drive a sword through another man's belly. Blood pooled around the sword hilt, staining the victim's white robes. She recoiled in surprise.

"Are you all right?" came Flintrop's voice.

Sara shifted where she sat, and blinked to shut off her power. "I must have been sitting on a stone."

He studied her. "Did you do something with your hair?"

Faith made a noise of disgust and got to her feet. "I'm going to my tent. I'll see you in the morning,

Sara."

Sara smiled and said good night, even though every fiber of her being was suddenly and instantly begging, *Please don't leave me with him if you love me at all, you traitor!* There weren't too many times she wished Faith could read her mind in return, but now might have topped the list.

Flintrop cleared his throat. "I know we haven't gotten on very well, Sara, but I do respect your work. I don't want you to hold South America against me."

She nodded in the direction of Faith's tent. "I think my sister holds it against you more than I do."

He sighed and tipped his flask again. "Faith and I never quite saw eye-to-eye on things."

"Is that what you call it?" Sara muttered.

"Look, I saw the reports that came back to Eurocon so far on this job, and they're brilliant. I'm not supposed to tell you, but Lambertson was even talking to Oxford about getting you a seminar, if this is as big as we think it'll be."

She gaped. "Really?"

"It's too early yet to make any sort of decision, obviously, but he was serious, and so am I. I back him one hundred percent. You deserve to get the credit on this." He smiled. "Call it my apology for South America."

She didn't know what to say. Gemini needed just the sort of publicity a seminar would promote.

Then again, credit for the dig wasn't his to give. What had seemed an expansive gesture began to smack of empty bribery. "You want something."

He chuckled. "I always did like your directness."

"You don't throw bones without expecting

something back, Flintrop. What is it?"

He touched her hand, only briefly, but she froze. "I want to be friends. Ever since I've known you, you've been running a race with me to see who's the best of the best. You don't need to prove yourself, Sara. I already know you're talented."

She shot him a scathing look. "I'm not proving anything to you."

"All right, that came out wrong. What I'm trying to say is, we've been working at odds with each other so long, it will be a nice change to work together on this project. With your skill and my resources, we're going to blow the lid off this thing."

She scrutinized him. He looked so enthusiastic, he almost convinced her he meant it. Then she noticed the way he leaned toward her...exactly the posture he'd presented to Faith while trying to seduce her in South America. Sara had enough experience—reading minds or not—to know that body language often gave away people's true intentions, no matter what came out of their mouths. She jerked backward with an uncomfortable ooze of dismay.

So much for goodwill.

A bag of coffee with a Waverly's label descended into the gap between them. Sara beamed and looked up.

Dangling the bag, Ian grinned down at her. "Saved from imminent sleepiness. This is from my private stash, I'll have you know. I took pity."

Delighted, she accepted the coffee. "Thank you."

"The keys are back in your tent. Thanks for the loaner."

Flintrop stiffened. "I take it you're the wildlifer."

Ian nodded. She noticed he didn't bother offering

his handshake. Impeccable timing *and* impeccable judge of character.

Then Ian turned his attention back to her, and his indifferent mask relaxed. "I brought you something else. I had a sweet tooth, so I made an emergency side trip." With a triumphant smile, he rummaged in his jacket pocket and withdrew a small paper bag.

She took the bag and opened it. Cinnamon drops. Pleasure swarmed through her. "I was almost out, too. How did you know?"

His smile was all genial charm, but something passed through his eyes that flushed her body with heat. Her memory shot back to searing kisses and skin on skin. She couldn't look at him, afraid that everyone could tell what was going on in her head. How could they *not* tell, when her thoughts were so loud?

"Know anything of archaeology, Waverly?" asked Flintrop.

Ian shrugged. "I'm familiar with the digging part."

"Ian spent part of a day helping us dig peat," Sara said, still distracted by the way her thoughts kept snapping back to the afternoon in Ian's tent.

"I'm sure that was enough to turn you off of archaeology altogether," said Flintrop.

Ian didn't look away from Sara. "Not entirely, no."

"Well, we're fully staffed now, so we won't be taking up your time any longer. I'm sure you have plenty of your own work to do," Flintrop added. He gave a plastered-on smile, then turned away from Ian and went back to tipping his brandy.

Sara stood. "Would you excuse us?" Without waiting for Flintrop's answer, she started away. Ian walked with her to her tent. "Sorry about him."

"Who is that guy?"

She sighed. "Alan Flintrop. I'm going to be working with him for the rest of the summer. I know he's a pain in the—"

"No, he's great. Must have tons of friends."

"Sure, if they're wealthy enough to be in his little club of worshippers." She waved her hand in the air. "That's not the point. We need his help on this project if we're going to get done on time and within budget...and why am I explaining this to you? You don't care."

He stepped closer to her, causing her to back up in surprise against the wall of her tent. His eyes bored into hers, as focused as a hunting raptor. "Oh, I care...just not about him."

Her heart thudded in her ears. Could he hear it? He bent his head. His breath warmed her face, and she leaned forward to close the distance, because for the love of God, it wasn't happening fast enough...

"Sara, may I have a word with you?"

Ian jerked back with his face completely blank. Lambertson stood nearby. Sara felt her face burn, and passed Ian a guilty look. "I—"

He smiled. "Don't sweat it. I have some birding notes to catch up on. I'll see you later." He turned and headed up the slope of the island. She watched him until he disappeared into the darkness, even now wishing him back. A charge of desire coursed through her and left her shivering with aftershock. How? *How*, when he hadn't even kissed her?

Lambertson approached her with an expression that made her feel like a wayward teenager. "I would venture to say he's *distinctly* interested in what's going on down here."

She gawked. "Are you being parental with me?"

"I am telling you to the point. I don't trust that young man, and I don't want him here. This project is confidential. His presence is a liability."

"Come on, Lamb—"

His frown cut her off. "I am the project supervisor, Sara. Don't make me employ that authority."

He'd never used that tone on her before, even during her undergrad years. Hurt, she zipped open her tent flap and stepped inside, shutting it before he could say anything further.

****

Several days after Lamb's reinforcements arrived, the peat and earth gave way to the first layer of stone marking the enclosure of their suspected Viking-era house. Sara couldn't feel more than a distant pleasure at the milestone. She hadn't seen Ian in almost a week. Whenever she found the time, Lamb managed to concoct a task that kept her at the dig. Moody and restless, she worked beside Faith at one of the plots.

"Now all we need from this mudpit is an artifact, and we're in business," said Faith.

Her sister seemed to have enough good spirits for both of them lately. Sara offered a smile and went back to scooping earth. Seconds passed.

At length, Faith hissed, "Quit moping and go see him. You're a grown woman."

Needled, Sara redoubled her efforts at removing soil from the house wall. "Lamb's already made it abundantly clear what he thinks of Ian. We can't afford to lose this project."

Flintrop approached. "We're having a bonfire tonight to celebrate," he announced. "I'm heading to

Unst this afternoon for some *aqua vitae*, if you'd like to come." He spoke to both of them, but his attention hovered on Sara.

Faith leveled him with a revolted look and moved away. He ignored it.

Sara stood and stretched her back. "Why don't you take one of your own crew?"

"Because," he said, moving closer and lowering his tone, "I'd really like you to come with me. Please? What's it going to take for you to accept my apology?"

Lamb's voice rose from the other side of the dig, hailing them all to midday break. Members of the crew shuffled off in the direction of the summons, leaving them alone.

Sara walked away and climbed onto the stone wall, preparing to jump down and follow the crew to lunch. "I don't think—"

The earth roared under her feet. With a shriek, she lost her balance and toppled headfirst down the other side of the wall. A fissure tore open and yawned beneath her.

A hand seized her ankle. She jerked to a stop above the crack in the earth. The amulet slithered from under her shirt and dangled from her neck over the crevasse. Sara gasped and clapped it to her chest. Open space gaped below her. The land thundered again. Flintrop's grip slipped on her ankle, and she screamed.

"Pull yourself up!" Flintrop shouted.

One-handed, she clawed at the ragged walls of the trench, refusing to let go of the amulet. Panic stabbed her.

And then she saw it.

At the bottom of the fissure lay a human skull,

half-buried in the dark soil. She froze. *I'll be damned.*

Flintrop's grasp slipped again. "Sara! Give me your hand!"

Another tremor issued from the earth.

Sara jackknifed her body and flung her free hand toward him. He seized her and jerked her out of the fissure just as part of the wall collapsed into it.

They ran for the edge of the dig and dove over the wall on the other side to a last, teeth-chattering quake.

The land settled.

Sara stuffed the amulet back inside her shirt, praying no one had seen it. She got to her feet, then hunched over with her hands on her knees, panting.

"Are you all right?" he asked. He glanced from her to the yawning tear in the earth.

She nodded. "Thanks."

Lamb came running toward them with Luis in tow. "Is anyone hurt?"

"No," she answered.

"Someone had better go check on Ian," suggested Luis.

"I will," she said before anyone else could reply.

Lamb shook his head. "Luis and Alan will go."

She opened her mouth on a burst of indignation. Lamb had never countermanded her in front of a team before. In front of Flintrop, it was a slap in the face. "Lamb, I know him."

"As does Luis, which is why I'm sending him. They will see to Mister Waverly. I want you here."

Her blood boiled. Humiliated and worried, she stalked away toward the rest of the crew.

She heard Lamb order Luis and Flintrop away, and then Lamb's hurried footsteps as he caught up with her.

He settled a hand on her shoulder.

She rounded on him. "How could you do that to me? Ian is my friend. Ever since you got here, you've been acting like—"

"Exactly as your father would have acted, had he known your house had been burglarized. What were they looking for?"

She stilled. "I don't know what you're talking about."

"Don't be obstinate. You and I both know it wasn't a chance occurrence. Your mother contacted me and said your father's stored research was decimated, a fact which I find curious when you and your sister are out of the country in Shetland itself. How well do you know this 'friend,' Sara?"

She struggled to maintain her calm. "It wasn't him. How could it be, when he's been here?"

"I don't take coincidence lightly. That young man followed you here. He knows something, and I want to know what it is."

With an effort, she kept her features neutral. Ian knew something, all right. Something she'd been hiding for twenty years, and God forbid the secret got any further.

She and Faith couldn't afford to trust anyone. Even Lamb, who'd been like a father. She stifled a queasy sensation in her gut. "Ian has nothing to do with this dig."

"I very much doubt that," said Lamb.

She forced her temper past the guilt. "Believe it, or don't—I don't care. But if you think upstaging me in front of Flintrop is going to bring me to heel, you're sorely mistaken."

Lambertson looked stunned. "I had no intention of doing any such thing. I'm trying to protect—"

"I do not need *protection*." She spun on her heel and stormed away.

Chapter Nine

The tremor happened while Ian hung halfway down the cliffside. The shake rattled a few pebbles loose from the rock face above and below him. Startled, he flattened himself against the cliff. Horus shrieked and launched into the air. Ian swung in his harness, wondering if the cliff would come down on top of him. Not how he hoped to end his career.

As soon as the tremor ceased, he started carefully back up the cliff. When he reached the top, Flintrop and Luis were waiting.

Luis gave him a hand up onto solid ground. "You all right? We just had a shakeup at the dig."

At once, he thought of Sara. A magnetic pull washed over him. He strove to ignore it. "I'm fine. Is everyone okay down there?"

"Another fissure opened," Flintrop reported. "Sara and I had a close call, but no one's hurt. We may need to shut the project down. The site's not safe like this."

Ian gave an inner growl at Flintrop's use of the words *Sara and I*. That reaction was harder to ignore.

Flintrop shrugged. "You might consider leaving as well, Waverly. It could get dangerous around here."

Ian snapped his gaze to Flintrop's. They held each other's stare. "I'll take my chances."

"I heard you were a bit on the stubborn side. Got a dislocated shoulder, and still stuck around. Tough stuff."

Ian unhooked his climbing belt and started coiling the ropes. "Some things are just worth it, I guess."

Flintrop's gaze never faltered. "I daresay you're right."

****

Sara glanced around at the assembled crew. They ate a restless lunch while Lambertson and two of his assistants took stock of the dig site. While they finished their meal, she leaned over to her sister and spoke in a hushed tone. "I saw a skull. In the fissure, when it opened."

Faith's eyes went wide. She glanced toward the trench and her mouth opened, but Lambertson's return interrupted her before she could reply.

The group shot to attention. Lamb held up his hand to silence the last of the conversation. "The structure of what we've unearthed so far is mainly intact. However, there's a new crevice, and I believe that for the safety of all, we're going to have to—"

"Can we brace it?" interrupted Sara as Flintrop and Luis returned to the camp.

"I don't think it's in the best interest of the crew for us to remain here," said Lamb. "We have no way of knowing if we'll get another earthquake."

"I found a skull, Lamb."

Everyone began murmuring. Sara stood up and spoke above the din. "It was in the crevice. If we can get it out, at least we'll have something to show for all this work."

Lamb frowned. "It might be possible to shore up the fault and continue working, but I can't guarantee our safety under those circumstances."

Sara glanced at her sister. Faith nodded, and Sara turned back to Lambertson. "Gemini will stay and finish the excavation."

"Are you telling me you're going to endanger yourself and your sister for the sake of this project?"

A mutter passed throughout the crew. Sara looked from face to face and found undisguised doubt. "Shetland was my father's labor of love. I'm not leaving the island until this dig is done, if I have to scrape away every bit of soil with my bare hands."

The mutter elevated.

"Are you kidding?" called a voice.

"This is insane," came another. "You heard Lambertson. The dig is dangerous."

"Who knows if there'll be another quake?" demanded a third.

And then, "I'll stay."

Sara blinked. Flintrop. *Flintrop* was backing her up? She stared at him across the group. The mutter became a collective argument until Lambertson shouted for quiet.

The crew settled. No one ever out-shouted Lambertson.

Flintrop tilted his head at Sara. "I think she's right. Any of my crew who wants to leave can do so, but if there are remains, it's possible there will be artifacts. I'm staying put."

Faith got to her feet and whispered, "Of all the people I thought would be an ally, he's the last."

"Me, too," Sara murmured. If Flintrop stayed, the money stayed. If the money stayed, that made things a lot less difficult. She almost found herself wanting to thank him.

Lambertson threw a hand in the air. "All right. You're all bloody well out of your minds. Those of you who plan to stay on will need to sign release forms. If anyone intends to leave, gather your gear, and then see me to make the arrangements." The group began to disperse.

Flintrop crossed the camp toward Lamb's tent. As he passed Sara, he said, "Some things are just worth it, I guess."

Sara watched him leave, struggling to stuff what she knew of Flintrop back into its neat little box. She met her sister's gaze, and even Faith looked shocked.

Faith shook out of it. "Leopard. Spots. I'm not convinced."

Sara grinned.

In the end, none of the crew wanted to leave the project in light of the found skull. That meant the project could continue at its present speed. Over the remainder of lunch, Sara decided she owed Flintrop a long-overdue apology. On the heels of that revelation came a good excuse for seeing Ian. Relieved that she'd found a point even Lamb couldn't argue, she packed up her mess kit, then marched to Flintrop's tent.

The door hung open. She ventured a look inside. He stood over his cot, stuffing a few articles into a duffel bag. She cleared her throat.

He turned. "Sara?"

"Yeah. I, er... Well, first, I wanted to thank you. Not just for staying with the project. For, you know, grabbing me before I fell into the..." She trailed off, wishing she'd thought more on how to apologize before coming to apologize.

A grin creased his handsome face. "You're

welcome."

Awkward moments passed. She hovered in the doorway, trying to decide how to proceed.

"Did you need something?" he added.

She flushed. "I just figured that since you were going to Unst this afternoon... If you still are—" She ground to a halt, toying with the cord that tied back the tent door. "I think maybe you were right when you said we got off on the wrong foot somewhere, and I'm sorry. I'll go with you, if you want."

There. Apology out. The fact that they'd have to go right by Ian's camp had nothing to do with her offer, of course.

"Yes, absolutely," said Flintrop. "I was just about to go. I'm glad you caught me."

She nodded. "I'll wait outside." She retreated as quickly as possible and heaved a sigh. After that, facing earthquakes ought to be no problem.

Flintrop joined her a short while later, and they started the hike up to the boat dock. They walked in silence for fifteen minutes before he spoke. "So, I'm glad you decided to come along for the ride."

She smiled briefly back and adjusted the backpack on her shoulder. He was going to drag this out of her, wasn't he? Blushing, she admitted, "I guess I have been competing with you a little. Ever since I started my undergrad work, I've been coming up against the Flintrop legacy. It's a little daunting."

"Try being part of the family sometime."

"Oh, right. Being the son and grandson of two of the field's most notable must have been terrible, growing up."

"I'm serious," he said. "There was a time, if you

can believe it, that I hated archaeology. I wanted to be a lawyer."

"Really?"

"My father almost disinherited me over it. God forbid the son of Nicholas Flintrop became anything but an archaeologist. Not after my grandfather Elliott had scratched out such a powerful legacy from nothing." His voice rang with sarcasm. "He finally agreed that I could study law for a year, and then we'd discuss it further."

"Obviously, law didn't make the cut, because here you are."

He shrugged. "My father offered me a job as vice president of his firm, and said eventually, he'd hand over the entire family business. I couldn't refuse. I didn't want it, but now I have it, and I'm good at it, so there was no point in stopping."

She thought about that. "I'd never have taken you for wanting anything but this life. I would have given anything to have what you have. I never got to learn from my father."

"Be glad you didn't learn from mine. He's good, but he's a hardass from a long line of hardasses."

There was a sharp, bitter undertone to his voice. Sara glanced up, but Flintrop's expression had gone blank.

They had reached Ian's tent.

As if he'd been summoned, Ian emerged with a camera tripod balanced on his shoulder. He stopped when he saw her, and smiled. "Hey."

She hadn't realized how much she'd missed his voice. Her whole body responded to the sound. She had to force herself not to move toward him. "Hi."

The corner of Ian's mouth curled upward. "Making another coffee run?"

She laughed. "No, just the usual supplies. Do you need anything? I could pick it up."

"No, I'm good here." He glanced at Flintrop. His eyes narrowed a fraction. "Flintrop."

"Waverly," Flintrop responded dryly. "Sara, we're losing good daylight. Shall we go?"

She saw Ian's jaw clench and she frowned, wanting more than anything to stay. "Yeah, I'll be right there."

Flintrop started away, clearly unwilling to do so. For a few seconds, Sara looked at Ian, expecting him to say something, but he didn't. With an inward sigh, she made to follow Flintrop.

Ian grabbed her hand. Surprised, she turned back. *The inlet,* he mouthed.

Her heart thudded. She lingered on his lips, remembering the way they had burned against her skin. She glanced around to see if Flintrop was watching—he wasn't, thank God—then nodded and jogged away. The whole time, she felt Ian's gaze on her, and her body pulsed like a sonar signal in response.

She stayed silent during the ride to Unst. To her relief, Flintrop followed suit for almost the whole trip. When they moored the boat at their destination, he asked, "So what's with this biologist, anyway? How'd he wind up on Hvitmar?"

She bit the inside of her cheek. She'd been waiting for that. "Why does everyone have such an abiding interest in him? He's here to study birds."

"Don't you think it's a little well-timed that he's here when we are?"

"Yes. It's all a conspiracy. He's here to rob us of

our nonexistent Viking treasure. We might as well just kill him." She threw her hands in the air with an exasperated growl, privately hoping it concealed her true feelings...and fearing that it didn't.

For the first time in her life, she'd lied to Lamb. Ian wasn't just a friend. What she felt for him went beyond friendship into something much more unsettling. She could hardly look at him without wanting to touch him. She could hardly touch him without wanting to find out where touching him led.

"A bit irritable, aren't you?" Flintrop asked.

She sneered. "Between you and Lamb expecting Ian to be at the center of some big plot, yes, I'm irritable."

Flintrop cocked his head. His cobalt gaze roved across her features. "You're attracted to him, aren't you?"

"What business is it of yours if I am or I'm not?"

He stepped around a group of fishermen heading out to the marina. "I've known you for almost ten years, Sara. You don't let people get close to you. What is it about Waverly? What's he got on you?"

Unease buzzed through her. "You've got some nerve, thinking you know anything about how I tick." Turning on her heel, she tromped forward down the dock.

"I do know. I've made it my business to know," he said, pursuing her.

She came to an abrupt halt. "What on earth is that supposed to mean?"

He sighed. "Dating Faith was possibly the worst mistake I've ever made. I didn't want to be with Faith. I never wanted *her*."

She stopped. Soaked that in. Kicked herself. "*You* and *me*? Nothing could possibly be more unlikely." Shaking her head, she started walking again.

He jogged in step with her. "Why not? We've worked together for a long time—"

"You mean you've been usurping my projects for a long time."

"Don't. Don't turn this into another pitched battle. I don't want to fight with you."

"You should have thought about that before you took *every single project* I started that Gemini didn't get to finish. You're a scavenger, Flintrop."

With a dark look, he grabbed her by the arms. She wrestled in outrage, but he held fast. "What other way did I have to get close to you? Everything you are is in your work, Sara. It was all I had to go on."

She dropped into a stunned silence. Her entire body flamed with embarrassment. She felt foolish even asking it. "Are you...in love with me?"

He didn't answer. A pained look crossed his clean-cut features.

"Oh, my God." She fled away down the dock.

During the awkward trip into town, their taxi driver kept up a stream of chatter that, to Sara's relief, distracted Flintrop from speaking to her. When they arrived in town, she paid their driver and they got out of the cab. She couldn't look at Flintrop. Without comment, she started for the first general store she saw.

Locals and tourists alike crowded the tiny shop. Two elderly women stood at a table along one end of the store, presiding over a large array of hand-knitted sweaters, jewelry, giftware, and homemade foodstuffs. "Is there a party going on in town this week?" Sara wondered, surveying the multitude of shoppers.

One of the women smiled in answer. "We're having a spring fundraiser. Would you like to try a tart?"

"No, thank you." Sara drifted along the table to the other end, where her gaze landed on a small rack of tour flyers. The one in front read *Hermaness National Nature Reserve*, and featured a large, mottled-brown bird on the front. She longed suddenly to rush back to Hvitmar, and Ian. Her imagination picked up where it had left off earlier. She was once again in his tent, kissing him, running her hands over his broad shoulders, lifting her chin so he could press kisses along her throat...

Flintrop passed behind her. She tore her gaze away from the brochure to a folded stack of sweaters resting nearby.

The second woman reached for the sweater on top and unfolded it. "These are all made right here in Unst. This one would look beautiful on you. Did you want to try it on?"

"Oh. Thank you, but no," she murmured, moving on.

Her gaze landed on an assortment of books, including a thin, garish softcover titled *The Sleeping Princess*. The cover bore an illustration of what appeared to be Sleeping Beauty, her long blond hair strewn across the stone dais on which she lay. Sara took it for a common children's book, until she saw what dangled from the prone woman's hand in the drawing:

The amulet.

Or, if not the amulet, a necklace that could have been its cousin. Sara glanced behind her. Flintrop stood across the shop, surveying the available grocery items. She pasted an expression of polite interest on her face and picked up the book.

The necklace in the drawing didn't exactly match the one hidden under her sweatshirt. No Celtic knot graced the pendant. The serpent didn't intertwine with anything; rather, it circled the outer perimeter of the discus, but its center bore a gold-colored oval. She flipped through the pages, not really seeing them, and smiled at the elderly woman. "I'd like this, though. And on second thought, maybe a couple of those tarts."

She waited on edge while the woman rang up her purchases. She had just finished putting the book in a paper bag when Flintrop returned to her side. "What did you get?"

"Just some touristy magazines," she lied. "Oh...and a peace offering." She handed him the small bag of tarts.

He shifted his groceries to one arm and looked inside the bag. "Snack food. How astute. Thank you."

She tucked the bag containing her book under one arm. "We'd better go. Are you finished getting supplies?"

He nodded and let her lead the way out the door. They returned to the boat, and she drove them back to the island. Sara spent half the ride with part of her attention on their route, part on the awkward pre-shopping conversation with Flintrop, and the rest hovering anxiously on the little book in the bag by her feet.

As they neared the island, Flintrop took out one of the tarts and bit into it. His gaze settled on her like a cement block. "Are you going to get all distant for the rest of the project now?"

"What do you think that peace offering was about?" she asked over the hum of the boat's motor.

He held up the tart. "While appreciated in its own right, pastry doesn't necessarily denote reciprocal sentiments."

It took a few minutes to find words. "Let me just say this," she said. "I've spent the past ten years not liking you. Right now, pastry is about all I've got to spare."

"What about Waverly? You never answered my question, earlier."

Ian again. She gritted her teeth. "Which question? Am I attracted to him, or what's he got on me that makes me want to be his friend?"

Flintrop shrugged. "Forget I asked."

"Forgotten." The boat drew close to the dock, and she cut the motor.

He stuffed the rest of the tart into his mouth, then jumped onto the dock to tie up the mooring lines. They secured the boat and pulled the cover on. As they gathered the supplies to return to camp, he said, "You just... I've been around you off and on for years, and I've never seen you so...animated."

She didn't know what to say to that. Had she been so withdrawn before that even Flintrop could notice the difference? *Was* there a difference?

Oh, yes.

"I'm just asking about him because I'm worried about you," added Flintrop.

God, he was like a gnat in her ear. She snatched her backpack from the floor of the boat. "Quit worrying. I'm able to take care of myself and whatever 'animations' I might have."

They started the hike back to the dig, passing once again by Ian's tent on the way. She scanned his camp, but it appeared he'd gone climbing. She looked away and caught Flintrop watching her. Pursing her lips, she hurried ahead of him.

She couldn't wait until cover of darkness that night, when she'd be able to steal away to the inlet. And, she hoped, to Ian's arms, because Flintrop was totally right. She'd never wanted anyone like this.

****

Faith sat reading in her tent, making notes in her new journal, and chewing meditatively on her pen cap. After the last journal disappeared, she'd gotten into the habit of keeping this one in her possession at all times. Rolling the pen cap between her teeth, she turned the page and continued her new entry.

Excavated the skull found in the fissure today. We haven't dated it, but I assume it's Norse due to its proximity to the house ruin. I haven't touched it, but I get a strange feeling about it. Maybe I'm just creeped out lately.

We also found a silver belt buckle. It's exciting to find our first artifacts. Too bad Sara went to Unst today.

She's been happier than I've ever seen her, here in Shetland. Probably equal parts respect for Dad's legacy, and the presence of Ian Waverly. He's been good for her.

Now the bad news: Flintrop showed up to help with the project. Can't say I am happy, but Flintrop supported us in the decision to stay and finish digging despite tremor activity. Wish there were a way to get his funding without having to work with him.

Sara interrupted Faith's account by dropping a bag into her lap. Faith jumped and shot her sister a glare.

"Open it," Sara demanded, looking grim.

Faith pulled the book from its bag. "A children's book?"

"Take a closer look." Her sister sat on the cot.

Faith did so. Her gaze landed on the lady's necklace. "What the...?"

"I just finished looking at it. Basically, it reads like your usual bedtime story. A jealous evil wizard puts a curse on a princess, and her prince has to rescue her. Which, unlike your usual bedtime story, he doesn't."

"Huh?"

Sara sat forward and rested her hands on her knees. "The wizard curses her into an eternal sleep, and the prince who's supposed to rescue her loses the battle against the wizard. The wizard gets mad and curses the prince, too. Prince and princess spend the rest of forever as a standing stone split down the middle, always together but never touching. Kind of romantic, in a tragic sort of way."

"What does the necklace have to do with it?" Faith wondered, flipping through the book.

"The necklace is what he uses to curse them."

Faith went through the pages again, pursing her lips. She stared at the cartoony necklace. "Okay, just for a minute, let's assume this is the amulet in the story. Since the wizard had it, my guess would be that's the druid from my vision. The prince in the story would have to be the man who killed the druid and stole the amulet. I don't get where the girl comes in."

"And you're the emotional one," scoffed her sister.

"Obviously, the guy in your vision killed the druid over the girl."

Faith frowned in thought. "God, this is familiar. *Why* is this so familiar?"

"I don't know. I thought the same—" Sara ground to a halt, and they gaped at each other. Faith knew her sister had reached the same conclusion as she had.

The fairy tale book.

Faith sprang out of her chair and searched through the trunk at the end of her cot. She retrieved the disheveled copy of *Fairy Tales of Western Europe*, the book they'd discovered in their father's safe box. She'd borrowed it from Sara to look for clues, and they had found it was the same book he'd read to them during their childhood bedtimes.

Frowning, Faith searched the book, then stopped short when she reached a damaged page. The top part of the page where a story title and illustration should have been was missing, torn out by a careless prior owner before the used book had even come to the Markham family.

She skimmed the story. "I think this is it. It mentions a wizard and a divided standing stone, but the necklace isn't in it. It just talks about the wizard calling a serpent demon." She met her sister's gaze and laid the book on her cot. "There's our serpent ceremony."

"Research from children's stories," Sara rumbled, toying with the amulet's leather cord. "What kind of wild goose chase was Dad leading us on?"

"Old stories and legends usually have some kind of metaphorical meaning, some basis in fact. Magic the way they would have seen it back then—"

"—could be what we're able to do now,"

interrupted her sister, looking startled. Her eyes turned green, and she floated the copy of *Fairy Tales* into the air. "Do you think the wizard—druid—was one of us?"

Faith recoiled. "I think we're in big trouble. You'd better take that thing back to a jeweler and have it dismantled. If someone like us is looking for that thing, I don't think I want him to find it. Especially if he knows how to use it."

Sara let the book come to rest on the blankets of Faith's cot again, and blinked her eyes back to hazel. "Did *Beardsley* give you anything on this?"

"No, but ley lines are nothing to kid around with. There's a lot of power in them, especially with the collective conscious of every ghost walking them. You saw what happened to me. I couldn't handle it."

Sara grabbed Faith's arm. "What if this druid could? What could he do with it?"

Horrified, Faith started imagining all sorts of things that could have linked the amulet to as much blood as she'd sensed on reading it. "Anything. If he could harness the power, if he wanted to do damage...anything. It would be the psychic equivalent of an atom bomb." She shook her head. "But it could kill someone, trying to control that kind of power alone. You'd have to be incredibly powerful."

"Or a whole druid order working together?" Sara suggested.

A chill seeped into Faith's bones. "I don't like this."

A commotion outside the tent interrupted Sara's reply. Voices rose in alarm. They rushed outside in the direction of the sound.

A knot of crew surrounded a figure lying prone on

the ground. Faith heard Lambertson's voice booming above the others, ordering them to lift. "What happened?" She bullied her way into the circle. Then she saw for herself.

Cameron lay pinned underneath a section of fallen scaffold. He groaned in agony, pushing at the heavy rigging and gasping for breath. Lamb and the rest of the crew struggled to haul it off the young man's chest. Horrified, Faith sprang to help.

Sara jumped in beside her and crouched down over Cameron. "Hang on, Cam," she murmured. Faith knew that her sister had called on her telekinesis, and her eyes changed, when Cameron's eyes sprang wide. Sara bent a shoulder to the scaffold and glared at it, pushing and using her power at the same time.

Faith jammed her shoulder against the bars and hauled upward with the others. The bulky steelwork dug into her body, resisting her efforts. With tacit understanding, she waited until Sara blasted it with another wave of telekinesis and gave a simultaneous heave, shouting for the others to do the same. It rose a few grudging inches. "Get him out, get him out!"

Luis and Dustin grabbed the young man by the shoulders and dragged him out from under the scaffold. Cameron gave a broken shout of pain. When he was clear, the crew let the steelwork slam back onto the ground.

"Dustin, the stretcher. Luis, my first-aid kit. Hurry!" Lamb shouted.

Faith saw them tear away in the direction of Lambertson's tent. She bent over Cameron, assessing the damage. The young man's ribs were crushed in on one side. Bile rose in her throat. All this from a scaffold that shouldn't have been that heavy to start with?

Sara crouched on Cameron's other side. Faith caught a glimpse of her sister blinking away tears and the evidence of her power. Cameron coughed. A reddish froth of sputum covered his lips. His glassy gaze fixed on Sara. "You— Your—" His chest heaved once, twice, then his breath hissed out and his stare turned blank.

Sara made an inarticulate sound and clapped a hand over her mouth.

Feeling sick, Faith checked for a pulse and found none. "Lamb. Radio the mainland for a helicopter." Lambertson was already walking as she spoke. She glanced up at Thomas and Michael and caught them staring, stone-faced, at Sara. Even without her sister's skill at reading expressions, Faith saw *It's your fault we stayed here* on their faces.

Flintrop's voice spurred them into action. "Someone get a blanket to cover him. The rest of you, help me put this goddamn thing back." Becky dashed off to find a blanket, and the others put their shoulders under the steel bars of the scaffold.

Faith watched it swing upright with less trouble than it had given moments ago. Suspicion raced through her. Thomas and Michael found sledgehammers, and secured the rigging with extra posts. Faith wanted to throw up.

Lamb returned. "They're on their way."

Sara got to her feet, swaying. Becky came back with the blanket, and swept it over Cameron's body. Sara swallowed convulsively, glanced once at Faith, then bolted away.

Lambertson made a move to follow. "Let her go,"

Faith said, stalling him with an outstretched hand. Lamb frowned, but stayed where he was.

Faith stared after her sister, sensing waves of guilt and anguish even from that distance. *Oh, Sara,* she thought, heartsick.

It would be no use telling her sister that she couldn't have saved him, or somehow done something to bring him back.

Sara had felt exactly the same when their father died.

Chapter Ten

Sara pushed the empty beer bottle onto the table to join its fellows. The bottle's lines blurred and swam in the lantern glow. How many drinks had she had since the helicopter had brought the police to investigate? They'd determined it an "accident," which was complete crap. That scaffold was rock solid. Her crew made sure of it every morning. She reached into the cooler at her foot for another beer, counting the chirps of a night insect outside her tent.

"Hey," came a hushed voice from the doorway.

Sitting in the chair facing away from the door, she couldn't see her tormentor. "Go away." She heard the person enter the tent in spite of her warning. "I said go away. Let me get drunk in peace."

The figure rounded the edge of the table. She recognized Ian from the corner of her eye and glanced up.

She must have looked as wretched as she felt, because his expression went from concerned to alarmed. His gaze fell on the throng of empty bottles. "You didn't show up at the inlet, so I came to see if you were all right."

Sara took a healthy swallow of her new beer. "Yessss. I am all right. I'm walking around... Sitting around. Talking. Breathing. Drinking." She saluted him with her bottle. "Drinking quite a bit, actually. And planning to do more drinking." She took another gulp and pursed her lips around the bite of the alcohol as it went down. Still not dulled enough.

Ian pulled the other chair around and sat beside her. "I saw a chopper today. What happened down here?"

She curled her lip. "What happened is, I'm the one who insisted we brace the fault and stay here. What happened is, twenty-three-year-old Cameron Leone got crushed under a scaffold, and it's my fault he's dead. What happened is, no one has let me get quietly drunk since six o'clock this evening, and it's beginning to piss me off. *That's* what happened today." She tipped the bottle up again, drained its contents in one long swallow, then slammed it down onto the table. "Between Lamb, and Faith, and Flintrop, I don't know why the hell I'm even here. I should find a way to open that damn ley line and walk right in. Maybe they'll give Cameron back in trade."

Ian stood, pushed the cooler away with the heel of his boot, and reached for her hands. "Come on, don't do this."

She lurched to her feet and flung his hands off. "Damn it, just go away! I don't want anybody here! I swear to God, I'll throw you clear back to your ca—"

"I'd like to see you try. You're plastered." He shot a look at the procession of empty bottles on the table.

Sara tried to hold his angry blue stare and couldn't. She took one unsteady step forward, pushing at him. "Just. Go. Away."

"Like hell I will. I'm not going to let you do this to yourself."

"Who's letting me? I'm a grown woman," she

snapped, turning away toward her cot. "I wish someone would tell Lamb that. Everyone seems to know what's best for me, and to hell with what I think."

"What are you talking about?"

She pivoted back toward him. The room swayed. She managed to keep her feet and muster another dark look. "I've been given an ultimatum to stay away from you until the dig is finished."

"Or what? They'll send you to your room without dinner?"

She thumped him in the chest. "You see my point, here. Pass me another beer."

He propped a boot on the cooler's lid and crossed his arms. "I don't think so."

"Don't be a jerk, Ian."

"I'm not. Give up on the beer for tonight. You're not getting it."

She threw her hands in the air and stumbled toward her cot, then dropped onto it like a stone. "Another asshole who knows what's best for me."

"Drinking yourself stupid is a better idea?"

Sara looked up at him. His figure blurred around the edges. *Tears. No tears. Stop it.* She screwed her eyes shut and pulled her knees up, hugging them and hunching on the cot's edge. "Please go away?" she begged into her arms.

The cot sank as he sat beside her. "Absolutely not," came his soft murmur.

She couldn't hold it in anymore. A long, broken wail tore from the center of her being. She covered her head with her arms and curled into a tighter ball, trying to disappear into herself. Tears flooded forth in a torrent that shredded her from the inside out.

His arm came around her back with a gentle tug. She gave up all pretense of hiding her anguish, shifted, and threw herself at him to sob into his shoulder. He held her tight while she went to pieces in his arms. Her heart unraveled. She couldn't stop it. She shook with terror at the force of emotion pouring through her. This—oh, God, this was why she never let her guard down.

Ian laid his cheek against the top of her head and stroked her hair, saying nothing as she wept.

The last vestiges of her self-control caved in on top of her. Guilt crashed down with it. She cried so hard her ribs hurt. She cowered against his body, clutching in desperation at his jacket, but the pain sought her out and laid her open. With no escape, she surrendered and let the tears come until none were left to cry.

Seconds, minutes, hours later—she had no idea—exhaustion crept up on her. Her eyes burned with salt and dryness. Her head ached. An empty hollow sat in the pit of her stomach where all the feeling had been. Still trembling, she pulled away from him and scrubbed at the tearstains on her cheeks.

He reached into his jacket pocket and withdrew a bandanna. He shook a puff of chalk dust out of it and offered it to her.

She took it and wiped the tears away. "I haven't cried like that in twenty years." Her voice sounded hoarse, nothing like her own. "Not since—"

"—your father died," he finished quietly. "I remember." He propped up the pillows on her cot, then slid backward to sit upright against them. Without a word, he reached for her.

She went, and rested her back against his chest. His

arms came around her again. Warm. Safe.

"You stayed late after school for something. I was there for baseball practice. I saw you crying in an empty classroom, but I didn't know why," he told her. "I wanted to do something. I should have."

She wiped at her face once more with his bandanna, then huddled on her side against him, gazing at the off-white canvas of the tent wall. "You just did."

****

Ian roused later to the sound of footsteps outside. The lantern had guttered out. Wide-awake in an instant, he squinted into the darkness. The footsteps paused in front of Sara's tent. He groped one-handed along the bedside table, but it held only the extinguished lantern. He searched along the bedside. His hand landed on a spare tent pole. Easing out from under Sara, he picked up the pole, then moved soundlessly to the tent door.

A sliver of starlight appeared as someone unzipped the door. A shadowy figure slipped into the tent.

Ian sprang forward and jammed the end of the tent pole into the intruder's gut. His victim wheezed and hunched over. He spun the pole around and swept the person's feet out with it. His adversary landed with a thud and another wheeze, and Ian brought his boot down on the figure's chest. There was a strangled grunt. Ian poised the tent pole to strike again if necessary.

"What's going on?" came Sara's panicky voice. Ian heard her fumble behind him, then the crash of the lantern falling to the floor. The tent flooded with flashlight.

Squinting against the sudden illumination, he looked down. The redheaded woman lay pinned under his boot with an expression of shock.

Sara lurched off the cot. "Becky. Oh, my God. Ian, let her up."

Ian took his boot away. The redhead heaved for air and rubbed at her chest. She struggled to her feet. He stepped back and planted the end of the pole in the floor with a suspicious glare. "What are you doing here?"

Sara took the woman's hand and tugged her to a seat. "Are you all right?"

"Yeah, more or less. I came to see if you were okay." Becky rubbed her stomach with a rueful moan. Her gaze darted around Sara's tent.

"I will be." Sara caught Ian's eye and he pasted a deadpan expression on his face. *Apologize!* she mouthed.

He didn't. Something in Becky's posture set the back of his neck prickling. He moved a little closer to Sara.

Sara laid her hand on Becky's. "I'm sorry about that."

"What's he doing here?" the redhead asked. "I thought Lamb told us to stay away from him."

"He saw the helicopter go over today, and came down to see if something was wrong," explained Sara.

Ian held the woman's gaze without so much as a twitch. She gave him a stare that said *How could you?* as plain as words.

Glancing back and forth between them, Sara blushed even in the flashlight glow. "Becky, I'll be fine tonight. Why don't I come see you in the morning and make sure you're still okay?"

The woman marshaled up a smile and rose from the chair. "Right. Sorry I woke you." With hunched shoulders, she fled the tent.

Guilty as hell, he thought, anger coursing through him.

Sara fisted her hands on her hips. "What was that all about?"

He tossed the pole tent corner with a clatter. "Why don't you ask her what she's doing sneaking into your tent in the middle of the night, instead of announcing herself like anybody else?"

"What, Becky? The poor girl wouldn't know *how* to sneak, Ian. She's got no poker face."

"You didn't happen to see her checking out your stuff a minute ago?" He waved a hand around the tent's interior.

Sara's hand flew to the necklace at her throat. The blush in her cheeks drained fast. "You don't think she was after—"

He strode toward her and laid his hands on her shoulders, when all he really wanted was to crush her against him. "I think it enough to worry about the same thing happening again. Enough to wonder if she isn't the only one who knows about the amulet. Please, come stay with me."

If possible, she went whiter. "I can't stay with you. I can't leave Faith. I have to go check on her. Right now." She broke away from him with panic screaming from every line of her posture.

He stalled her with a hand on her arm. "After, then. Just for tonight. Sara, if they can't steal it, they're going to try to kill you for it. Get rid of it. Something. Please. I'll take it."

"No!"

"Sara—"

She shook her head and hurried out the tent door.

Ian cursed under his breath and followed.

Before they could reach Faith's tent, Lambertson intercepted them, striding forward with Flintrop, Michael McGrath, and Luis Rivero close behind. Their expressions, hostile even in starlight, gave them all the appearance of a lynch mob. Becky was nowhere to be seen.

"Waverly!" Lamb shouted.

Ian stopped. Sara came to a halt beside him, dancing with agitation and looking in the direction of Faith's tent.

Lambertson reached out and seized the front of Ian's jacket. The older man shook it, surprising Ian with his strength. "What in hell do you mean by attacking one of our crew?"

Sara rushed forward, separating them. "Lamb, not now. Becky's fine. It wasn't Ian's fault."

The man rounded on her. Ian saw her shrink back in astonishment at his fury. "Don't cross me on this. I run this dig, and I want him gone. If I have to have him arrested for assault, I will do so. Alan, get him out of here."

Flintrop stepped around Lambertson, seething. "I'd like nothing better."

Ian glanced at Sara, who shot him a worried look. He stood his ground, unwilling to leave her.

Flintrop advanced until he stood nose to nose with Ian. "Don't give me an excuse to pummel you. I haven't liked you since day one, Waverly."

Ian's attention snapped to Flintrop's leering face. Hostility churned under his skin. "While we're on the subject, the feeling is mutual."

Flintrop showed his teeth. "If you so much as set a

foot down here for the rest of the summer, I'll have you landed in prison by any means I can use."

Ian bristled, but stayed put.

Flintrop lowered his voice to a hiss only Ian would hear. "What's the matter? Don't like being shooed away from her?"

In the same venomous tone, Ian said, "You aren't worth my time, Flintrop, and you'll never be worth hers." He turned and walked away, forcing himself not to look back at Sara as he went.

****

Sara unzipped her sister's tent flap and ducked in with her heartbeat thumping. "Faith!"

Her sister jerked in her seat. "What!" She whirled around and relaxed when she saw Sara. "Don't sneak up on me like that."

Sara's brow furrowed. "You didn't hear me unzip the door?"

"No. Zip it back up."

Sara did, then took a seat beside her, only beginning to relax now that she saw her sister in one piece. She swept the table with a glance. On it sat the skull and belt buckle from the fault. "What are you doing?"

"I was in a divining trance. I didn't think I was going to have company in the middle of the night." She favored Sara with a worried look. "Are you okay?"

"I will be. We have to talk."

"That's an understatement," said Faith. "You first."

Sara took a breath and plunged in. "Ian came down and stayed part of the night." Leaning forward, she dropped her tone to a whisper. "Faith, he caught Becky sneaking into my tent. I think she tried to steal the amulet."

Faith opened her mouth in what was sure to be an anxious tirade.

"She didn't get it," Sara interrupted, "but Lamb just came out with a couple of the guys saying Ian attacked her. Ian went back to his camp, but I'm worried. I think the three of us should leave. I don't know if we can trust anybody right now."

"We can't. I told you I read these..."

Sara cast a suspicious look at the skull resting on her sister's table. Reading artifacts had always been a risky business for Faith. Reading human bones was categorically dangerous. "Faith..."

"After what happened today, I'd just as soon learn everything I can about this dig site, as fast as I can learn it. That scaffold didn't stay down by itself today."

Sara frowned. "Are you saying someone was pushing down on it? Like, with telekinesis?"

"That's exactly what I'm saying. I saw Flintrop and some of the others put it back up like it weighed nothing. Someone was holding it down in the first place. And that's not all." She picked up the skull and put it into Sara's hands. "Say hello to Hakon Ivarsson."

"Hakon?"

"Our druid-killer from the vision was a Viking, and not just any Viking. Sara, I've had dreams about him since I was a kid. Just flashes, mostly, but I think he wants me to do something. Help him. He's the ghost I've been sensing since we got here, even without my power."

Sara eased the skull back onto the table as if it were radioactive.

"I've spent all night trying to communicate with

him," Faith added. "Something's keeping him from talking to me. I can only catch bits and pieces. He's here right now."

"Did he bring up the amulet?" Sara cast a suspicious look around as if the ghost would appear from thin air, though she knew better.

"I haven't used Old Norse since college. I'm trying. He said something about the moon, the next full moon. He mentioned a sword, but I can't make out what." Faith sighed. "We have to stay on Hvitmar until I figure this out."

"The next full moon isn't for three weeks. If Becky knows about the amulet, others must know. If whoever wants it is like us and can use the amulet—if someone today pushed that scaffold down on Cameron—we are all in serious trouble," Sara said.

"I don't like it any better than you do. I don't make the rules. At this point, I don't even *know* the rules."

Biting her lip, Sara thought of Ian's father. "I—I think I'd better tell you something." In halting words, feeling guilty for betraying Ian's confidence, she related his father's murder to Faith.

When she finished, her sister sat still as a marble obelisk. Sara watched her go through the same succession of emotions that she'd had. Shock. Horror. A twisted sense of kinship that there were others out there with proven supernatural abilities...and the worry that not all of them might be good souls.

Finally, Faith pursed her lips and picked up the belt buckle from her table. "I trust Hakon. I think he may be able to help us. I'm going to keep trying to speak to him."

"Alone?"

"We haven't got time to argue about it, have we? Besides, he won't hurt me. I don't know why I know that, but I know that." Sara gave a doubtful murmur, but Faith cut her off. "He won't leave tonight. If anyone comes, he'll warn me."

Sara paced the tent, realizing Ian had been right in his warning. "If Becky tried stealing the amulet tonight, what's to stop her from sneaking into my tent again over three weeks? Your tent?" She felt the color leave her cheeks. "Ian's tent."

Faith's gaze went sharp and alert. "Out the back."

Worried now, Sara launched herself at the back wall of the tent and pulled up the stakes that pinned the canvas to the tent floor. With a last look at Faith, she slipped out.

She shapeshifted into the wolf and ran full-tilt up the slope of the island. As she came within sight of his camp, she slowed to a trot and then a cautious walk, approaching it from the back.

Ian's scent drifted toward her on the cool air. She pricked her ears forward and sniffed again, but no hint of other company reached her. She rounded the corner of the tent. Lantern light glowed from within.

When she reached the door, she released her hold on the shapeshift. The shape of the tent blurred, then took on the more indistinct lines of human night vision, and the change completed. "Ian?"

"Come in."

She did so, and found him sitting on his cot cleaning a rifle. Sara pulled up a chair and sank into it with her heart thumping. "You should leave."

He lowered the rifle to his lap. "Are you kidding?"

"Take the boat tonight and go to Unst. Call a ferry,

I don't care. You don't have to stay here. This isn't your problem."

"Let me tell you why it is my problem. I've had recurring nightmares since I got here about something happening to you, about how I'm supposed to protect you from God knows what or who, and they're only getting worse. You know who I see in these damned nightmares, who tells me this stuff? Your father."

She blanched. Her mouth fell open, and she struggled for something to say. Nothing came.

Ian went back to cleaning his rifle. "He died in an office, right? There was a wooden desk, and a brass lamp, and a big silver picture frame on the bookshelf with your family in it? Leather books? Stuff in display cases? An old map of Shetland on the wall?"

His words hit her like a spray of bullets. She cringed in the chair. "Stop, stop! How are you seeing all this?"

"Tell me again how it isn't my problem."

She hugged herself and whispered, "He never comes to me or Faith."

"I guess I'm just lucky."

Wounded, she stared at him.

Regret flashed across his features. "Sara, you don't want to see him. Not like this." He looked back down, wiping the small parts of the rifle and piecing them back together. "Anyway, I'm not leaving. Not unless you do. Don't ask me why he picked me, because I don't know."

"We can't leave. Faith and I found something out about this amulet. It's connected somehow with a druid ceremony that manipulated the ley lines. The order that used it... We think they were like us."

Ian looked up. "Like you? With the floating objects and shapeshifting?"

"Yes. Except this druid order, if they really were a druid order, was able to control the ley lines and use their power. Faith said it would be like having possession of an atomic bomb."

"And you want me to leave without you?"

"We found a skull at the dig, from a Viking who killed one of the druids." Her body screamed for motion. She lunged upright to pace back and forth. "Faith read the skull, and she found his ghost, and he wants us to stay here. Something about the next full moon and a sword, and he's guarding her, and I came up here to see you because I'm worried that something is going to happen to you—"

Ian set his rifle aside and stood up. He caught her in his arms. "Now you know how I feel. Don't you think I'd go out of my mind with worry if I left?"

She shook her head violently. "I don't want you staying here because of some dream—"

"It's not just about that! Are you blind? I—"

She gaped. Had he just meant to say...?

Ian looked away, but not before she saw the torment in his eyes. He circled like an angry wolf, twice around the tent, then he gripped her shoulders and gave her an angry shake. "I've wanted you almost from the minute you got here, and I can't even explain why. Then I find out what you are, and I have no idea what I'm doing, feeling the way I am, because *my father* was killed by one of you—" He broke off and lunged away, raking both hands through his hair.

Old pain tore through her, suddenly fresh again. "Freaks? Is that what you were going to say?"

He glanced back, then away, hunching his shoulders. "I didn't mean..."

"No, you did!" She shot across the tent to stare him down toe-to-toe. "Say it. Get it out. I want to hear you say it!"

He gave her a desperate look. "You have no idea what this is like. I was ten years old, and I saw my father murdered, by a man who—who could—"

"Do what I do? Telekinesis? Shapeshifting? Mind-reading?" She flung the words at him, seething when he flinched. "Do I look like a murderer, Ian? Does having this power make me a monster?" She shuddered. "I didn't ask for it."

He sighed explosively. "Jesus, Sara. You don't... I can't..." He turned his back on her. "I've been making myself crazy ever since I got here, knowing what you are."

"Then why did you come? You can't stand what I am unless it helps you with your goddamned research, is that it? Is that all this was? You're using me? And to think I came up here to warn you." She wheeled toward the tent door.

He spun back and caught her by the wrist. Writhing with ferocity, she tried yanking it away, but he held fast.

His expression shifted; she saw him fighting with himself. The pulse pounded in his throat. "Don't go."

Chapter Eleven

Sara glanced at the door, hovering like a wild creature on the razor edge of fight or flight. *Idiot,* he cursed himself. *You've screwed this all up from the first second you opened your mouth.* The hurt in her eyes knifed him.

Once more she moved to leave, and his entire being railed against it. He lunged forward and kissed her.

She gave a muffled sob and pounded his chest with both fists. Her cry resounded in every nerve of his body and tore at him. She tried to wrench away. When he didn't release her, she hid her face in his shirt and gave another thin cry, thumping his chest again. He held her hard against him.

Little by little, her trembling subsided. Her tears dampened his shirt. He pressed his face into her hair. "I'm sorry, I'm sorry. I didn't mean to hurt you, I swear. Please believe that."

She turned her face up to him at last. The hurt pride cleared from her features. In its place came a cool wariness that cut him worse than her tears had done.

She'd closed herself off...gone where he couldn't follow. And he never would have believed it, but that pained him still more.

She wiped moisture off her cheeks, then pushed out of his grasp. "You want what you can get out of me, like everyone else who would turn me and Faith into lab rats if they knew about us."

He spread his hands. "Sara, I have told *no one*. I wouldn't do that."

"Oh?"

He saw it in her eyes; she expected a fight. Probably even welcomed it, because then he could leave her, and she'd be just as alone as she'd looked in that tavern on the mainland.

Oh, no. Not this time. Not when his insides were roaring at how she pulled away.

He stroked her hair. She remained immobile, unresponsive.

Distrustful.

"What's it gonna take, Sara?" he whispered, stepping back toward her. Gently, he kissed her again. He slid his arms around her, telling her with his body what he couldn't say, and what he knew she wouldn't accept.

She lit like a dynamite fuse, seizing his shirt in both fists. But she would have none of the slow, soft caresses. She dragged at his shirt, demanding fire.

And, God help him, he gave it.

When she took his lip between her teeth, his body ignited. He swept her mouth with his tongue, drinking in the taste of her. He couldn't pull her close enough. She pressed against him along the entire length of their bodies, and still she was too far away. She gasped against his mouth as his searching hands reached the soft skin under her shirt.

Christ, she burned.

He broke the kiss long enough to pull his shirt off and throw it on the floor. Her hands explored the muscles of his back. Blood boiling, he reached between them to undo the first button of her shirt, and placed a kiss there. She made a low sound, and the skin of her throat vibrated under his lips. The earthy scent of her flooded his senses.

Another button, another kiss. Her fingernails dug into his back. He fought to keep from tearing her shirt open to get to the rest of her. With painstaking slowness, he undid the remaining buttons and drew the shirt off her shoulder, planting still more kisses on her satiny skin.

She straightened her arms. Her shirt fell to the floor. Her hazel eyes glowed in the lantern light. Separated from him only by her bra and pants, she was more beautiful than he'd ever seen her in any form.

His control slipped. He molded his hands to her and she arched against him, her body molten with desire, but her eyes...

Cold as gemstones.

No, he thought fiercely. *Answer me. Answer this.* He reached up to grapple with the hooks of her bra and it fell away, leaving her bare under his hands. When he cupped her breast, skin to heated skin, she moaned and pressed closer.

With an inward hiss of triumph, he crushed his body against her, reveling in the feel of her skin on his. He urged her to the cot with fervent kisses. She went, willing under his touch. He lay beside her and drew his fingertips along a taut nipple, teasing it with his thumb.

She inhaled, sharp and surprised. Ian lowered his head and took the nipple in his mouth, drawing hard on it, grazing the edges with his teeth. She whimpered, and he wrestled for restraint. He pushed aside the amulet at her throat to touch his lips to the hollow between her breasts. Her heartbeat thudded against his mouth. When her nails grazed the skin of his back, he sucked in a breath and looked up at her. "Are you sure you want this?"

She answered by cupping the back of his head and drawing him down to her. He kissed her again, groaning when her tongue swept into his mouth to imitate the strokes he made with his own. His erection strained against his pants. Ian broke away and took another breath, trying to cool his raging blood. *Slow down,* he told himself.

Hell, no, demanded another, more primal part of him. He wanted all of her. Here, now, before another second went by. He stroked the burning skin of her belly and she sighed, lifting her chin. He bent his head to her throat and savored her with gentle nips. Her nails dug into his shoulders.

Ian blasted apart. With a possessive snarl, he unzipped her pants and almost tore them off. He stretched out over her with triumph scorching through his body. The feel of her skin, hot and satin-smooth, tore another snarl from him.

Sara dug her nails into his skin again, pinning him there, though he'd have died before leaving her. Naked, she lay beneath him, watching him with eyes that blazed now with the need echoing in her body. Ian memorized every curve and hollow, then swept his hands along each contour, lingering with kiss and touch.

He stroked a hand along one slender thigh to the curls between her legs and found her center hot and moist. When he slid a finger into her, she moaned. His thumb found the sensitive bud between her folds, and he stroked her. She arched off the cot with a soft cry. "Ian!"

He drank in her reaction to his touch with ferocious greed. His senses reeled with the sweet musk of her arousal. Every time she gasped, his tenuous control unraveled faster.

Her fingertips brushed along the top of his pants. His belly clenched. He felt her reach for the button and realized she was following his example. She wrestled, and he closed his hands over hers to help her. He pushed his pants off and lay naked beside her, letting her look at him, hardly able to keep his patience when his entire body ached to be touching her.

She gave him the same thorough appraisal he'd given her, then glanced up at him. At last he saw her come back from that distant place—no longer unreachable, but somehow both intense and shy. He reined in his need and took her hand, pressing it to his chest. "Touch me."

She did. Her hands swept along his skin, searing him wherever they landed. He trembled under her questing fingers as he'd never done with any other woman. Her hands closed around his rigid manhood, stroking feather-light along its length. "Sara," he ground out, teetering on the brink.

"Now," she whispered. "Now, Ian, please."

The rest of his self-control shattered. She urged him down and opened herself to him. He pressed his hips into hers, and eased home in a long, slow, blissful stroke.

And then she was his. Completely, finally. No more secrets. No painful pasts. Only the two of them, here at this moment with the rest of the world far away. *Mine*, repeated his primal self.

She arched underneath him, urging him still deeper. He cupped the back of her head in one hand and slid the other along the length of her body. "You're beautiful," he said. "So incredibly beautiful."

Her gaze found his again, glowing with passion. She kissed him, pulling him into her, gripping him harder with each stroke. Her breath came faster in his ear. A moan caught in her throat and drove him higher. Every nerve sang where she touched him. Her breath, her skin, her heat, the very smell of her struck him like a storm to a lightning rod.

She gasped out his name, and her body arched like a drawn bow. An electric hum seized him and burned along his spine. He buried his face in her hair and swept over the edge with a groan. The charge reverberated back up his spine, then faded.

****

Sara's skin resonated with liquid flame. *Yes*, her body echoed, as if it had known all along that this moment was inevitable. This time, this place. Him.

Ian's breath rasped in her ear. She drew her hands up his back, tracing her fingers along the sweat-slick skin.

He was shaking. So was she. "Are you all right?" she whispered.

He arched onto his elbow, still panting. "Your eyes are green. What did you just do?"

Her powers. "Oh, God, Ian, I'm sorry."

He cupped her face and shushed her with a kiss. "No, don't be sorry. Don't be," he urged, then kissed her again. "I'm fine." He withdrew and rolled onto his back, curling an arm underneath her to pull her close again. He kissed her hair.

She let her hand hover a second before settling it on his chest, then she huddled in the hollow of his arm. "I think I might have let go of my power. I didn't mean to."

Ian rocked onto his elbow. "Is that what that was?"

"I think so." Her face burned with guilt.

He flopped back down and grinned, scraping a hand through his sweaty hair. "Jesus. Do that whenever you want."

"Are you sure I didn't—"

He rolled on top of her. "Whenever. You. Want," he repeated, punctuating the words with kisses. "You didn't hurt me. In fact, you *adamantly* didn't hurt me."

Another blushing wave heated her cheeks and she smiled, somehow shy after what they'd just done. It had never been like that before. But there was no before, now. No after. Just Ian, here in her arms.

She must have been staring, because he chuckled and stroked her cheek with his thumb. He rolled to his back once more, and slipped an arm around her. One-handed, he reached up and put the lantern out.

Sara laid her head against his chest. She drew a long sigh, and he pulled her close against him. His hands stroked her cooling skin, warm and rough and pleasant. He pressed his lips to her hair. And for the first time in twenty years, she felt at peace with herself.

****

Against her will, Sara's eyes fluttered open. The gray of pre-dawn had stolen into Ian's tent, shattering the veneer of sanctuary in which she had slept. She wanted to go back to it. Back to believing she could shut the world out and lie there in his embrace. Reluctant, she shifted toward the edge of the cot.

Ian's arm tightened around her. "Not yet."

She burrowed into the warm hollow of his arm and stretched her own across his belly. "They'll be up soon."

"I know." He rubbed her back. "How did you get up here last night without them knowing?"

"The wolf," she answered, tracing her fingers through the dusting of hair on his chest. "It's faster and quieter, and I can see better in the dark."

They lay still for a few minutes more while the traitorous light increased.

"So, with the shapeshifting," he said at last.

She tensed, wondering for a moment whether he would bring up her accusation that he was using her.

He shook under her fingertips, and she realized he was holding in laughter. "This has been killing me. How do you do that with clothes on?"

Startled into giggles, herself, she answered, "I don't know. I've always been able to do it either way. Whatever I'm wearing just becomes part of the change. It's all matter."

He laughed now, and it rumbled against her cheek. "I guess I thought it would be more like in the comics, with shredding clothes and stuff."

At that, she lifted her chin and smiled at him. "God, no. I'd have to buy a new wardrobe every other week."

"No, you wouldn't. Walk around naked."

She groaned in mock outrage and pushed up onto her hands.

He reached up to stroke the back of her neck. His

eyes clouded with regret. "I am sorry, Sara." His hand slid from under her hair, and he touched the amulet swaying between her breasts. "Be careful down there today, okay?"

Uncomfortable, she turned from his gaze. A look like that was too dangerous to contemplate. She'd offered him her body last night, and he'd taken it without hesitation. She didn't dare hope there might be more to it.

You are *a freak. Face it.* She shoved into a sitting position. "If it gets much lighter, they'll see me coming back." She reached for her clothing and pulled it on. "You be careful, too."

Ian swung his legs over the edge of the bed and scooped his jeans off the floor. She paused to admire his naked body and the way the light trailed across his skin. The same way her hands had done the night before.

He caught her looking and grinned.

She flushed and went back to dressing. She'd meant their night together to be a one-time thing, a way of proving to herself that something of her truly mattered to him...but oh, she wished they had just a few more hours.

Last night hadn't been enough.

They stood up together, and he gave her a gentle kiss. She leaned into him, breathing him in, fearing she'd never have another chance.

"I'll see you later," he murmured. With a last caress, he released her and went to the door to open it.

She called on the wolf. As soon as she slipped into its body, she sprang out the door and loped away.

The journey back to camp didn't take long in her

lupine shape. With all her senses alert, she crept around the back of her tent. She heard movement in some of the other tents; she'd gotten back just in time. Making sure no one saw, she shapeshifted back into human form and rounded the tent, then ducked inside.

The interior looked undisturbed. As she saw the profusion of beer bottles on the table, Cameron's image punched into her mind, blatant shock in his expression. What good were her gifts if they couldn't save him? Cam hadn't had a chance to live. How could he die so young?

She forced away the guilt and snatched a fresh set of clothes. Pulling on a lightweight jacket against the cool air, she emerged from her tent.

Dustin, Flintrop, and Lambertson had already begun morning preparations, moving about in subdued silence. Sara sucked in a breath and went toward them.

Lamb noticed her and left the others, meeting her halfway. "Are you all right?"

She marshaled a smile. "I'll be okay." She saw lines of grief in his face, and felt her smile disappear. For the first time, Lamb didn't seem like the invincible, brilliant doctor of archaeology that she'd known since childhood. He looked tired. "You?"

"Cameron was the best student I ever taught, excepting you girls. I know his family well." He sighed. "I have to go back to England to see them about this. After that, I'll be staying at Eurocon to take care of some business matters. I'm leaving you and Faith in charge here. Sara, be careful. I don't want any more accidents."

"You aren't coming back?"

"As soon I'm able." He took a step toward her, and

she saw by his posture that he wanted to comfort her, but didn't know quite how. For that, she loved him all the more.

She studied the laces of her boots. The amulet weighed heavily around her neck. Her heart thumped, and she teetered on the point of telling him everything. "Lamb?"

"Yes?"

She lost her nerve under his somber, pale-blue gaze. "Have a safe trip," she mumbled, then stepped around him to join the others.

As she approached, Flintrop looked up from his position at the sieve box. "Hello."

The sympathy in his voice pricked at her. She remembered asking Flintrop if he was in love with her. He hadn't answered, but he hadn't needed to.

Tilting her head, she gave him a critical look. He was handsome enough, the sort of man who could make grimy jeans and a T-shirt look appealing. Smart. Successful. Powerful.

But cold. Distant in the way of a beautiful artifact, unreachable behind barriers of velvet rope and glass.

Ian was different. Warm and real and immediate, and he set fires in her that no one else ever had—fires that burned well after the lovemaking ended. Was that why the look in his eyes this morning had made her ache so much?

She sat down in front of the camp grill, where Dustin had started a pot of coffee. "Good morning."

Flintrop sat beside her. "Are you doing okay?"

"I will be, as long as people stop asking me how I am." She accepted a cup of coffee from Dustin when it finished brewing.

"You know what happened to Cameron isn't your fault, Sara. I made the decision to stay, too."

"I know."

Becky emerged from her tent wrapped in a blanket, looking pale. She sat on the other side of the grill, avoiding eye contact.

Flintrop cleared his throat. "Becky? Do you need to talk?"

The woman shook her head. Her gaze flicked everywhere but at them.

"You sure?" Flintrop prompted.

Sara ducked into her coffee mug until her hair swung forward to hide her face, then let loose her telepathy. Becky flushed red and murmured something about not feeling well, but Sara caught a fragment of her thoughts:

What was I thinking? I can't take that thing. I don't want to do this.

Startled, Sara blinked and raised her head. Not good. She took a huge gulp of coffee, then choked on it as it scalded its way down her throat.

Flintrop pounded her on the back. She waved him off. "I'm fine, I'm fine."

"Between you choking on breakfast, Becky not feeling well, and Lamb leaving, I think we're going to be on light duty today," he muttered.

"I said I'm fine. We'll keep working."

He flashed a brief smile. "I remember when we were in Iceland, and you got the flu. You still wouldn't stop working. Do you ever quit?"

"There's a lot to be said for persistence," she told him, half listening, and half furtively studying Becky, who stayed silent.

"That's very true," Flintrop said softly.

Sara gave him a wary look and ducked into her coffee again. Right now, there just wasn't enough room in her head and heart to sort out what to do with that.

Faith exited her tent and started across the moor. Sara heaved an inward sigh of relief. She caught her sister's gaze, and Faith gave an inconspicuous shake of her head. No further contact with Hakon, then. Sara downed the rest of her coffee, then poured herself another.

Hard work helped turn her thoughts from Cameron's death, and Becky's unwitting admission of attempted theft. She threw herself into the labor, clearing her plot faster than any she'd done since arriving there. Still, each hour ticked by as though it were an eon. While she worked, she stole looks up the slope of the island toward Ian's camp, wondering if he was thinking of her. All of her crew's expressions of concern for her last night had not gone nearly as far as his silent embrace while she broke to pieces in her tent. Had he known that she needed, for once, to feel like she wasn't alone?

When midday break rolled around, Dustin called them to lunch. She didn't realize she hadn't moved until Faith grabbed her elbow. Sara jerked back to the present.

Faith waited until the crew had moved off in search of food. "What's the matter with you?"

"I... Nothing."

"Don't give me that. Is Ian all right? You've been staring up there all morning."

Sara felt her cheeks burn and blurted, "What's with this ghost of yours? Did you talk to him?"

Her sister raised a slender brow.

"Never mind," muttered Sara. "Becky did try to steal the amulet."

"Are you two eating, or not?" called Thomas.

"We'll talk later. At the inlet," Faith murmured.

Sara nodded understanding, and they went to join the others.

****

Sara waded into the inlet up to the bottom of her shorts. The cool water washed around her legs, a relief after the sweat and toil of the dig site. She sank to her neck with a grateful sigh.

Faith splashed in beside her. "Now that we have ten seconds where no one's hovering, can I quietly panic about this Becky thing?"

Sara followed her sister into the inlet until they were both waist-deep. "I heard her thinking this morning. She said, 'I can't take that thing,' which pretty much tells me she was planning on stealing the amulet when she snuck into my tent."

"It can't just be her, acting alone," Faith said. "She couldn't steal a paper clip."

"Faith, we can't stay here for three weeks. I feel like a sitting duck. Even if I go to Mainland and have it dismantled, what are we going to do with the pieces?" Sara touched a hand to her T-shirt, where the amulet hung hidden underneath.

Faith dunked into the water and came up dripping. "I need your help tonight." Her sister's golden-blond hair floated on the water's surface. She pushed a sodden lock out of her eyes. "I'm going to try and read the dig wall."

"The whole wall? Are you insane?"

"We have to know what happened here, and fast," Faith explained. "Hakon told me about a sword, that we need it. I know it's here somewhere. I think I can find it if I do this."

Sara hissed. "This dig site is over a thousand years old! You'll never make it through a divination of the entire thing. You'll pass out, or get lost in it, or worse!"

"That's where you come in. You're my tie to the here and now. I need you to anchor me."

Sara swallowed back the anxious knot in her throat. What if she couldn't get Faith back? She hunched in the water. "Are you sure there isn't another way?"

"Don't you think I've checked? This is the only other thing I can think of, the fastest way we can find this sword before someone else uncovers it. Are you helping, or am I doing this alone?"

Ian's words came back to her. *You're not alone, Sara.* A sudden, visceral pull in the direction of his camp filled her, and oh, how she wished his words were true. Aching, she dropped her gaze to the surface of the water. "I can't let you try this by yourself."

Nodding, Faith said, "I'll come get you at midnight. Everyone should be asleep by then."

"Faith, what if this Hakon is wrong?" Sara asked. "What if he's misleading you?"

"Even if he is, he knows something about that amulet. Right now, all we've got are old stories, and a couple of vague paragraphs in *Beardsley*. I have to believe this is going to work."

Sara wanted to feel as confident as her sister sounded, but an ominous prickling at the base of her spine warned her it wouldn't be as easy as she hoped.

Chapter Twelve

The sky clouded over soon after dark, obliterating all traces of the stars and the waning moon. Sara had put out her lantern an hour ago. One by one, the other lights in the crew tents had also winked out. She hovered in the doorway of her tent, peering at the sky with a mixture of gratitude and unease.

Thunder growled. The rising wind battered against her body in fitful gusts and lashed her hair about her shoulders. The atmosphere bristled with the electric scent of oncoming lightning. A storm would keep the crew inside the shelter of their tents. No one would see them flitting about the dig site in such weather. She wished it would discourage Faith from this reckless plan.

It wouldn't.

The restless drafts of air brought her snatches of Flintrop's voice from inside his tent, then the sound faded, giving way to another boom of thunder. The first patter of rain sheeted across the moor, bringing Faith with it, bearing a shovel over her shoulder. Sara didn't see her until she was almost close enough to touch. She grabbed her rain slicker, and followed her sister to the dig without a word.

They walked along the dig wall until they came to the edge of the new fault. "Right here," Faith said, setting her shovel down. "This is where you found the skull, isn't it? It's as good a place as any."

With her belly churning, Sara sat cross-legged on one of the large, flat stones. Rainwater had already soaked to her skin in spite of the slicker. "How do we do this?"

Faith sat opposite her, mirroring her position. "I'm going to lay one hand on this wall, and you're going to hold my other. Give me ten minutes. If I pass out, or don't come out of it, I want you to pull me off the wall. Don't let go of me, no matter what."

Sara held her breath and gripped Faith's hand in response. "Be careful."

Faith smiled. The first flash of lighting arced across the sky and illuminated her eyes as they melted into silver. "See you soon." She laid her other hand flat against the wall, and fell into silence.

Sara began to count off seconds. The chill of the storm started seeping into her bones. Water trickled down the back of her neck. *Ten, eleven, twelve...*

Seconds lengthened into minutes, and still her sister gave no sign of coming out of her trance. Sara counted on.

Just past seven minutes, Faith shuddered, and her hand went slack in Sara's. Sara shot off the wall and yanked on her sister's hand. Slick with rain, Faith's hand slipped out of her own. "No. No!" She threw her arms around Faith's waist and pulled her bodily off the wall. They tumbled to the sodden ground. Sara snatched up Faith's hand and squeezed. When that didn't work, she slapped Faith's cheek. "Wake up. Faith! Wake up!" Still nothing. Sara shook her by the shoulders. Rain hissed around them.

Faith's features contorted into a scowl. Her eyes

fluttered open to blink against the downpour.

"Oh, thank God!" Sara gasped out. She fell back with a moan of relief.

Shielding her face from the rain, Faith heaved herself into a sitting position. "Thanks for the pull."

"I lost my grip," said Sara. "I thought I wouldn't get you back."

"You let go? I still felt a buzzing. I thought it was you."

"Where's the sword?"

Faith shook herself out of her post-vision haze. She swept a hand across her face in a futile effort to clear it of rainwater, and they got to their feet. "There, under the opposite corner. Help me clear away the wall stones." She brought her shovel to the area she'd indicated, then dropped it to grasp the top stone. She gave it a heave. It dropped with a thud to the earth beside the wall. "We have to hurry. I'm almost out of energy."

Sara nudged her sister. "I'll do it. Watch the tents for me."

Faith stepped aside and shielded her eyes against the rain, looking in the direction of the tents. Lightning speared the heavens, followed by another angry roar of thunder. The storm was almost on top of them. "Not that I can see much in this," she said. "Make it quick. If a tent blows down, they'll come out to fix it."

Sara concentrated on the stones at the corner of the wall, shivering as her power flowed in. She held out a hand and took a few steps back. The top layers of stone trembled and shifted. She focused harder. Her breath quickened, and even in the chilly rain, she began to sweat with exertion. Her heartbeat thudded against her ribs. The weight of the stones resisted her. She pushed again, gritting her teeth. The stones gave way at last, and toppled off the wall.

Just four more layers. Sara stepped back to make more room. Mud sucked at her feet. She shook her head, flinging locks of dripping hair off her forehead, and started again.

This was going to be a long night.

Ten full minutes passed before the next three layers of stone gave way, tumbling on top of the others. Sara exhaled, and her shoulders slumped. "I'm just about tapped. That's all I can manage."

Faith knelt in the mud. "You got the worst of it. We'll do the rest by hand." She seized one of the stones and hurled it aside.

Dropping beside her, Sara bent to the task. The storm whipped the rain, stinging, into their faces while they worked. Lightning and thunder continued their fierce argument overhead.

When they pulled the last of the stones away, Faith took up her shovel and began digging while Sara kept watch. The way the wind howled, she worried that someone's tent would fall victim to its fury.

A little more than a meter down, the shovel *thunk*ed against something solid. "I hope that's a sword, and not bedrock," Faith said. "Have you got enough left to help me lift this thing out?"

"I can try. Let's see what we're working with."

They scraped out handfuls of mud and tossed it away, fighting against a slide of earth and rainwater that filled the hole almost as fast as they emptied it. Sara's fingers brushed the pitted surface of weathered wood. "I've got it. Quick, help me find the edges and lift."

Together, they managed to heft one end of a long wooden box from the hole. Sara struggled to levitate it while Faith hauled on the other end. The wet earth dragged at the box, sapping the last of Sara's power. She pulled harder. "I didn't get this far to quit now," she snarled.

The box gave way at last with a squelch of mud. She and Faith fell back, and the box landed on top of them. Panting, they clambered to their feet and raised the box up onto their shoulders.

"Your tent, quick. It's closest," said Faith, taking the lead while Sara stumbled along behind her.

They reached the shelter of Sara's tent, and ducked inside as another volley of lightning snapped. Sara zipped shut the tent flap while her sister set the box on the table. She went to the lantern and turned it on as high as she dared, just enough to see. Any higher, and it would attract the notice of other crew members.

Standing over the table, they examined the dig site's third find: a battered oak box, splitting with decay. Judging from how long it had lain hidden in the peat, Sara couldn't believe it had survived. She touched the amulet hidden under her sodden shirt and wondered if, as with the necklace, there might be a reason it hadn't aged faster.

Fragments of cloth stuck to the brass hinges and lock. The box must have been wrapped in an oilcloth before being laid in its resting place. She traced her fingers over the lid, and felt regular, shallow depressions where carved runework had worn to near illegibility. The archaeologist in her screamed for a tape measure and notebook. "I hate to open this thing without cataloguing it."

Faith gaped at her. "Put this in writing? Are you nuts?"

"I know, I know. Let's just open it before I lose the nerve."

Faith picked up her shovel and smashed it against the lock. The soft brass split in two and fell to the table. "Hakon, I hope you know what you're doing." She opened the latch and lifted the box's lid.

Inside rested a cloth bundle. Touching it, Sara felt a greasy residue. She'd been right about the oilcloth; whale or seal fat, maybe. "How is this not decomposed? All of it should be rotted away after a thousand years in the ground." She lifted the bundle out. Faith set the empty box on the tent floor.

Sara laid the bundle on the table, then unwrapped it, holding her breath. She turned back the final corner of canvas. She and Faith gasped in unison.

It gleamed, even in the diffuse light of a low lantern. The sword blade reached almost three feet. In utter defiance of its age, it bore a mirror shine. The hilt's grip sparkled with inlaid brass and copper bands. The pommel bore another inset of copper. Then Sara noticed the gently curving guards at the base of the hilt. "Serpent heads," whispered Faith.

Sara brushed her fingers along the hand guard.

The amulet sizzled under her shirt. With a yelp, she snatched her hand back and grappled with the necklace, pulling it out and holding it away from her body. "It burned me!"

Brows aloft, Faith laid one hand on the sword and, ignoring Sara's objection, touched a finger to the amulet. Hissing, she took her hands away from both objects. "Not burning...buzzing. That's what I felt when

I was searching for the sword and holding your hand. I felt it through *you*. They're connected somehow."

Sara pulled the neck of her shirt down. Her skin bore no burn marks. "*You* handle the sword. I'm not touching it again."

"It's almost angry," Faith murmured. "I've never felt an object express emotion before." She folded the canvas back over the sword, then picked the bundle up. "I need to take this back to my tent and try to reach Hakon. With any luck, he'll tell us what to do with it now that we have it." She bent and placed the wrapped sword back in its box.

"What about the hole at the dig? Someone's bound to notice in the morning and start guessing."

Faith frowned and shoved the box under her sister's cot. "We'll have to refill it."

"I used almost everything I had. There's no way I can rebuild that wall."

Retrieving her shovel, Faith unzipped Sara's tent door. "Then we'll make it look like it collapsed. Grab a shovel."

Thunder rumbled as they left the tent. Through the driving rain, Sara spied an approaching figure. She shouted a warning. Faith swung the shovel.

Her adversary caught it by the shaft, and its arc stopped short. Lightning speared the sky, throwing Ian's features into sharp relief. "We have a problem. Becky's at my tent."

"What?" Sara peered over her sister's shoulder at him. Alarm raced to every nerve in her body.

Ian let go of Faith's shovel. "Becky. At my tent. I need your boat keys."

"Are you okay? She didn't—"

"I'm fine," he responded. "She, on the other hand, needs a hospital as fast as she can get there."

Faith lowered her shovel. "What happened?"

"I have no idea. I'm lucky I didn't shoot her when she burst into my tent. She's been burned pretty bad, but she won't say how it happened. We're losing time talking."

Faith glanced at Sara. "Have you got the strength left to get Ian back to his camp?"

Sara hesitated. "I'm almost finished as it is. Any shapeshift big enough to carry him wouldn't last long enough."

"Are you hurt?" Ian turned to Faith. "What happened?"

"She's tapped, and me, almost so. We've used too much of our power at once. Sara, can you get yourself there? Will you be able to drive the boat?"

Uneasily, Sara glanced southward, into the darkness. "A sparrow," she murmured, "if I can fly in this wind."

"All right, go," said Faith. "Ian, I need you. Take her shovel and come with me. I'll explain everything."

Ian looked back at Sara. Another bolt of lightning sizzled above, and she saw worry on his face. He laid a hand against her cheek and kissed her, brief and fierce. An ache just as fierce rushed through her. "Come back safe." He pulled the shovel from her hand and headed away with Faith.

She stared after him for a few seconds before realizing she was wasting time. Later. She would think about that look on his face later, because it had almost looked as if he didn't want to let her out of his sight.

She sprang back into her tent long enough to douse

the lantern, snatch her boat keys from the table, and stuff them in her pocket. Back outside, she called on the sparrow. For a few agonizing moments, she grappled to hold onto even that small demand on her power. The shape came in a flash that surprised her. She took off into the storm, fearful that she would lose the shape now that she had it.

The storm railed around her, hammering the small bird's body with merciless power. She flew low, but even the lesser winds close to the ground forced her to fight for every inch of distance. She lost hold of the shapeshift fifty feet from Ian's tent. Sara slipped out of the sparrow's shape and into her human one, tumbling to the ground with a grunt of pain. She rolled to her feet and stumbled the rest of the way, then opened the tent door, dreading what she'd find.

Becky lurched off Ian's cot and shrank back against the rear wall of the tent. She grappled for the rifle leaning against the table.

"Whoa, whoa!" Sara held up her hands and staggered into the tent. "I'm here to help. I'm taking you to the hospital—" She ground to a halt as her gaze landed on Becky's face. Three blistering, russet burn marks crossed the redhead's cheekbone. Another burn glared from her opposite forearm, blackish and peeling. "Oh, my God."

Instead of speaking, the young woman dropped the rifle with a thump and began to cry. She fumbled for the bandage that had fallen to the cot and tried to rewrap her arm.

Moving closer, Sara took Becky's chin in one gentle hand and turned it to see the burns on her cheek better. "This looks like...finger marks." With her mind spinning, she glanced down at the woman's arm. "What happened to you?"

Becky threw her off, shaking her head and sobbing harder.

Sara backed away a step. Part of her had trouble reconciling this tearful woman with the one who had tried breaking into her tent. Becky looked so...vulnerable. She saw why Ian had been moved to help her, and could do no less. "All right, all right. Don't cry. We're going to fix this. Come with me."

Becky hunched backward, clearly unwilling to take one step out of the relative safety of Ian's tent.

One of his windbreakers had been draped over a chair. Sara picked it up and eased it around the redhead's shoulders. "I won't let anyone hurt you—I promise—but we need to go now, if we're going to get help for those injuries." She glanced around the tent and found a protein bar lying on Ian's nightstand. She snatched it up and unwrapped it, then took a large bite. She'd need the strength to steady the boat on the way to the hospital. The storm had lessened, but not by much.

It would be a long night, indeed.

"Come on," she said, walking to the door.

Becky gave a shudder, but nodded and followed Sara outside.

Sara plodded along, rubber-kneed. She reached the boat by sheer stubborn will. "I may need you to drive it, if I lose consciousness."

Becky's brows shot up.

"I'll be all right. It's just exhaustion. I ran all the way up here." When Becky answered with a look full of questions, Sara bit her tongue. She turned aside to pull back the boat cover. No time—and no idea where to start—for explaining how she'd raced almost a mile to get to Ian's tent.

The ocean raged. She wondered how on earth she and Becky were going to get to the mainland in this tempest. Better that than linger on the island, but she worried about Ian and Faith every second she was away from them.

She and Becky hadn't gotten very far into open water before Mother Nature made good on her promised ferocity. The boat pitched to and fro like a child's plaything. Sara clenched her fists on the steering wheel and called on her power again, using telekinesis to stabilize the craft as best she could. It had scarcely any effect against the tumult. Her head swam. Lights danced before her vision. She couldn't lose it now. What would happen to Ian and Faith if she didn't get back to the island?

Becky stretched a bandaged arm toward her. The redhead's hand clapped over her own on the wheel. A surge of power ran through Sara's hand, and the boat steadied in the churning water. She looked up in amazement.

Becky's eyes were silver.

Sara passed out.

****

Light. Silence. No rain. *Am I dead?* Sara struggled to make sense of her surroundings. "Becky?"

A white-coated figure ducked into her frame of vision. The bleary image resolved into a smiling brunette. "Hello, there. You had us worried."

"Becky," she said again. Her head reeled with jumbled images of the Viking sword, Faith, lightning, and Ian. She sucked in a defiant breath and forced herself into a sitting position. "Where is she?"

"You should get more rest. Can you tell me your name?"

Sara felt the shivery influx of her powers beginning to return. Some of her strength came with them. "Where is Becky? I need to see her."

"Miss, please get a little more rest. You were very dehydrated—"

An alarm beeped, and the hospital P.A. system kicked on. *"Code Blue, Unit One-Four. Code Blue, Unit One-Four—"*

The nurse moved toward the door. "I have to leave. We have an emergency on the unit. If you need anything, you can put your call light on, and one of the aides will respond as soon as possible."

Sara nodded as if this sort of thing happened to her every day. The nurse hurried from the room.

As soon as the woman was out of sight, Sara swung her legs out of the bed. She wore a hospital gown. An IV tube had been attached to the back of her hand. She touched her fingers to her throat.

Her *bare* throat.

Trying not to panic, she ripped the IV out of her hand, then launched herself out of bed. Her clothes were nowhere to be seen. She wondered with a thudding heart whether they'd gotten rid of the amulet, too. What the hell had happened when she passed out?

She crept into the hall, but it looked like everyone had raced off to handle the emergency. The woman at the nurse's station was on a call. Sara crept around the desk for a peek.

The amulet rested on top of a phone book with its leather lace coiled around the stone pendant. Sara's breath spilled out of her in rushed relief. She picked it up with a silent prayer of thanks, and looped it back over her head.

Now what? She paused, uncertain, expecting the nurse's station attendant to see her and chivvy her back to her room.

A nurse emerged from a staff room down the hall, and hurried away in the opposite direction. Making sure no one noticed, Sara eased into the room and closed the door.

Phew. Now the little matter of the hospital gown.

She found an open locker and—oh, thank God—a folded set of scrubs within. Once changed, she ducked out of the room and started down the hall.

She found a directory listing the location of the burn unit, then followed the signs to another wing of the hospital. Becky's name wasn't on the board at the burn unit's main desk; not surprising, if she hadn't been able to speak. Sara snatched a lab coat from its hook in another staff lounge, then proceeded to check each room as she went down the hall. Some of the patients looked up in curiosity as she passed, and she murmured greetings that she hoped sounded professional. Any second, someone on staff would fail to recognize her, or notice her lack of a badge—or a patient would code— and her hunt would end in a sedated return to bed.

She found Becky at last in a room near the end of a hall. The young woman lay sleeping in the midst of an army of machines at whose purpose Sara didn't want to guess. Her arm and face had been bandaged. Sara crept toward the bed. "Hey."

Becky's eyes flew open. When she saw Sara, her shoulders slumped in relief.

"What did you do to me on the boat?" Sara whispered. "You did do something, didn't you?"

The redhead gave a faint, groggy nod. She lifted a hand to her throat and tapped it with a regretful look.

"You can't speak?"

The woman shook her head. Wayward, flame-red curls fluttered against the pillow. At a sound in the hallway, her features contorted in fear, but it was only a cart going by. She turned back to Sara with the same anxious expression, and it took on a pleading note.

Sara laid a hand over Becky's ice-cold one. "Do you know what a 'conduit' is?"

Becky frowned.

Sara pursed her lips, deciding how to continue. "A conduit is a person who has no paranormal ability of her own, but can amplify the power of others. Do you realize that's what you are?"

The young woman nodded.

Sara paused. Her insides echoed that look of anxiety on Becky's features. She took a long, shuddering breath, then asked, "How did you know I had telekinesis?"

Becky shook her head this time, which Sara took to mean that she hadn't known until their speedboat ride. A thousand questions clamored to be asked at once. She struggled to remain calm. "All right, this is very important. I won't say a word, but I need to know. Was someone forcing you to use your ability when Cameron was killed? Is it the same person that hurt you?"

The young woman's frightened gaze flashed around the room as if she expected her assailant to be there. Her eyes welled with tears, and she looked back at Sara with her breath hitching.

A cart rumbled outside the door. She and Becky jumped in unison. A nurse entered, pushing the cart ahead of her, and stopped when she saw Sara in the lab coat. "I'm sorry. I didn't realize you were in here, Doctor."

God, I need to get back to the dig and make sure everything's okay, Sara thought. "I was just on my way out," she said. "Miss Palmeter, I want you to contact my office as soon as you're discharged, and speak to Holly Robbins. She'll arrange for your further care. Don't forget."

Becky nodded, conveying that she understood she was to go to the Gemini offices upon her release. Sara backed away toward the door, wishing desperately that she knew more of Becky's side of the story.

The redhead turned her attention to the nurse. Frantic for more information, Sara made sure neither of them saw, then let her eyes change.

What she read in the frightened woman's thoughts made her back hastily out the door into the hall. She pulled off the lab coat and dropped it on the floor. It couldn't be.

Oh, God, Faith and Ian, alone at the dig with this.

A step, and another, and in the next moment she broke into a flat run.

****

Ian stripped off his muddy shirt, brooding, staring at the rifle propped against the table. Thunder still pounded the heavens outside. Three weeks. Three weeks of cat-and-mouse on a remote island until they could do anything at all.

He hadn't felt right about leaving Faith alone, but she'd sworn she was under protection, and that she had work to do with the sword she'd found. Ian had his reservations about how much protection a long-dead Viking ghost could provide. Restless, he paced the length of his tent.

Through the rumble of the storm, he heard the thump of fast-approaching footsteps. Picking up his rifle, Ian went to the door flap and drew it back.

Sara stood there shivering, hugging her arms close against her body, teeth chattering. "T-Thomas Callander."

Ian grabbed her by the arm and pulled her inside. "Callander, the guy who's working on your team?"

She nodded breathlessly. Rainwater dripped in steady rivulets down her face. "Just before I left the hospital, I read Becky's mind." He saw her hesitate, and then she plunged ahead again. "Ian, Tom Callander's a telekinetic. I think he's behind Cameron's death."

Ian stiffened as the implications hit him full force. He remembered his father and the horrible day that had wrecked his disillusioned, young life.

And then he thought of the woman standing before him now. *Oh, God.* "Sara, Callander works for Lambertson, doesn't he?"

"What are you saying?" she asked, icy warning in her tone.

"I'm saying that if he's involved, how do you know Lambertson isn't? Callander is on loan from Eurocon, am I right?"

She shook her head fiercely. "No. Lamb wouldn't do this. He wouldn't. He's a friend of Cameron's family. A friend of *my* family."

Ian bristled. "I don't trust anyone anymore, and that includes Lambertson. He was there with everyone else when Cameron died, and now he's conveniently gone home."

She stepped back toward the tent door. He took a corresponding step forward. "Sara, listen to me. Faith told me he got you the job here because he knew Shetland was your father's life's work. He was one of your father's best friends. He's in a perfect position to know about that amulet, and maybe the ley lines, too."

He reached for her hand, but she snatched it away. The words he didn't say hung in the air between them: *Maybe Lambertson is responsible for your father's murder.* Pained, Ian raked his fingers through his rain-damp hair and moved away from her. "You'd better go see Faith. She's waiting."

Chapter Thirteen

By the time she arrived back at the dig, Sara felt feverish with chills and exhaustion. She'd run most of the way as a wolf, but even its heavy double pelt could not withstand this much rain. Her stomach twisted with dread that Ian might be right, and that there was no longer anyone whom she and Faith could trust.

The lantern in Faith's tent threw a dim glow. Sara approached with caution and opened the flap.

Her sister looked up from a pile of books and released a long, weary sigh. "Becky?"

"Hospital. She'll be all right." Sara went to Faith's cot and sank down, holding her roiling belly. She lowered her head until wet locks of hair swung, dripping, into her face.

Before she could add anything more, Faith stood up. "I was able to find out a little more about this druid serpent ceremony." She came to the cot with a worn leather book, and sat beside Sara. "A sect of druids created the serpent ceremony to allow them to travel the ley lines in a kind of half-life, drawing knowledge from the ghosts already walking the lines, and bringing it back with them when the lines closed again."

Faith ran a hand through her hair. "It made them powerful, but the ceremony got more and more unstable as time went on. To balance it, they had to sacrifice people in increasing numbers. Eventually, even the sacrifices weren't enough, and the ley lines shut down for all but twice a year, on the days of the spring and fall equinox."

Sara looked up as the weight of her sister's words sank in. Faith's expression sent a new chill dancing down her spine. "Where did you get all this?"

Hands shaking, Faith slid the book into Sara's lap.

With a concerned glance at her sister, Sara opened the book's tattered cover. Drops of water from her sodden hair fell onto the dog-eared flyleaf, smudging the ink of the inscription: *Robert Markham, 14th April -*

No end date.

Sara slammed the book shut and hugged it to her chest, feeling the blood drain from her face. "W-What is this?" she gasped, even though she knew the answer.

"Dad's last journal. He started it the month before our tenth birthday. It was in with the stuff I threw together from his research before we left for Shetland." Faith's voice shook.

Sara reeled. Her churning stomach threatened to bring up what little food she had eaten that day. "Do you think he knew about us, about what we would be able to do? Do you think that's why he gave us the lockets?"

"If he did, he never mentions it in there. He wrote all that in the context of a legend. I don't even know if he believed in it himself. I was afraid to use my power to read it." She reached anxiously for the book again.

Sara released it. Faith cradled it in her hands, and added, "He must have found the amulet and tracked down its history, or the other way around. I've looked everywhere for information on this serpent ceremony and the amulet, and found nothing until now."

Distracted, Sara rubbed at her forehead. "The druids didn't keep written records. They passed their culture on through spoken word. We'd be lucky to get anything in scattered pieces, like the fairy tale books. Which don't mention anything about druids, anyway."

"I know that." Faith stood up. "Dad knew something about all this, but where are his sources? He doesn't reference any in his journal." She paced the length of the room, holding the book close. "He doesn't say how the ceremony goes, either. I'll have to try to reach Hakon again."

The mention of the Viking's name brought the sword back into Sara's thoughts, and then Becky's recent confession. Her stomach turned over again. "Faith, Becky's a conduit."

"She's what?"

"A conduit, she's a conduit. She amplified me when I was trying to use telekinesis to steady the boat. She saw what I was doing, and *wham*!"

"Conduits don't exist. They're just a theory!"

"So are we," Sara reminded her acerbically. She sobered, grasping at the last threads of her focus and self-control. "I told her to go to Holly as soon as she's out of that hospital. She needs to be somewhere safe."

Faith began to look frantic, pacing faster around her tent, scanning the interior as if looking for an emotional anchor.

"There's more. Faith, sit down. I'm still tapped, and you're making it hard to think."

Her sister dropped onto the cot's edge, but her eagerness for action screamed from every muscle.

Sara drew a long breath. "Tom Callander is a telekinetic. He used Becky to push that scaffold down and kill Cameron. Ian thinks Lamb is behind it."

Faith froze. "How are we going to prove any of this? What do we do?"

Sara fought a surge of anger. Could Faith believe so readily that Lamb might be involved in Cameron's death? There had to be an explanation—*any* explanation—to absolve the man who'd been a second father to them all these years.

As bitter a task as it was, she forced herself to consider the possibility. "We need to keep this quiet. Until we're off this island, everyone is suspect." She swayed, and propped herself up where she sat.

Faith laid a hand on her arm. "God, you're like ice. Get out of those wet clothes. You're going to get sick." She reached for the blanket at the end of the cot and shook it out over Sara's lap, then rummaged through her trunk for a clean, dry sweatshirt.

Sara took it and peeled off her soaked shirt. "You can stay here," she heard her sister say. She gave a groggy nod, only half hearing, and lay down. Faith pulled the Viking sword out from under her cot, and Sara fell fast asleep.

****

Faith turned her lantern down as low as possible. She sat at the table and laid the oilcloth bundle across her lap, then unwrapped it ever so gingerly. When she drew back the last layer of cloth, the sword blade shone in the dim light.

She stared at it, holding her breath, sensing the anger flowing from the weapon without having to touch it. She lifted her hand and let it hover over the blade with a frown, dreading what she'd see.

No help for it...and no choice. She let her hand fall

210

on the sword hilt, and released her power.

Fury like an ice storm swept all around her. Shuddering, Faith clutched at her power with single-mindedly determination. *I am here, and you will not push me out,* she ordered the maelstrom.

As if just now sensing her, the anger subsided. The presence inside the sword darted around her, questing, wondering who she was and what she was doing there.

Then it swallowed her.

Longing gripped her, so fierce that it forced the breath from her body. Tears stung her eyes.

Love. Aching, desperate, passionate. Any emotion she'd ever had felt hollow and soulless by comparison. The sword hilt sizzled under her fingertips. She warred with the need to let go of it. There was bitterness, too, that a sword—an artifact of action—had been made useless by becoming its own wielder's prison. "H-Hakon?"

The tempest of emotion lifted. She stood at the edge of the dig. The night sky draped its velvet cloak overhead. Light from the moon and stars enabled her to see a man approaching. For the first time, she looked on the face of the Viking warrior.

He was tall, broad-shouldered and clean-limbed, with a catlike surety in the way he carried himself, even in a worn tunic. His long, blondish mane was tied back, drawing her attention to the strong edges of cheekbone, jaw, and nose.

As she approached, she saw him more clearly, more brightly, as if he glowed, himself. His eyes broke her heart. Clear blue-green, like the warm southern seas. In them swam an ages-old pain that echoed in her bones. Tears burned down her cheeks, and she wasn't even sure why she cried.

His gaze landed on her, and he made a strangled sound. The bronze of his skin went ashen white. She heard him speak a name, something soft and lilting. He came forward—one swift step, two—and then crushed her against him.

Frightened, she pushed at him, gasping for air. "Let go! Let go of me!"

He jerked away as if she'd slapped him across the face. He flung a stream of words at her that she didn't understand, and wouldn't have remembered if she had taken Norse only yesterday. His eyes hurled all other thoughts from her mind.

Something in her clicked. "I've dreamed you before," she told him.

The realization that he didn't comprehend her words came when he gripped her arm with terrifying strength. He shook her, demanding, the pitch of his voice rising in furious questions. He took her chin and stared hard at her.

She flung his hands away. "Back off!"

More angry Norse words. She caught the knife edges of them, and raced to follow his meaning.

Sorcery. Trickery.

"Wait!" she snapped. "Just hold on a minute. Let me think, damn it!" She turned in a circle. The air, still and hot, seethed with Hakon's anger and distrust. Her skin stung in empathy.

She had held the time-weathered skull of this man in her hands, and here he stood before her, whole. Vertigo settled in at the thought. She wanted out of this vision, even as she knew there were questions to be asked.

A word from Hakon, calmer now, sounding like an inquiry. She looked back at him. He seemed to be coming to some sort of understanding, and his expression relaxed.

"That makes one of us, buddy," she muttered. Drawing a breath, she placed a hand over her heart. "Faith."

He hesitated, giving her a doubtful look, but nodded and said "Faith" in a perfect imitation of her American accent.

She bit her lip. A thousand questions sprang forth, only to be bottlenecked by her hazy recollection of the language. After a panicked moment of wondering where to start, she fumbled for the threads of long-unused Norse. "I am a friend. I am the one who has been speaking to you through..." Through what, exactly? Would he even grasp the concept of psychic power? "...through the veil of dreams."

A look of relief at understanding her speech passed across his face. The firm line of his mouth softened. "I am sorry I have hurt you."

For a moment, she wondered if he meant the way he'd squashed the breath out of her. Even now, he seemed reluctant to touch her, let alone get close to her.

Her confusion must have been evident, because he laid a hand on her shoulder. A weak buzzing radiated from his fingers. She remembered her experience on Beltane when the ghost had touched her. She remembered the knifing sensation in her belly.

So she'd been right. It was him.

Hakon lifted his hand away. "It was not my desire to cause you pain. If I had known you would look—" He broke off and changed direction in a rush of words she almost didn't catch. "You must help me avenge the murder of my wife."

Her mouth fell open on several different replies, none of which she had sufficient command of his language to make. "Why?"

He met her gaze again. The pain in his own reached inside her and gripped her by the heart. "It must be you. You have her face."

She felt the blood drain from cheeks. In its place came an unsettling prickle. She found her mind racing back to the half-remembered dreams she'd had as a young girl, when her power first made itself known. They came back to her now, vivid as ever.

Here. She had visited this place in her dreams, years ago. A house of wood, thatch, and stone. A man tilling the land. A woman carrying water, and laughing at a pair of kittens tumbling across the grass. She had never seen the woman's face, but the man...

That was Hakon.

He stood beside her now, waiting for her reply. Everything jumbled together on her tongue, trying to get out all at once. She cleared her throat and fought to sort coherent words out of the mess in her head. "How must I do this thing?"

Seeming to sense her turmoil, he continued slowly, pausing to be sure she understood his words. "Finish your digging. Reveal the house I built when I reached this land. There, destroy the stone disk and close the serpent paths."

She shook her head. "It cannot be 'destroy'... destroyed."

When he spoke again, his words came so fast she could hardly follow. She caught "moon" and "sword" among the flurry of sounds. Cursing her faulty memory, she held her hands up to get him to slow down. "When the moon shows all her face," she repeated. Switching to English, she muttered, "That much I got. I have a damn deadline, and no instructions." She changed back to Norse. "What of the sword?"

"I swore on it that I would not rest until I have vengeance for her death. The sword will break the stone disk when the first spring moon, riding at its highest point, looks upon them both. It must be done using sacred wine."

Just what the hell does that mean? If I had a bottle of wine handy at the moment, I'd probably drink it, and to hell with this serpent thing. "Blessed wine?" she guessed aloud.

Hakon jerked a knife from his belt, then raked it across his palm. Faith flinched. Blood, bright as rubies, welled in the weathered creases of his hand. "Sacred wine," he repeated.

"Blood?" she murmured in Norse. The words "blood" and "wine" were different enough in his language that there could be no mistaking the two. She wondered if it were a metaphor.

Then she wondered how a ghost could bleed.

"Not the blood of common men," Hakon said. "It is no longer powerful enough." He gripped her hand, spreading her fingers so that it lay palm-upward in his. "Sacred blood that carries the gift of the druids must also be their downfall."

Reeling, Faith shook her head. "You're crazy," she spat in English. "I want out of this. Let go." She struggled, trying to pull her hand from his. "Let go!"

She woke from the vision sweating.

Faith threw the folds of oilcloth back over the sword, dropped it into its box, slammed the lid shut, then shoved the whole works under her cot and out of sight.

Gifted blood. The blood of the descendants of druids. He wanted her to avenge a thousand-year-old murder because she carried gifted blood, and somehow just happened to look like his dead wife. In addition to which, she'd been dreaming of him her whole life.

Nausea gripped her. Could this get any better?

The storm raged on outside. Faith bent toward her cot and prodded at her sister. "Hey, wake up."

Sara mumbled something and opened glassy, unfocused eyes.

"I talked to Hakon. Sara, come on. Wake up." Faith nudged her again.

Sara's gaze fixed somewhere over Faith's head. "Dad?" she whispered, a brittle, hollow rasp of sound that gave Faith chills.

She clapped a hand over Sara's forehead. Her sister's skin felt icy and fiery hot by turns. "Sara, don't do this, not now. I need you. I've gotta tell you this."

No response.

Yep. It could get better.

Faith spun around to get her first-aid kit, and started praying.

****

Rainwater dripped sulkily from the edges of Flintrop's tent as he opened the flap. The storm had spent the last of its energy by dawn, but the sky remained gray and moody. Today's weather promised to be little better. Pulling on his jacket, he headed outside.

Michael emerged from his tent. "Morning. Such as it is."

"Yeah. Start setting up. We'll see how far we can get today with the ground being so soft."

His assistant nodded and moved off in the direction of the dig.

Flintrop crossed the moor to Sara's tent to find the door flap already open, and the tent unoccupied. He turned toward Faith's tent instead. Hers was also open, but sounds of activity came from within. He ducked his head inside. "Looks like we— What's going on?"

Faith sat in a camp chair beside the cot with slumped shoulders. She squeezed water from a rolled towel. Sara lay prone on the cot, murmuring in her sleep. Faith pressed the damp towel to her sister's forehead. "She has a fever. She hasn't been coherent all night."

Flintrop gestured outside. "I'll get a couple of the team and a stretcher. We can take her to Mainland."

"No. I can take care of her."

Flintrop watched the way Sara shifted restlessly on the pillow. Her damp hair stuck in tendrils to her forehead. "Faith, don't be ridiculous. I'm not going to let you endanger her health because you think you can han—"

"I said I can take care of her. Please, Alan. Can you manage the dig today?"

His given name. That was a change. Reluctant, he nodded and left the tent.

Michael, Luis, and Thomas met him halfway to the dig. "Part of the wall must have broken down overnight," Michael reported. "We'll have to shore it up before we can continue working."

Dustin jogged up to join them. "Becky's gone. Has anyone seen her since last night?"

Flintrop rubbed at the stubble on his chin. "She has to have radioed for a ferry to Unst or something. Michael, I want you to go to the dock and see if the boat's still there. The rest of us will do what we can with the dig site until you get back."

"What about Faith and Sara?" Dustin asked.

"Sara's not feeling well. Faith's watching her. Luis, call my office and see if Becky's checked in. Eurocon, too. Let's get moving before the rain starts again."

Michael nodded, then hurried away. Flintrop looked up to watch him go, and found Ian approaching. "Start work," he barked. "I'll catch up in a minute."

He intercepted Ian at the edge of camp. "What in hell are you doing here, Waverly?"

"I didn't come to see you, for starters."

Flintrop blocked his progress. "You've been warned to stay away from this dig site. I didn't think you needed reminding."

Ian's eyes flared. He stepped forward until he stood inches from Flintrop's nose. "I'll bet it just burns you that she might rather be up there with me than spend every waking minute with you, doesn't it? Tough guy like yourself with loads of money could probably buy almost any woman he wants. *Almost.*" He veered around Flintrop. Before Flintrop could stop him, Ian headed, not for Sara's tent, but Faith's.

Faith looked up when Ian appeared in her doorway. "Hey."

He stepped inside.

Flintrop barged in right behind, seething. "Get him out of here, Faith."

She sighed. "Will you two stop bickering?"

"These are not my orders. They're Lambertson's," Flintrop spat.

Faith surged out of her chair. "And Gemini is in charge until he comes back. Since Sara's not functional, that leaves just me. He stays. Get over it. May I take care of my sister now?"

Flintrop shot Ian a look that should have knocked him over—and he wished it had done worse—and then stormed out.

****

"Arrogant bastard." Faith turned back to her sister, and replaced the dry towel in her hands with a damp one.

"What's the matter with Sara?"

She heard the urgency in Ian's voice and looked up. "She has a fever. Nothing I can't take care of."

He started toward the cot, worry in his eyes, but stopped. "Faith, I need you to listen to this."

She frowned at the way he balanced on his feet—light, edgy. Just his posture was enough to send pinpricks of unease skittering down her back. "What is it?"

He reached into the inside pocket of his coat and withdrew a rolled sheet of paper, then spread it out on her camp table. "Shut the door." He took a pencil out and clamped it between his teeth long enough to grab a pair of binoculars, a bottle of water, and two glasses to weight the corners of the curling sheet. He took the pencil from his teeth and sketched furiously without bothering to sit.

The unease on her skin multiplied. Faith zipped her door shut and hurried back to the table.

The large sheet of graph paper hung off the edges of her table. In the right margin, Faith recognized a drawing of the outline of Hvitmar, criss-crossed with penciled lines that met, if the hand-sketched map was right, exactly at the dig site. One line, bolder than the others, made her cringe just looking at it. It ran from the dig straight down the island through Ian's camp. "You had another dream, didn't you? You saw the ley line."

"I saw ley *lines*," he corrected her, still drawing with reckless speed. "There used to be more. They faded and died out."

Faith followed the sweeps of his hand in the center of the sheet. He'd drawn a large rectangle with interrupted lines at the top and bottom ends. Other lines had been sketched inside it, as well as a rough circle in its center. Outside the bottom end of the rectangle were four bold *X*s. "What is this?"

"This is your ruin."

"Come again?"

"Your Viking house. I saw it, the whole thing." He tapped his finger on the circle. "This is where they killed her."

"Killed who?"

"The Viking's wife. The druids slit her throat when he wasn't home, while she was cooking at the hearth." Ian's gaze traveled up and down her figure as if to ascertain who he was seeing. "She looked like you. I thought it *was* you."

"I know, I know. Hakon told me about her," Faith said, suppressing an empathic shudder as she recalled Hakon's pain. "What else did you see?"

Ian turned back to the paper. "I saw them doing the snake ritual. I don't know what they said, I couldn't understand them. Four of them, they stood here." He pointed to the Xs. "One of them dripped her blood into some stone bowl. They smeared her blood over the amulet, and the ley lines opened, and then... Then, I woke up."

Agitation rolled off him in such sharp waves that Faith wondered what else he'd seen. She turned her attention to the Xs on the map he had drawn. North, South, East, and West. There had to be four. "You saw the ceremony? Ian, can you repeat anything they said, anything it sounded like?"

He shook his head. "I could hardly even hear them. There was this noise, this buzzing. It was so loud, it almost drowned everything out." He spun away from the table to pace her tent like a trapped panther. "I can still feel it burning in my guts."

She shuddered. "I know. I've felt it, too."

He turned on his heel and flew to the cot, sitting on its edge to lay a hand on Sara's cheek. "I can't stand this waiting."

She studied his hasty rendering of the ruin. "We need to dig it out. We need to end it where it started."

He swept her with a suspicious look.

"I talked to Hakon last night," she added. "He said we can destroy the amulet and close the ley lines for good, but it has to be done exactly at the height of the first full moon after Beltane...and it can't be done without gifted blood."

"No," Ian said at once.

"You saw it yourself. Blood is what opens the ley lines, and it can close them down. Regular blood doesn't work anymore. It has to be gifted blood."

He rose to his feet and strode toward her, then

snatched her by the arms. "Just whose blood are you planning to use? Yours?" He jerked his chin at the cot. "Hers?"

Trembling now, she murmured, "There is another one."

He jerked her closer. "Callander? Are you crazy? What are you going to do, kill him?"

"You felt it!" she burst out, wrestling against his grasp. "Even in a dream, you felt the ley line. Do you know how much worse it will be in real life? How much worse it *is*? I felt it for real, Ian. I still feel it roaring around inside my head!"

"You are not doing this. We'll find another way."

She managed to throw his hands off. "What do you suggest? I'm out of ideas."

"I don't suggest murder!"

"It didn't stop Callander!"

"Stop shouting," interrupted Sara.

She and Ian turned as one. Her sister struggled to a sitting position on the cot. Faith seized the water bottle from the table and launched herself across the tent.

Sara took it with an exhausted, grateful look, and downed its contents.

"Are you feeling any better?" Faith asked, holding a hand to her sister's forehead.

Sara dropped the now-empty bottle on a chair. "No." She divided a glance between them. "Do you two want the whole camp to hear your conversation?"

Faith gripped at the woolen blanket. "We need to clear the dig, and we have three weeks to do it. How much can you pull out with telekinesis?"

"I haven't got that kind of power. Even healthy, I haven't." Sara dropped her legs over the side of the bed.

"We'll have to find another way. I just need a little more rest." When she struggled to get to her feet, Ian crossed the tent and put a bracing hand under her elbow. She swayed there. "Right now, we have to assume that whoever's working against us wants the same thing. To clear out the dig. We're going to help them. Then we're going to stop them."

Chapter Fourteen

Coming out of her fog, Sara leaned against Ian's solid frame. Her strength began to return in halting, miserly increments.

He curled an arm around her waist and turned to her sister. "Please tell me you're not going to try anything stupid."

What's that about? Sara wondered.

Faith sighed. "I'm sorry about the argument. I don't know what to do. We have no data, no sources—"

Ian's arm tightened around Sara. "You have Hakon."

"I'm almost as tapped as Sara. It's going to take me at least a couple of days to recover before I can make any contact worth getting. This is just crazy. In three weeks Callander, or whoever else, could do anything to us and make it look like an accident. All the while, we're helping him excavate the dig and get closer to opening the ley lines."

"That's if they even know where the amulet is in the first place," said Sara.

"Either you're coming to stay with me," Ian said, "or I'll stay down here."

"I'm not leaving my sister," she said.

"Then I'll stay."

Sara knew he meant to guard her, but even weakened, her body responded as though he'd offered her seduction. She couldn't halt the images of their night together flitting through her mind.

Faith pushed aside the glasses and binoculars on her table. The large sheet of graph paper lying there rolled up of its own accord. "Bad idea. Flintrop's gunning for you as it is, and he's not the kind of guy who puts up with people he doesn't like. I know how he is, I dated him."

Ian snorted. "Why?"

Faith threw her hands in the air. "I don't know. It didn't work out. A few months later, he dumped me for no particular reason, and acted like we'd never—" She broke off and cleared her throat. "Is this need-to-know, or can we get back to the big problem?"

"Fine." Ian looked back down at Sara. "I'll walk you to your tent."

She nodded, and they started together toward the door.

Faith snatched up the graph paper and crumpled it into one fist. In a flash of silver eyes and a burst of flame, the map withered to ashes in her hand.

Ian tensed, quick as reflex. Sara pushed him out the door ahead of her.

On the way to her tent, she asked, "What was all that about back there? Why were you two arguing?"

"It's nothing," he said. "Does she do that a lot?" He made a flicking motion with his hand, imitating Faith's burst of flame.

"Often enough." She cast a look around camp, but no one was outside at the moment. They entered her tent. "She's right about Flintrop."

He slid his arms around her. "I couldn't care less about Flintrop. Do *you* want me to stay?"

Oh, yes. Her body vibrated with it. "You shouldn't."

His lips trailed along her cheek. Heat sizzled from his touch into her skin. He molded his body to hers and kissed her, swallowing her moan. The rigidness of his growing arousal pressed against her abdomen.

Her head spun, but it had nothing to do with fever. "Please," she whispered, not knowing if she meant him to stop, or to keep going.

He kissed his way down the side of her neck. "I worried about you last night," he said, his breath warming her ear.

She shivered with pleasure. "I'll be all right," she said, then gave a soft cry as his teeth closed over her earlobe. She fisted her hands in his jacket and jerked him closer.

He hissed and pressed his hips into her. The sweet pressure of it rebounded through her and left her breathless. She arched against him.

He kissed her again, again, again. "The inlet. Tonight," he whispered, then pulled away with reluctance in his eyes.

She stood there for several moments after he left, touching her fingers to her tingling lips as if she could preserve the feel of him.

Weariness won out. She went to her cot and lay down, intending only to get another hour's rest before joining the crew. But when she woke again, she realized by the dimming quality of the light that she'd slept the entire day.

The sounds of clanking dishes reached her, and the faint smell of dinner made her empty stomach rumble. She hefted herself into a sitting position and touched a hand to her forehead. Well, at least it didn't feel like she'd bake alive anymore.

She heard the zipper of her tent door being drawn back, and turned to look. Flintrop ducked in with a thermos. "Good, you're awake."

"Just," she said.

He stepped inside. "I brought you some soup. Thought it would help shore you up. Doing better?"

The rumble of her stomach intensified at the thought of food. "Probably look like hell, but yes, I feel better."

He handed the thermos over and sat on the cot. "You couldn't look like hell if you wanted to."

She chose to ignore his comment, and unscrewed the cap of the thermos.

"Lamb called," he added. "There's some snag at Eurocon that he's got to stay and sort out. We haven't located Becky, even though the boat's still here."

Pouring a cup of soup, Sara said, "Really? She must have caught the ferry out. I'm sure she's all right, but she should have called."

What Becky really should have done—and was currently doing, if she possessed any sense—was to flee as far as possible from Hvitmar and everyone on it. If she was lucky, she'd already be on her way to the Gemini offices. Safer than they were, and no one would use her like that ever again. Sara felt a pang of remorse for the young woman. She'd had her sister. What about others who possessed paranormal gifts? Who did they turn to?

Had Callander found himself alone and scared as a gifted child, and then gone horribly wrong?

With half her mind on the morning's events, and

the other half wondering how to finish the dig in three weeks under the strain of constant danger, it took Sara a minute to realize Flintrop was staring. "Did you want something else?"

His cobalt gaze mellowed. "Are you sure you want me to answer that honestly?"

She leaned away. "We've been over that, Flintrop."

"We have." He chuckled. "We never quite addressed what we were going to do once we got past the pastry level."

"That's because we aren't past it, and we are never going to be past it," she said, raising the thermos cup to her lips. She closed her eyes. A sudden flash of Ian's naked body and scorching storm-blue gaze insinuated itself into her thoughts.

She choked down the swallow of soup and slapped the empty cup down, then stood. "I've got to get out there. I've wasted a whole day. Excuse me."

He rose to his feet beside her, and blocked her escape. Frustrated, her mind still full with Ian, she said, "We're finished here. If you don't mind—"

He raised a hand to her cheek. The gesture surprised her into stillness. "Don't leave. You've been sliding away from me for years," he said. He leaned forward until his breath misted her face. "Stay."

Her heart pounded. She stared blindly, seeing a different pair of eyes. *Focus!* She wrestled her senses back to the present. Realization of what Flintrop was asking dawned on her. Before she could react, he kissed her.

Her senses blasted into static. The back of her neck prickled. Her skin hummed so loud she couldn't think. Sara froze, immobilized, even as her body screamed to fly out the door. His palm stroked along her cheek and down the curve of her neck. "Be with me," he whispered against her lips. His fingers threaded into the thick hair at the back of her head.

His fingertips brushed over the leather lace of the amulet. With her blood fizzing, she put a hand on his chest and pushed, breaking the kiss with an effort of will. "This isn't going to happen, Flintrop. I-I'm sorry. Excuse me." She grabbed a jacket and rushed out of the tent, confused and unsettled and needing to be anywhere but near him.

Dusk had fallen. The crew milled about the camp, packing up tools. Sara fought a moment of guilt at having missed a day's work, but her feet moved as if they had a will of their own. Rather than turning toward the camp, she walked straight across it, heading for the inlet.

Faith met her halfway across the moor. "What's wrong?"

"Nothing. I've just got to get out of here. I can't think straight."

"Sara—"

"I'm fine, I swear. I feel a lot better." A lie, if there ever was one.

Faith looked over Sara's shoulder. Sara followed her stare to find Flintrop emerging from her tent with a too-composed expression. He didn't look toward them, walking instead toward the dig. "What did he do to you?" Faith demanded.

"I just need to get out of here, okay?"

Her sister looked unconvinced, but Sara didn't stay to explain. She strode away from camp without looking back.

Coward. She'd never run from anything in her life.

When she reached the inlet, dusk had passed, and the stars scattered across the sky. The wind carried the sound of surf crashing on the rocks offshore. She hugged herself against the cool evening air, burrowing deeper into her jacket. The temperature seemed to have plummeted in the last five minutes. Her breath steamed in front of her.

She picked out Ian's darker shape against the starry sky, sitting on a boulder near the water's edge. She walked faster. Her walk became a jog, and then a run.

He turned and slid off the rock to meet her, catching her in his embrace. His kisses rained across her cheek and down her neck. "I'm glad you're all right," he breathed, holding her face in his hands. "You have no idea how much I wanted to stay with you today."

She threw her arms around his neck and held on, welcoming the feel of his mouth on hers and the way it erased the disquieting hum that had been plaguing her since Flintrop's kiss. "Can we just stay here like this for a minute?"

He answered by holding her harder against his body. "You're shaking. What happened?"

"I'm okay. I'm fine now." She pressed against him, as much to ward off the chill of night as the chill that had settled along her spine.

****

Ian threaded his hand into her hair, letting the silken strands glide through his fingers. He kissed her again, pulling her with him as he leaned back against the rock. He'd known something was wrong the moment she appeared, but as soon as he touched her, everything except the feel of her against him swept out of his head.

She still shivered. God, she felt like ice. He opened his jacket to pull it around them both, willing his warmth into her.

Her hands slipped up the back of his thermal shirt to trail along the hollow of his lower back. Ian forgot his worries. He hissed softly at the touch, then louder when her nails grazed his skin. Urgency radiated from her.

His body reacted like a lightning strike. He dropped to the sand and pulled her down with him, needing to bury himself in her. They grappled at each other's clothing in a mad rush. Jackets, shirts, and pants fell away unheeded. They came together in a surge that drowned out everything else. Ian rocked his hips against hers with a groan of satisfaction.

She gave a broken moan, pulling him into her, propelling him upward. "Please—Ian, please."

He sensed the storm raging in her and answered it with a primal growl, meeting her thrust for thrust. A charge built at the base of his spine with each stroke until he could hardly take it, then it burst along his nerves in a shower of sparks. She sank her teeth into the skin of his shoulder, muffling a hoarse cry that echoed his own.

She went limber in his embrace, and drew a long sigh that seemed to come from the center of her being. He drifted back down with her in a tangle of arms and legs and rasping breath.

He kissed her, gently now, then breathed in the scent of her. "Hi," he whispered.

She dimpled. Her gaze slid away from his to rove

along his chest. "I'm sorry. I just...I wanted you so much...I needed..."

"This is me, not complaining."

Her dimple deepened. He couldn't resist kissing it.

Sara curled her arms around his neck, and then cringed. "There's a rock digging into my back."

With a grin, he rolled until she lay on top of him, then dragged his jacket over them. A rock jabbed him in the back. He flinched and dug it out. "Ouch. Christ. Sex on the beach isn't everything it's cracked it up to be."

"It's perfect," she murmured into his neck. With a long sigh, she settled against him.

His body changed his mind for him, already responding to her again. Yep, he agreed. Perfect.

Circling her waist with his arms, he looked up at the blanket of stars. A thin slice of waning moon rode low overhead, spinning out the hours before sunrise.

His nightmare about the Viking's wife barged in uninvited. In his mind, he heard Hakon's wife scream as the hooded men broke into their house. A second scream, cut short as they slit her throat. Blood poured down the front of her dress.

Buzzkill, he told the image, but it persisted.

Someone was trying to reconstruct the ley line ritual. Someone who now needed gifted blood to perform it. What would happen if they found out about Sara?

He turned his face into Sara's hair. Her warmth, the steadying beat of her heart against his, and the faintly musky, earthy scent of her urged him away from the nightmare.

Not her. Not while he breathed.

He must have tightened his hold on her. She tilted her head to look at him. "Something the matter?"

He grinned again, forced now. "Sand and rocks notwithstanding, a man could get used to this naked-woman-on-a-beach thing."

She smiled, and the nightmare washed away as easy as that.

They lay silent for a long while. Ian let his blood cool while the sounds of surging waves and chirring insects filled the air. When her hands skimmed along his sides and down his belly, he gave a throaty rumble and trapped them with his own. "Unless you plan on spending the night on this beach, I don't recommend you do that."

She sat up, tugging him with her into another kiss. His jacket slithered off them to drop on the sand. He made out her curving silhouette against the moonlight flashing on the water, and contemplated spending the night on the beach anyway. In spite of everything going on around them, all he wanted was to pull her back down and repeat what they'd just done.

The breeze picked up, fluttering in her hair. She broke the kiss with a violent shiver. "When did it get so cold out?"

"What cold?" he deadpanned, reaching for his pants.

Kneeling, she clapped a hand over her own pile of clothing, then dressed hastily. She turned back to him as he shrugged into his shirt, and stopped to raise a hand to his cheek. A troubled look crossed her features. "I don't want to go."

His gut clenched. He snaked his arms around her and pulled her close against him. "I don't want you to, either. I'll come back tomorrow. If you can get away from the dig—"

"As soon as I can," she said between kisses.

Ian helped her to her feet. He let go of her, trying not to dwell on the reluctant expression in her eyes that made him want to pull her back. A few seconds more of that, and he might be spending the night with her on the beach—and damn Flintrop and the dig and everybody else sticking their noses into other people's business. Sara held his hand until they were too far apart to do so, then jogged away.

When she had gone, he looked up at the moon again to find it bloodred.

Startled, he blinked and looked once more, but the moment had passed. The moon hung silent and white as a ghost.

****

When dawn broke over the camp, Sara was already bent in concentration over the large mesh box beside the dig, sieving earth. Stones rattled as she shifted the box back and forth, searching. She picked chunks of peat, stone, and grass from the box and tossed it into a wheelbarrow, hardly acknowledging it before moving back to sieving again.

The task was perfunctory, something to put down on paper when—and if—they wrapped up the excavation. It also occupied her mind just enough to keep her from racing to Ian's camp the way she wanted. Lying naked at the inlet with him in the middle of the night, she'd felt safer than if she'd been at home, locked in her house. Even now, she ached to be with him.

But she couldn't leave Faith alone here. They needed to watch each other's backs until this was ended, however it ended. Her sister hadn't been able to reach Hakon since that last time when she'd tapped herself. If Thomas Callander was plotting something involving the serpent ceremony, he'd decided to bide his time. How could Lamb not know the man he'd hired, the man he'd known for a good ten years, was capable of murder?

And he wasn't alone. Couldn't be alone, if he were bent on doing this. No one had the kind of power it would take to open and control the ley lines himself. *Stone, stone, grass, stone...*

"Good morning."

Sara spun on her heel, fists raised to swing.

Thomas hopped backward. "Whoa! A little edgy today, aren't you?"

Forcing a smile, she lowered her fists. "Don't sneak up on me like that."

"How should I sneak up on you, then?" He laughed.

She tried not to stare. She'd never seen his eyes change, even once. Did they change, or was it not the same for everyone? Could he lift as much as she could with her gift? Did he feel that shiver when he used his power?

Cameron's terror-stricken face sprang into her mind. She gripped the edge of the sieve box, and fought back the bile rising in her throat.

"You all right? It sounded like you were pretty bad off, yesterday."

"I'm fine," she murmured, no longer able to meet his gaze. "Just working. Preoccupied."

She felt his gaze on her for a moment, and implored her body not to tremble. She scanned the dig, looking for something he might use against her. What would happen if he suspected she knew about his gift? Would she be strong enough to stop him?

"You're up early," came Flintrop's voice.

She couldn't keep the relief from edging her tone when she saw Flintrop and Luis coming toward the dig. "The better to wade through a few tons of dirt."

Flintrop handed her a corn muffin. "We're eating cheap this morning. Dustin and Michael are making a supply run."

Frowning, she kicked dirt off the toes of her boots. "Both of them? We need all the manpower we've got today."

"What's your hurry?" Flintrop angled his head at her. "Iceland all over again. You're half-dead yesterday, and look at you." He did look then, and lines appeared between his brows. "Did you sleep at all?"

She turned back to the sieve box, and began shaking it again one-handed while she bit into the muffin. "I got enough sleep yesterday."

"All right, let's get a move on," Faith sang out. She strode toward the dig with a bucket of tools.

Flintrop made a noise of amusement as Luis and Thomas went to start work. "A pair of slave drivers, the both of you."

Sara eyed him. "You're in an awfully good mood today."

He bent closer to her ear. One tawny brow arched. "I'm always in a good mood when I go after something I want."

She opened her mouth on an acid response, but Flintrop jogged away, whistling, to join the others in the pit.

The crew worked through the morning. Sara felt charged with energy. The faster she worked, the more every nerve willed her to keep going. She barely registered Michael and Dustin's return. Only when Faith called a halt for lunch did she come out of her trance. Even then, she was the last to leave the pit.

During lunch, Faith sat beside her with a set of charts in her lap, eating her sandwich with one hand, and flipping through the sheets with the other. "We made good time. We can do this."

"I hope to God Hakon is guarding you at night," Sara muttered. "I don't know how we're going to keep this up for three weeks. I'm jumpy as it is."

Her sister shot her a look of appraisal. "Even for you," she agreed with a note of concern. "Just sitting next to you is giving me the jitters. Can't you tone it down?"

Sara snatched one of the charts off her sister's lap. Restlessly, she folded and unfolded it. "I don't like this. I don't. I can't think." The paper crinkled in her hands.

Faith clapped a hand over Sara's, stopping her torture of the chart. "What's the matter with you? No bullshit."

"You don't think what's going on around here is enough to make me a little haywire?"

Dustin strolled over, brandishing a wax-paper bag. "Cookies and other sugary bad stuff. Any takers?"

"Sure," Faith said, reaching for the bag.

"I'm going back to work," Sara said, jumping up. She marched away to the dig site, feeling Faith's gaze on her every step of the way.

She worked through dinner in the pit, and then at the sieve box, pawing through its contents by the light of the lowering sun. She murmured along with a half-heard tune from someone's radio, and rearranged the rough granite rubble without actually seeing it. A flurry of thoughts skimmed the surface of her consciousness, but like the earth and stone in the box, nothing stayed put long enough to be examined. Just work, work, work, and when she paused, she wanted only to get back to work again.

Maybe because if she stopped, even for a second, she'd have to consider how insane this game of spider-and-the-fly was.

"Hey. You're making the rest of us look bad," Dustin joked, coming toward her with a lantern.

"Sorry."

Laughing, he rested the lantern on the post beside the box. "Are you going for a world record?"

"If we're going to finish the excavation this summer on the manpower we have, we need to buckle down," she said.

"At the rate you're going, you'll finish it next week all by yourself."

She glanced around. "What time is it?"

"Damn near bedtime. Are the rest of us required to keep up with you?"

For a few seconds, her drive lifted, and she relaxed just enough to smile. "You could help me finish this batch, and we can call it even."

Dustin rubbed his hands together. "Step aside, and let a real grunt show you how the work is done."

Sara shrugged, and stepped back from the box. While Dustin worked, she cast a surreptitious look at the sky. Ian had said he'd be at the inlet. He hadn't said when. She hoped he'd still be there when she arrived.

They'd come together so fast and furious last night. The memory still hummed on her skin. He'd smelled of sunshine and chalk dust, and even though he'd sent her spinning into breathless ecstasy, she wanted him again as soon as they had finished. And what about the way he'd looked at her afterward? The way his arms had tightened around her, as if he meant to keep her there with him, safe and wanted, forever?

All at once, the urge to go to him became too much to bear. She picked up her bucket of tools, then strode toward her tent to put them away.

Flintrop intercepted her on the way. "Sara, have you got anything else from Lambertson on that skull and belt buckle we found?"

"Just the lab results, and what we've already catalogued on them. Why?"

"Nothing," he said, looking displeased. I was hoping we'd have found something else by now."

"Well, what is it you're looking for?"

"I'm working on the pitch for Oxford. Can you show me what you have so far?"

Sara felt her chance to see Ian, possibly uninterrupted, slipping away. She stifled a painful sigh and gestured toward her tent. "All right, come on."

He studied her with a stare like a buzzard. "Got something else to do?"

"No."

He said nothing, but allowed her to lead the way back to her tent. She discovered then how much easier it was to deal with Faith's stare on the back of her neck than his.

Chapter Fifteen

Faith gathered up the last of her dinner dishes and handed them to Michael. She stood and fisted her hands at the small of her back. The day had been productive not only in digging, but in aching muscles. A hot bath would have been a dream come true. Right then, she'd even have settled for a cold one.

Sold, she thought, heading to her tent for swimwear, a towel, and a change of clothes.

When she emerged, Dustin was still working. "Swim?" she offered.

He waved her on. "No, thanks. Camp shower. I'll tell the others where you went if they want to join."

Shrugging, Faith headed away to the inlet.

When she got there, she found Ian sitting on the beach, bent over a notebook and absorbed in writing. A folded pile of clothes, a rumpled towel, and the remains of what appeared to be his dinner sat beside him on the sand. From his damp chestnut hair, she guessed he'd already had his swim.

At her approach, he looked back over his shoulder. "Hey."

"Hey, back. Why do you not seem happy to see me?"

He flashed a brief grin. "Sorry. I thought you were Sara."

She mirrored his grin and sat beside him. "Taller.

Blonder. She's finishing up some lab work, I think."

"Did everything go all right today?"

"Yeah, all things considered. Working beside Tom Callander has become a new experience in walking on eggshells."

His gaze swept her figure as if to assure himself she was in one piece. She shook her head to forestall his concern. "We're okay. He acted completely innocent, like he hadn't...done what he did."

Lines appeared in Ian's brow. "Maybe he's waiting."

"Thanks for that cheery thought." She drew up her knees and hugged them while creepy-crawly sensations migrated through her body.

Needing to change the subject, she studied the notebook in his lap. In the margins of his field notes, she caught a sketch of a wolf's face. The markings matched those of her sister's shapeshift. "You don't think they're going to question that when you get back to the college?"

"They don't read these. They get the edited version from a computer." He closed the book, then stuffed it into his inside jacket pocket.

Faith got the impression that it wasn't the only drawing of Sara that he'd done in that notebook, lupine or otherwise. She held his gaze just long enough for him to respond with a look that said, *Forget it, you can't see it.* She giggled, and he shook his head.

Time passed in companionable silence while they gazed out over the water. The waves of the inlet whispered at the shore. Faith watched the few clouds pick up threads of champagne pink and sherbet orange, prelude to the sun's fiery descent.

Without warning, Hakon sprang into her mind. *Aesa,* he'd called her, before she told him her name was Faith. She'd pondered on that while caring for Sara's fever. Among its other possible derivatives, "Aesa" in Old Icelandic meant "to incite war." How very prophetic. What was she, the Viking Helen of Troy?

A thousand years down the line, Faith had been born with the exact same face as this Viking woman. Heck of a coincidence. She'd been charged to fulfill a mission that Hakon could not: the downfall of some rogue druid sect and their serpent ceremony. Might as well have asked for the Brooklyn Bridge, while he was at it.

Thinking back on Hakon's first reaction to seeing her, she gave her ribcage a discreet rub. For a ghost, he was awfully good at dealing out bone-crushing hugs. Bleeding, too. That he could touch, and bleed, and at other times disappear without a trace from her senses, made her head spin with questions.

He's not completely a ghost, she thought, startled. That explained why she couldn't always hear or feel him. His soul had been trapped on Hvitmar, one foot in this world, and one in the next, because he'd never finished his quest. He'd vowed himself into a half-existence for the love of a woman.

But Aesa had gone on. Why couldn't Faith sense her here, trying to be with Hakon however she was able?

A frisson flew down her spine. She gripped herself. *Oh, my God. She's me.* A strangled whimper escaped her. How could she have failed to make the connection all this time?

Ian's head snapped up. "What's the matter?"

Air refused to reach her lungs past the constricted knot in her throat. She felt the blood drain from her face, chilling her further. "I loved him. I cried for him. I'm her. She's *me*."

"Faith, you're starting to scare me." Ian gripped her shoulder.

"Hakon's wife. I'm her, a thousand years later."

"What the hell are you talking about?"

"Her name was Aesa. She loved him more than anything in the world. I felt it when I saw him." The depth of passion Aesa and the Viking warrior had felt for one another brought tears to her eyes, even now, in a mere echo. She'd never imagined love like that existed. She fisted a hand on her chest. "I felt it like it was my own emotion."

Ian started shaking his head. She cut him off before he could deny her words. "You saw her," she protested. "It's me! I have to finish this. I was meant to."

"I hope to God you aren't saying what I think you're saying. If you think your sister's going to let you sacrifi—"

"Ian!" Faith felt the shiver of her eyes flashing into silver. She wrenched his hand from her shoulder and dug her fingers into the coarse denim of his jacket. "If you say one word to her, I swear I will make you regret it. I don't need you scaring her." She shoved his hand away. "Hakon said *gifted blood*. He didn't say *sacrifice*. It could take one drop, for all I know."

Ian bared his teeth. "Or everything you've got. Damn it, Faith, this is insane. Even considering it is insane. You don't know what that ley line will do to you if you try this."

"You don't, either. We haven't got many options.

It's Callander, or Sara, or me." She blinked again to let her eyes return to their normal color, then gave him a sardonic smirk. "Do you want to walk up to Callander and say, 'Excuse me, but I know you're a telekinetic and a murderer. Can I use some of your blood to ruin your chances at absolute power?'"

A muscle worked in Ian's jaw. He sat back to push a hand through his hair. "Don't you think Sara needs to know about this? If something happens to you, it'll kill her."

The knot in her throat tightened a little more. "You love her, don't you?"

He looked away then, his expression irritable...but he didn't deny it. Faith grinned.

She heard the shuffle of footsteps and looked behind her. Sara came toward them with a towel slung over her shoulder. She'd changed into her red bathing suit, with a beach wrap tied around her waist. Faith felt a surge in the air beside her. Another look at Ian confirmed him sitting up straight now, all attention. She smiled again. When he noticed, he glared back with a look that said *shut up*, which only made her smile wider.

Her good humor vanished when she saw Luis and Flintrop trailing behind her sister. "Great. I was just saying to myself how I needed a raging headache." She scrubbed at her face, angry now that Alan Flintrop might catch her teary-eyed.

"Yeah. My day didn't suck enough, either," Ian agreed, getting to his feet and helping her up. He pulled a bandanna from his back pocket and handed it to her.

Sara reached them, beaming. "Found a bone comb." The exultant smile died on her face when she saw Faith. "You okay?"

"Fine." Faith marshaled her features into an easygoing expression.

Luis passed them with a quick hello, then plowed straight into the water. Flintrop approached and laid a hand briefly on Sara's shoulder. "Faith, I take it back. She's worse than she was in Iceland. I think she's on auto-pilot." He took a closer look at Faith. Damn, had he seen the tearstains after all?

Ian shoved his hands in his pockets. "I was making her laugh."

Faith warmed from the toes up, and officially named Ian her new best friend. He and Flintrop continued to hold each other's gaze. Mutual dislike hummed in the air.

Time to return the favor. "Alan, I need to talk to you about one of the charts we printed out this afternoon," she said. "Do you mind if I borrow you for a few minutes?"

He looked at her like she'd just given him a violent shake. She stifled a smug chuckle. *Yeah, normally, I wouldn't volunteer to chat with you, either. That's because you're a complete weasel.* With her liveliest smile, she beckoned him away and headed off down the beach.

She didn't really give a damn about the slight rise in electromagnetic readings that the charts had shown that afternoon. It could have been put down to the ley line itself—which she had no intention of pointing out, in any case. She'd have told him to come inspect one of the beach rocks, just for the satisfaction of getting him away from her sister and Ian.

With Flintrop in tow, she sat at the water's edge on

a flat rock. She glanced back over her shoulder to see Ian flash a grin in her direction. He bent his head toward Sara and murmured something that made her giggle. A split second later, she caught the glimmer of annoyance on Flintrop's face. *Go, Ian.* She couldn't suppress a broad smile.

"What are you so happy about?" Flintrop demanded. He plopped beside her on the sand.

"Nothing. About the chart... The electromagnetic readings came back a little on the high side. I wondered if we shouldn't look into that."

"I'll take care of it. Probably just a false reading, or the equipment might need adjustments. Are we having a conversation, here? I was just getting used to your undying hatred."

Touché, weasel. "Let me make it clear that the only reason I'm at this dig with you is because my firm is in control of it," she said. "If it were up to me, I'd have scrimped and saved for every penny this project is costing, rather than involve you. Your being here was Lamb's decision."

"All right, all right." He held up his hands.

Faith fumed at the way he laughed, and then at the way she let him annoy her. She caught him glancing over at Ian and Sara again. "What? He's not at the dig site. You going to commandeer other parts of the island, too?"

Flintrop sighed. "I don't know how long this is going to go on between you and me, but I'd like to get past it. You and I just didn't work out together. It's nothing you did."

"Careful. That almost sounded like an apology."

His cobalt stare bored into her. "Are we through?"

he asked.

"There is no *limit* to how 'through' we are."

He stood. She remembered she shouldn't be antagonizing him, when her goal had been to guarantee Ian and Sara a few minutes free of Flintrop's interference. She vaulted to her feet. "Don't go getting into a pissing match with him. He's got as much right to be here as you have."

"Birds being more groundbreaking and crucial than a thousand-year-old ruin."

"Listen to yourself. You're jealous!"

"Are you?"

"Of you, wanting my sister? You're just conceited enough to believe that, aren't you?" She struggled to compose herself, when all she wanted was to punch him repeatedly in the nose for being the biggest jerk in the universe. "You know what? This is ridiculous. We have a job to do, and like it or not, we're stuck together. After this project, I pray to God I won't have to work with you ever again." She shook her head and walked away to join Luis.

****

Ian watched Faith stalk into the water. Flintrop sat back down and withdrew a sheaf of folded papers from his coat pocket. He snapped them open with an aggravated flourish, and began to read. Ian wondered if the bastard had come just to chaperone Sara. "Does he have a talent for pissing people off, or something?"

Sara worried her lower lip between her teeth. "I'm sorry. I tried to come alone. Luis heard I was coming, and then Flintrop got in on it..."

He took her hand. "I don't care. I'm just glad you're here."

She blushed and evaded his gaze.

He angled his head. "What? You worried about the watchdog over there?"

"He's looking," she protested.

"Good." Taking her face in his hands, Ian planted a thorough kiss on her lips.

She squeaked as if in surprise, but when he drew back, she beamed, even as her cheeks reddened. "We're in *public*."

"So? When we get home, I plan to do a whole lot of kissing you in public."

Her mouth opened, but whatever she meant to say gave way to a look that hovered between a smile and underlying anxiousness.

Ian's stomach lurched with a disappointment that startled him. "You didn't think this was just a passing thing, did you?" He searched her face. "You did think that."

"I don't know what I thought. I've been trying not to think past the next few weeks." She hugged herself, rubbing her arms in spite of the evening's balmy air.

Ian stuffed his unwelcome dismay into a mental corner. He stroked a hand across the soft curve of Sara's cheek, then cleared his throat and lowered his hands. Looking her up and down with appreciation, he asked, "Going for a swim, or did you just come to flaunt that bathing suit at me?"

"Are you complaining about my bathing suit?"

Banter. Much better than that anxious look. He waved a finger between them. "I've come to realize, the less clothing separating the two of us, the better I like it."

She blushed, and he fought the urge to throw her

over his shoulder and carry her off to the nearest secluded spot. She glanced furtively around, looking like a teenager who'd been caught staying out too late. "I'm going to swim now."

He groaned. "You *are* flaunting it."

She smiled again, untied her wrap, then handed it to him with a sly smile. "Now I'm flaunting. See you in a bit." She strolled off to the water.

Ian allowed himself a pleasant view of swaying hips as she walked across the uneven sand.

A shadow fell over him. He looked up.

Flintrop gave him a cold blue stare as he passed on his way back toward the camp. "Don't get too used to it, Waverly." He sauntered away before Ian could reply.

The rest of the evening went well enough, though Ian wished he'd carried Sara off, after all. By the time he got back to his camp, he couldn't think straight for wanting her. The erstwhile cold bath of the inlet had done nothing to alleviate that. He stayed up most of the night writing in his journal, though none of the entry mentioned a stitch of his wildlife research.

Faith had asked him flat out if he loved her sister.

God, yes. Since he was ten. Even when he didn't want to.

But then Sara had given him that look. Did she think this thing—this whatever-it-was between them—was temporary?

That thought bothered him almost as much as the gathering apprehension whenever he thought of the amulet around her neck.

****

The next week and a half went by in a blur of full-speed work. Ian spent his days on the cliffside. During the nights, Sara came to his camp, and they made love. Always passionate, always intense, and over far too soon. Each time, she stole away well before the sun rose. And each time, something stopped him from confessing the way he felt about her. He sensed an uneasiness in her, but put it off to the looming dig deadline.

This morning, he'd started climbing early and spent most of the day on the rock. Halfway down the cliff, he thrust his fingers into a handhold and angled sideways on his rope. A flock of terns rested on a craggy outcrop below, jabbering amongst themselves. He took a rough visual count of the flock and raised his camera, focusing the lens, aiming, and shooting the photo without conscious thought.

Horus soared by, chirping in what Ian had come to understand as his greeting. "Hey, hotshot, can I borrow those wings?" Smiling, Ian edged the instep of one foot onto a thin crease of rock for a moment of rest.

Then he saw the second falcon.

For a moment, he wondered if Sara had paid him a visit, but Horus shot past him again with a drawn-out wail and rose into a dizzying spiral. The two birds whirled around one another. Ian recognized a courtship flight. His mouth fell open as he followed the roller coaster circling of the larger bird.

Definitely not Sara, by the way Horus was reacting.

Grinning, he raised the camera around his neck and hurried to focus. "Sweetheart, I think you just got me my tenure." He snapped a rapid series of photos, running the battery almost all the way down before the birds circled away together. He started back up the cliff, eager to get his observations down on paper.

He had to tell Sara.

When had thinking of her become such second nature?

He gave a soft laugh. Since forever, really.

His memory spun back twenty years to the first time he saw her. Shaking, her eyes a startling grass-green, she'd braced herself against the oncoming punch of a boy almost twice her size. Ian recalled a bright flash of anger and his blood surging in his ears. He'd been about to jump between them when the bell rang, and the teachers came to herd them all back from the playground into the school.

Those eyes had burned right down inside of him. After twenty years, in spite of all that had happened since then, they still did. He suspected, twenty years from now, they still would. *If we ever get the chance to find out,* he thought, grimly returning to the present.

A fitful burst of wind rocked him in his harness, reminding him that he'd better get topside. With the breeze picking up like this, he expected another storm to follow on its heels in the next day or so. He climbed back up the cliff, feeling out each crevice before continuing the push upward. Birds scolded him from their niches in the rock far below. The wind gusted up the cliffside, smacking against his body.

He had just gained the edge when a shadow blotted out the sunlight overhead. Ian swore and slid downward a few feet. He gripped harder on the rope, wincing against the burn, and jammed the toes of one shoe in a foothold. He jerked to a halt with pebbles rattling their way down the cliffside, and looked up.

The shadowy figure bent down out of the sun glare.

Ian recognized Luis. "Need a hand, greenhorn?" the man asked, then laughed.

"Jesus, Lu. Could you not do that when I'm dangling from a two-hundred-foot cliff?" Ian hauled on the rope, regained the last few feet, then reached for his friend's hand.

Luis pulled him upward over the cliff edge. Ian unbuckled his harness and started winding the rope. "What's up?"

"I just came up to say hello."

"How about a hello and a beer? It's damn hot down there with the sun pounding on the rock," Ian said, wiping a hand across his sweaty forehead.

"Lead the way, *amigo*."

They headed toward Ian's tent. Freshly armed with a cold six-pack, they sat in a pair of camp chairs outside. Ian propped his feet on an empty crate. "I was just hurting for a break. You came along at the right time, buddy."

Luis beamed, and they clinked bottles. Time stretched out while they settled into the wordless male communion of sunshine, the outdoors, and fermented beverages.

Luis swept a look around Ian's camp. Some crates had already been packed for shipment home, and covered with a tarp. "It looks like you're going to be done around here pretty soon."

"Yeah, another few weeks, maybe. Got most of the data, and about a thousand photos."

Luis gave him a broad smile. "So, you and Shark Markham, huh?"

"Me and *Sara*."

"All right, all right. She's not so bad, I guess. At

least she pulls her weight on a project. She was in a good mood this morning, so I figure she must have gotten an hour of sleep instead of the usual half."

Ian wondered if they knew about her sneaking out to see him. "What do you mean?"

"I mean, she'd rather work than eat. She's going to wear out before we finish, unless she's part machine." Luis set the heel of one work boot on the crate.

Ian picked at the label on his beer bottle. "How are things going down there?"

"We've almost got the perimeter dug out, and we've started on the interior. You need some peat bricks for a campfire, you know where to find them."

Ian flashed a quick, preoccupied smile. A little over one week to go. He itched to do more than sit up here waiting. He kept his gaze on his beer bottle, peeling its label back bit by bit. "I guess you guys are ahead of schedule, seeing you were planning for this to take all summer."

"Yeah. Lambertson is going to be late coming back, but I think we're going to finish without him." Luis drained the rest of his beer, and stood up. "That is, if I get back down there and help, instead of sitting around up here with layabouts like you."

"It's a dirty job. See you." Ian waved his friend off, then went reluctantly back to work.

Chapter Sixteen

Ian spent the rest of the afternoon catching up on his notes. After that, he decided to pack one last crate for the day. Unused tent gear joined extra camera lenses in their padded case. He wedged a few books in the remaining space, then hammered the crate shut.

That about covered anything he could do to occupy himself with something other than ritual sacrifices. Hour by hour, he found himself more convinced that he, Faith, and Sara should be as far away from Hvitmar as possible. Even his work couldn't distract him anymore.

When he turned around, his gaze landed on a wolf standing at the edge of his camp. He flinched reflexively, even though he knew it was Sara. "Hey, gorgeous."

She twitched an ear, and her tongue lolled in a brief lupine grin. She loped forward with her muzzle to the ground. Ian watched, fascinated, as she wound between the camp chairs and nosed at the beer bottles. In spite of her disparate lack of fear around a human establishment, he almost forgot she wasn't a real wolf. She moved like one, sounded like one, and sure as hell looked like one. He resisted the urge to grab his camera.

Finished with her explorations, she padded over to him. He took an instinctive step backward. She laughed that toothy wolf laugh again and slowed to a stealthy walk.

What the heck was she doing?

In the next instant, she dodged closer and snatched his pant leg in her teeth. She jerked on it, then bounded away with her tail high in the air.

Ian stumbled, but stayed upright. "Hey!"

She bolted around the camp chairs and came to a skidding halt beside one of the large crates. To Ian's amusement, she lowered her forequarters to the ground in the quintessential canine play-bow.

Laughing, he stalked toward the crate. "This isn't fair. You've got four legs." He feinted a jump around one side of the crate. When she raced around to avoid him, he flung a hand out to grab at her from the other side. She sprang into the air and disappeared around the corner of the large shipping box again.

Ian crouched behind it and peered around the corner.

Nothing. "Where'd you go?"

He felt a tug on the back of his T-shirt and spun around.

The wolf bounced backward. He lunged, and caught her by the forepaw with a laugh.

It occurred to him then that he was holding onto a living, breathing, untranquilized wolf by its leg. Startled, he let go of her.

She must have seen the surprise in his face, because she cocked her ears forward, and her tongue lolled again. Lowering her shaggy head, she thrust her nose under his hand.

Ian almost yanked his hand back without thinking. He let his fingers skim along her muzzle, over the broad forehead, and behind her large, triangular ears. He took a deep breath. She even *smelled* like a wolf—that dense, dusty scent of heavy pelt and wilderness. He laced his fingers through the coarse guard hairs of her ruff, and into the soft, wooly undercoat.

Never, never stare down a wolf, he remembered someone telling him when he'd volunteered with the Yellowstone packs. But she looked up at him, and in her eyes he saw only Sara. He smiled. "This is unbelievable. Sara, you're beautiful."

She slipped out from under his hands and backed away. Ian watched the lupine shape blur around the edges, then resolve into that of a crouching woman in a faded navy sweatshirt and jeans. No matter how many times he saw her do that, it amazed him.

Sara beamed at him and sat back on her heels. "You're not so bad, yourself. When was Luis here?"

"Luis?"

"He's all over the camp. In the chair, on the beer bottles—"

"You smelled him?"

"Yeah. People smell, much as they'd like to think otherwise."

Ian gaped at her. "Do you have any idea how cool that is?" Then, because the curiosity was killing him, he asked, "What do I smell like?"

She dimpled. "Like chalk, sweat, and beer, right now. Been climbing?"

"That's flattering."

"If it's any consolation, you smell good to me." She got to her feet. "How about one of those beers?"

"Sure." He got up and dusted off his jeans.

They moved to the camp chairs. She took a beer from the carton, then popped it open. Ian propped his foot on the makeshift stool, then removed his climbing shoes. "Tag, huh?"

"I used to play tag with Faith all the time. She got so she'd tag me just before climbing a tree, so I couldn't reach her."

He laughed. "Well, good. Now I know how to beat you."

"I don't see any trees around here," she pointed out, looking smug.

"I'll figure something out," he shot back, just as smug. He settled back into his camp chair. Recalling what Luis had told him earlier, he studied her face. She looked paler than usual, with dark smudges under her eyes. He frowned. "You haven't been sleeping."

"I'm all right," she said, fast enough for him to realize she wasn't.

He wondered if he might not be contributing to the problem. He *had* been keeping her up nights, but no power on earth could make him part with that. The more she was with him, the less he worried what was happening to her when she wasn't. "Sara."

"I'm fine. Just unsettled about finishing on time."

A pair of specks wheeling in the sky distracted him. "I meant to tell you," he said. "We've got a Hathor."

She looked up at once. "Where?"

He stood and motioned for her to come closer. He drew her in front of him and stood at her back. Instantly mindful of her nearness, he hesitated. His thoughts fuzzed into a tempting vision of her ensconced in his camp bed, not birdwatching.

Later, he ordered himself. Scanning the approaching falcon pair, he reached over her shoulder and traced a finger in the sky. "That's her. The bigger one."

Sara did a little dance on her toes. "Ian, this is wonderful!"

"Yeah. I think I just got myself a permanent job, thanks to her." The wind changed. He caught a hint of cinnamon, and inhaled deeply. She'd been eating those candies again. He revisited the image of the two of them in his tent, and pulled her back against his body. "You're here early today."

"I got a reprieve, on account of Flintrop being too busy to annoy me. No one's been out of their tents all afternoon."

Ian slid a hand beneath her sweatshirt and up her belly to her breasts, stroking the soft skin under the edges of her bra. "What do you say we forget about him and the birds, and think about something else for a while?"

She turned in his embrace to curl her arms around his neck. He loved the way she melted against him. "What did you have in mind?"

He grasped her hand and lowered it from his neck, then towed her toward his tent with an inviting chuckle. "Come with me, and I'll show you."

****

Another seven days passed in a flurry of activity. By now, only the hearth of the Viking ruin remained to be cleared. Numb with exhaustion and increasing worry, Sara couldn't feel any pride in the speed of their progress. She hadn't slept more than a handful of hours in the past few days. Work continued without incident, as if Cameron's death had never happened. The thought made her sick.

She put her tools in a bucket and lifted it to move to the next plot. Several feet away, Faith stopped her work and stood upright. Sara felt her sister's stare even before she turned to look. "What?"

"You need sleep," Faith said.

"I'll sleep after this whole thing is over."

Faith stepped over a marker, and came toward her with a frown. "Look, I know we need to get this done, but you're teetering on your feet."

Sara spoke in a harsh whisper. "We have exactly three days until the full moon, or didn't you notice that?"

"And you're no use to me half-dead like this. Go lie down."

Sara let her shoulders slump. "I can't. I've tried."

Faith cast a look around the dig, but the others were working steadily. She laid a cool hand on Sara's forehead. "Are you sick again?"

Sara backed away. "No. It's not like that. I just... Whenever I try to get any rest, I jump right up again and have to do something. Nervous energy, or whatever it is. I just can't lie around."

"Well, take a break long enough to go ask Flintrop where he put the electromagnetic charts. He's in his tent."

Sara nodded and climbed up the scaffold, over the dig wall, then headed down the slope toward Flintrop's tent. Finding it empty, she entered, then flipped through a sheaf of charts on his camp table. Nothing there. She turned to the smaller table beside his bed, pushed aside a bottle of saline solution, then picked up a stack of pages.

"Sara. Nice of you to drop by."

She jerked and looked to the doorway. Flintrop stood silhouetted in the late afternoon sun, wearing a smug expression that made her want to throw the papers at him. "I was looking for Faith's E-M charts."

Flintrop stepped into the tent, moved around the bed, then retrieved a folder from an open box. He brought the folder to her with an aggravating smile. Sara noticed his gaze lingered on his bed before meeting hers. She tried not to shrink away from him as she held out her free hand for the folder.

"I'm not going to bite you," he said. His voice held a maddening note of purely male amusement.

She tossed the other pages on his bed, then grabbed the folder from his hand. "I might bite *you*, if you don't stop staring at me."

He laughed.

She waved the folder at him. "Did you figure out whether these were misreads, or not? They keep popping up, and I'm starting to get a little concerned."

"The equipment is fine." He reached an arm around her back to urge her toward the tent door, and this time, she did jerk away. "Easy, Sara. You came into *my* tent."

"I'm not looking for a liaison! I want my sister's charts. While we're at it, I want to know why these readings keep getting higher." She thrust the folder at his chest.

He favored her with a long-suffering look. "Is this the way the rest of the dig is going to go? You've been barking at me the past two weeks. I am on your team, you know. We both want the same thing."

Sara fixed him with an icy look. "I don't think we want *exactly* the same thing."

He threw his hands in the air, and plopped down on

his bed. "All right. I've made no secret about the fact that I'm interested in you. Does that mean you're going to be hostile to me for the rest of this dig?"

"I'll tell you what," she said, moving toward the door. "You be nice to Ian, and I'll be nice to you."

"Him again."

Incensed, she spun back toward the bed. "What is it that bugs you about him, Flintrop? It can't possibly be that he has more money and fame than you do."

Flintrop rose to his feet. He stalked forward with a sudden, serious look that made her freeze where she stood. When he reached her, he leaned close enough for her to feel his breath on her face. His eyes gleamed. "He only has one thing I want."

Sara felt the hair on the back of her neck stand on end, and backed toward the door. "I'll see you later."

She wasn't certain, as she left, why it seemed more like she was fleeing than walking out.

Work continued at a killing pace the final three days of the excavation. The crew had given up trying to chide Sara and her sister away from their work, and did their jobs without comment.

Sara forgot everything but the mindless routine of trowel, brush, and sieve. Instead of being an amorphous mound of earth, the dig now showed the lines of wall and doorway, the contours of sleeping areas, and places where food and livestock had been stowed. She could almost see a house where the ruin stood, a familiar sensation that still gave her a chill to this day.

In the beginning of her career, as a field assistant, she'd felt like an intruder into the private lives of others. As time went on, she grew accustomed to the feeling of being watched and judged by the ghosts of the past.

She wondered offhand if Hakon was watching them now.

The thought gave her the jitters. Everything gave her jitters lately. What little sleep she could catch sapped away with simpler and simpler tasks. On hands and knees, she shook off her apprehension and continued scraping away at the circular patch over the hearth at the center of the house. The earth blurred beneath her, and she shook her head. *So tired. If I could just rest for ten minutes...*

"Sara."

She jerked to attention and looked across the hearth, where Faith had paused in her digging. Her sister dropped her tools and sat back. "Why don't you go up to Ian's camp?"

For a moment, Sara just looked at her sister without absorbing the question.

Faith's brow furrowed. "Ian. Remember Ian? Sara, I'm worried about you. You need to sleep."

Guilt oozed down Sara's spine. She'd been working through the night without telling her sister. And Ian... She hadn't seen him in days. The only rest she'd gotten in weeks was the too-short space of time she had spent in his arms after making love to him.

Did he have any idea how she felt when they lay together in the night, silent and peaceful while the wind drifted and the ocean sighed outside?

She loved him.

I love him.

I have to tell him. She lunged to her feet.

The motion made her head spin. As her legs buckled underneath her, she registered only distant surprise.

"Whoa, easy." Firm hands hooked her by the elbows and pulled her onto her feet.

She shook her head and looked up. Flintrop stood behind her with a concerned expression.

Faith hurried over. "All right, that's it. Go lie down before I make you. I'm not kidding."

Flintrop frowned. "Faith's right. You need to take a break, even if you don't sleep, Sara. Exhausting yourself isn't going to help us finish the project."

Sara heard her sister give a *hmmph* of surprise at Flintrop's support. "Never thought we'd agree on something."

Shaking her head, Sara tried pulling her arms away.

"We can get it done without you." Flintrop hooked his hands under her arms and pulled her up. "Come on."

She took a step and tottered again. Flintrop caught her. She didn't have the stamina to resist as he swung her into his arms and carried her toward her tent. She fought to block out the head-spinning motion. "Will we finish in time?"

"In time for what?"

"I want to finish by tonight."

"Yeah, I think so. What's the hurry?"

She felt him step up onto a scaffold, then down the other side. "I will be fine," she said. "Give me ten minutes, and I'll be back out there."

"You're your own worst enemy. Did you have a reason for this deadline and the way you're trying to kill yourself?"

She forced one eye open, but closed it again when the motion of his walking made her dizzy. She wanted to tell him she could get to her tent without help, but arguing took too much effort.

She'd been about to do something just before the collapse. What was it? Her head ached with trying to remember. Her thoughts drifted.

"You're a lot more approachable when you're half-asleep," Flintrop murmured, bringing her awake again.

Lacking enough energy to glare at him, she settled for a long look of disgruntlement before closing her eyes again.

He pulled a blanket up over her, chuckling. "One of these days, you're going to figure out I'm not half bad."

Several minutes passed, and sleep danced just within her grasp. She forced conscious thought out of her mind, and reached hopefully for oblivion. Just as she hovered on the threshold of rest, it slipped away from her as it always did. Her body thrummed with the need to be awake, to be active, to *do something*. She whimpered in desperation.

"What's wrong?"

Her stomach turned over with the nausea of fighting to still her singing nerves. In her turmoil, she forgot that the voice belonged to Flintrop. She curled into a ball on her side. *Can't sleep. Can't be awake. Can't function. What's wrong with me?* When had this started?

She saw a man's shadowy face in her mind, dark-haired and blue-eyed. With her thoughts roiling in the middle ground between sleep and wakefulness, she couldn't remember who he was, except that she wanted wildly to go to him. *Safety.* "Help," she whispered.

The cot sank as someone sat beside her. A hand stroked her hair. "I'm right here, Sara," the voice soothed. "What is it?"

The buzzing sensation rang in her ears, and she clamped her arms over her head, trying to squeeze it out. "Stop. Please make it stop," she begged the shadowy apparition. "Help me."

Whoever sat beside her gripped her shoulder. "Sara. Come on, snap out of it."

His voice distracted her from the buzz surging through her body. Was that him? Shaking, she turned blindly toward the voice.

"Flintrop, I've got her. Go back to the dig," she heard a new, female voice order.

Clarity swept though her. She seized it, fearing it might slip away again. "Faith. Jesus, Faith."

Flintrop stood up, dividing a look between her and her sister. "I'll radio for a chopper. She doesn't have a fever, but she's losing it, Faith. She needs medical attention."

"She needs me. Just go back to the dig."

"Are you nuts?"

"I've got it handled. Go," Faith demanded.

"Like hell."

Sara cradled her aching skull. "Stop. Please." She teetered on the edge of the cot. "He's not... He was helping me. I think."

Both of them turned to stare at her.

Faith recovered first. "Flintrop, if you want to help, clear the hearth. Let me worry about my sister."

He cast a doubtful glance in Sara's direction. With an irritable jerk of his shoulder, Flintrop spun and left the tent.

Faith sat down as soon as he was gone, and laid a cool hand on Sara's forehead. "I don't know how much use this is going to be, but here goes nothing."

Sara struggled to shut out the bass-drum pounding of her head. "What are you doing?"

"Hopefully not asking for trouble. Sit still. I'm going to read you."

Sara seized her sister's hand and yanked it away from her forehead. "Don't!"

"What do you mean, 'don't?' This isn't funny anymore. You're scaring me."

"It's not... You shouldn't. Just don't."

"Sara, you can't keep this up. It's not like you, even when you're working hard. Something's wrong."

Sara shook her head, sliding back onto the cot away from her sister. She lay back down with a sigh. "Just give me a little while, and I'll be back out to help."

"You're staying put if I have to strap you down. I'm getting Ian."

Sara didn't hear her leave.

****

Faith headed up the slope at a fast walk, hugging herself. *What's the matter with her? If it's the ley line, why isn't it happening to me?* She chewed at her lip, wishing she could contact Hakon for help. She'd been unable to reach him for days, and that made her almost as uneasy as Sara's mysterious illness. She should have let Flintrop radio a chopper, but she couldn't afford to be without her sister tonight.

"Where is she?" came Ian's voice, snapping her out of her thoughts.

She looked up to see him marching down the slope toward her. "How did you know—"

He kept walking, and she turned back toward the

dig with him. "Is she hurt?" he demanded.

"She's exhausted, Ian. Tonight's the deadline, and—"

"Are you still planning on going through with this insanity?"

"What choice do we have? It's too dangerous *not* to close the ley line. Why do you think we've been working so fast?" She broke into jog, outstripping his lengthy stride. "It hasn't been for fun."

They went on in silence for several yards. When they reached camp, Faith went to her sister's tent without stopping.

"What's he doing here?" asked Flintrop from his position inside the dig.

"Don't start," Faith snapped. "He's here to see Sara."

"She's asleep." Flintrop stood upright, brushing earth from his hands. "Finally."

"Oh, thank God." Faith could have kissed him. Almost.

"Hopefully, she'll stay out for at least a few hours, if no one disturbs her," Flintrop added, casting a pointed look in Ian's direction.

Faith felt a charge of sheer hatred in the air around Ian. She winced in empathy and took his hand. "Don't."

Ian hissed outward through his teeth.

Flintrop came toward them through a gap in the ruin that had once been a doorway. "Faith, the crew's got something up at the hearth I think you should look at. We found a bowl."

A bowl. Forgetting their feud for a moment, Faith headed toward the ruin, urging Ian with her.

"What are you doing?" Flintrop asked, seeing her

propel Ian into the confines of the dig.

"Never mind what I'm doing. He's not bothering Sara, is he?"

"What *are* you doing?" Ian murmured in her ear.

Michael turned around, cradling the bowl in his hands. Faith reached for it.

Ian sucked in a breath, and then covered it with a cough. Puzzled, she caught him staring at the bowl. He shot her a warning look and glanced around the ruin. Faith saw him taking quick measure of the layout, and realized that he was comparing the modern-day structure to the house he'd seen in his dream. His gaze swept back to the bowl.

She realized then why he didn't want her to touch it. This was the sacrificial bowl he'd seen in his dream. The one that had held Aesa's blood.

The world went off-kilter for a few seconds.

Faith pulled a cloth from her back pocket and unfolded it, then held it out for the bowl. Michael gave her a long look of bewilderment, but set the artifact in the cloth. She folded the edges over the bowl, trying not to notice the discolored stains on its rough concave surface. With a curt word, she sent the crew back to work.

"Waverly," Flintrop called, coming up behind them.

Faith saw Ian tense for another battle.

Flintrop dusted his hands off on a rag. "Why don't you stick around this evening? We're almost done, and we were going to celebrate."

"You're giving me permission to be here?" Ian's voice remained even, but Faith felt waves of hostility radiating from him.

"Look, I know we haven't gotten on well, but it's the end of the project. I'm willing to let bygones be bygones if you are. Stay, if you have the time." Flintrop held out a hand.

What's this? she wondered. Ian must have been thinking the same thing, because he stared at Flintrop's hand as though he were contemplating a venomous snake. After a tense moment, he shrugged and shook Flintrop's hand. The two didn't take their eyes off each other, in spite of the friendly gesture.

Flintrop released Ian's hand, then stepped around them to continue work. Faith adjusted the wrapped bowl in one arm and took Ian's sleeve with her free hand. "You can help me."

"Sure."

Faith headed away from the ruin with him in tow. "This is the bowl, isn't it?" she asked once they entered her tent.

"Yeah."

Faith grunted and set the bowl on her camp table. She turned to her trunk for a pair of work gloves.

"Sara hasn't been up to camp lately," he said. "What the hell's been happening down here, Faith?"

She sighed. "I've never seen her work this hard. She doesn't sleep, she barely eats. For once, I find myself liking Flintrop, since he's managed to get her to rest for the first time in God knows when. I've been wondering if it isn't the ley line affecting her—"

"It would do something to you, too, wouldn't it?"

"I thought so, too, but so far I haven't felt a thing. You'd think today, of all days..." She trailed off with her skin crawling.

"What do you need my help with?"

Sitting at her camp table, Faith pulled on the work gloves, then unfolded the cloth from around the ceremonial bowl. "I want everything you remember about your dream. Between you and this bowl, I might get enough information about closing the ley lines. I need you to anchor me while I read it. This is important, Ian. Do not let go of me while I'm reading this thing. It's a sacrificial relic, and without an anchor, I might not make it back."

His eyes went stony. "Bullshit."

"Either I do this with you, or I try it by myself. Your choice."

With a dubious look at the uncovered bowl, Ian sat down and began recounting the nightmare.

Chapter Seventeen

Later that afternoon, Ian helped the crew clear the remainder of the ruin. The closer it got to completion, the edgier he got. Every now and then, he stood up to look in the direction of Sara's tent. Everything in him ached to go over there and see her, if only to be sure she was safe.

As safe as could be, anyway. He'd told Faith all he could recall of the serpent ceremony. Telling it had been easy enough; the nightmare hovered on the edge of his thoughts every waking minute. He remembered the vision of Aesa's death, and stared across the dig at Faith with a troubled frown. How could he just stand around and let her guinea pig herself on the ley line? What if it didn't work?

What if it did?

He looked toward Sara's tent again. His worries flooded back to him with teeth-grinding intensity. The reopening of the ley lines required a sacrifice of gifted blood, and Callander—it had to be Callander—was already bent on murder to accomplish that. Ian stole a look toward the man, wondering how Sara and Faith had stood working beside him for three weeks, knowing what he was and what he intended to try. Did he suspect anything of Faith or Sara's gifts? Would he try to kill them?

Ian didn't give a damn. It absolutely wasn't going

to happen.

"All right, Ian?" asked Luis.

He shook himself out of it. "Yeah, fine."

"Good, 'cause you've been staring into space for the past fifteen minutes."

With a rueful look, Ian turned back to the peat bricks he and Luis had been stacking beside the ruin's outer wall. He could have been working on his own project...at least, wrapping it up. But the later it got, the less he wanted to leave Sara and her sister to whatever was coming.

The sun lowered in the sky. Sweat trickled down the back of his neck, along with an increasing sense of dread. He could almost hear a clock ticking under the lonely whoosh of wind and clink of tools.

At last, Flintrop's voice boomed across the moor. "Pack it up, guys. This dig is done!"

Ian's stomach wrenched the moment Flintrop said it. He doubled over in surprise and clamped an arm against his belly. His knees buckled. He wheezed, feeling like he'd been kicked in the gut.

Luis said something, and then Faith was there, pulling Ian onto his feet. "Get up," she said in an insistent whisper. "Get up." She waved Luis off. "He's fine. Just give him some breathing room."

Ian struggled to regain his breath. "What the f—"

Flintrop's hand descended onto his shoulder, and a canteen loomed into his field of vision. "Easy, Waverly. Take a drink."

Ian grabbed the canteen and downed a mouthful of water large enough to make him choke.

"Out of here. Come on," Faith said, tugging on his sleeve.

He dropped the canteen and staggered along with her, away from the dig. The screaming in his head faded. He clenched his teeth and gripped his belly again. "It's...fucking...*alive*."

"I know." She rushed him toward her tent with worry in her eyes. "I can feel it. What I want to know is, why can you?"

"You're the expert."

Once they were inside her tent, she pushed him into a seat. Sweating, he braced his elbows on the table and cradled his head, half expecting it to split apart. He took a few breaths, and the stitch in his midsection eased. "Is that what it always feels like?"

"More or less. Now do you see why we have to do something?"

He said nothing for several minutes, panting through nerve-jangling surges. He gritted his teeth against a final wave of pain. "Sara."

"I'll go check on her. You stay put."

Ian lurched to his feet anyway, fully intending to go to her himself.

****

Blood. Oh, God, the blood.

Waves of it crashed against Sara. She struggled to breathe, but she was drowning in it. Her chest burned. She thrashed against the gory tide. Every time she tried to call out, the surging waves forced her back under. *Help!*

A hand descended onto her forehead. She came awake with a scream.

Flintrop snatched his hand away. "I just came in to check on you. How are you feeling?"

Sara sat up and cast a look around her tent. The

dig. Shetland. Panic seized her. "Is it finished?"

Flintrop chuckled. "Yes."

She tried getting out of bed, but he sat on the cot, pushing her back down. "Sara, you've worked hard on this project, harder than I've ever seen you work. No one appreciates the magnitude of that more than me, you know that. But you're really running yourself into the ground."

"I'm all right now. I feel better." She rubbed her eyes. "I had the most horrible dream."

"About what?"

She ran her fingers through her hair. "Blood. God, it was awful," she murmured, more to herself than to Flintrop. She thought about the countless druid sacrifices that had been done to open the ley lines, and shuddered.

Flintrop raised a hand to her face. She felt the gesture and looked up at him, but the nightmare still held her attention. "You're going to be fine."

She didn't feel fine. Nausea was still doing the backstroke in her belly.

The door flap swept back, and there stood Ian. He froze when he saw Flintrop with his hand on her cheek. His expression turned icy. "Is this why I haven't seen you in half a week?"

Sara came into the present. "What? I don't even—"

Flintrop released her and stood up. "There's nothing going on here. She just woke up."

Ian moved into the tent. Sara noticed her sister hovering outside the doorway. Ian stepped back and left just enough room for Flintrop to leave. "Bygones, huh? Don't let me stop you from not being here."

By the set of his shoulders, Flintrop was about to

say something nasty. Sara shifted and swung her legs over the edge of the cot. "Alan, don't."

Both Ian and Flintrop stared at her.

"He wasn't doing anything wrong," she said.

Ian stiffened. The two gave each other a long look, then Flintrop left the tent.

Faith hurried inside and sat down on the cot. "We found the ceremonial bowl that they used for sacrifices."

"Just give me a second," Sara murmured. She ran her fingers through her hair, trying to order her still-scattered, still-agitated thoughts, then shoved the blankets aside.

"Sara." Faith laid a hand on her knee, and Sara looked up. "We need you. Are you well enough for this?"

Sara felt for the amulet hidden inside her shirt. "I'll have to be. What do we need to do?"

"I read the bowl."

Sara gripped her sister by the shirt. "You did *what*?"

Faith pushed her hands away. "I'm fine. I'm here, aren't I? There are some incantations. We know they needed blood to open the ley line, and we'll need blood to close it. And—"

"And what?" Sara prompted.

Faith shot a glance at Ian before adding, "I'm going to use my blood."

"The hell you are!" snapped Sara.

"Hakon said gifted blood can close the ley line," her sister said.

Ian stepped forward. "Faith, I said we'll find another way. This isn't it."

Sara turned on him. "You knew she was going to try this? When were you going to tell me?" she demanded.

He bristled and came forward another few steps. Every hair on the back of her neck stood on end in response. "If you want to talk about telling people things," he said, "why don't we start with Golden Boy out there?"

Her skin prickled as though a mass of ants were crawling down her spine. Surprised, she backed toward the door.

"We haven't got time for this." Faith stood up and planted herself between them. "Ian, I need you to help me reconstruct the map from your dream. I need to know exactly where everyone stood. Think you can help me with that?"

"Why didn't we do it earlier?" he shot back, still glaring at Sara.

"Just help me. The more prepared we are, the better. Sara, the amulet?"

Sara touched the leather lace at her throat, then nodded.

"All right. I have the sword," added Faith. "Let's hope that's enough."

Sara backed out of the tent before either of them said anything further.

****

Ian sat beside the campfire with Faith, who picked at the last of her dinner. He cast a suspicious glance at the twilight sky. The moon rode ever higher, full and yellow as ancient bones. Everyone around the fire went about their business as if it were a typical night.

He pulled his journal from his coat pocket, then

flipped it open, angling it toward the fire to see it better. The first several pages overflowed with birding notes and sketches. He flipped ahead and came upon a shadowy silhouette of Sara as she'd looked the night they'd made love at the inlet, with her hair blowing around her shoulders and the curves of her body outlined by the moonlit water.

Even on paper, she made him crazy to touch her.

Tonight, she had flopped down as far from him as possible, still furious at him for not telling her of Faith's ridiculous plan for shutting down the ley line.

Worse, she sat beside Flintrop. Ian wanted to jump across the fire and pummel the son of a bitch just for looking at her. He saw Flintrop brush her knee, and all but growled. She didn't seem to notice. What the hell was wrong with her? She hated him...so she said.

Ian set his jaw and turned to a fresh page, then started sketching a rough outline of the ruin.

Faith leaned toward him, whispering, "Where was the one with the bowl?"

He turned his attention back to the page long enough to put a star at the correct position, then looked back across the camp. Since waking up, Sara had avoided coming any closer to him than shouting distance, but Flintrop seemed to have an all-access pass.

Bastard.

Michael and Callander went by behind them. Ian closed the book and set it down beside him. "What else do we need?"

"Nothing, I hope," Faith answered. "I've done everything I can think of. Now, all we can do is wait."

Wait. For a death sentence.

Flintrop's laughter brought Ian's gaze back across

the fire. He and Sara had stood up. Flintrop's arm curled around her back, and he made a sweeping gesture in the direction of the ruin. She smiled at something he said, and then caught Ian looking. Ian held her stare. Her expression went flat, as though she were looking at a stranger, and then she looked away. Flintrop touched her arm, and she headed away from the fire to her tent.

Flintrop's gaze slid away from her to Ian...and he smiled.

A white-hot surge of fury hijacked Ian's senses, and before he knew it, he was on his feet.

"What are you doing?" Faith demanded.

"Settling this," he snapped, marching toward Sara's tent.

She'd already disappeared inside. Ian crossed the moor at a fast walk and burst into the tent with his blood boiling.

Sara shot up from her cot, knocking a stack of books off her table in the process. They thumped to the floor by her feet.

"What the *hell* was that all about back there?" he demanded.

She scowled, then bent and piled the fallen books into her arms. "I don't know what you're talking about."

"Bullshit, you don't. He's all over you!"

She met his glare with an expression of outrage. "Are you out of your mind?" She stood and shoved the books back onto the table so hard that they knocked over a bottle of water. She didn't bother to catch it. It bounced onto the floor to create a spreading puddle in the tent corner.

"Why don't you tell me how, all of a sudden, he's

able to have his hands on you whenever he feels like it, and you won't let me near you?"

"You think I'm *sleeping with Flintrop*? After what we...? How dare you!"

Oh, he dared, all right. His temper blazed again as though she'd poured gasoline on it. He crossed the tent in two steps and reached for her arm.

She shrieked in pain before his fingers even landed. The air flared in a blue arc and snapped with static. Ian hissed and snatched his stinging hand back. He stared in disbelief at his fingers, and then at her. The taste of copper filled his mouth.

Sara clutched her arm, panting. Her eyes, fear-wide and liquid hazel, raked him from head to foot and back again.

Ian flexed his numbed hand. The electric smell in the air prickled in his nose. "What the hell was that?"

She didn't answer. He hated the distrustful way she watched him. Contrite, he stepped toward her again, reaching out. "Sara..."

She sprang backward like a spooked deer, still gripping her arm close to her body. "Get out," she whispered, trembling.

She might as well have screamed it. Ian backed away with his mind spinning. *Was it me? Christ. It wasn't her.* He turned on his heel and strode out of the tent.

Finding the camp empty, he crossed the dig and barreled into Faith's tent.

She spun out of her chair at his entrance, looking ready to pummel him flat. "Jesus, Ian. Are you trying to scare me?" She must have noticed the worried look on his face a moment later, because she stood and reached for his arm. "Are you—"

He sidestepped her grasp, flinging his hands in the air. "Don't touch me!"

"What?"

"I just shocked Sara. I don't know what happened. I went to touch her arm and *zap*, like I hugged a frigging transformer. It wasn't her, I know it wasn't. Her eyes didn't change." He thrust his smarting right hand under her nose, palm up.

She examined the angry red marks already developing across his fingers. So did he. His throbbing fingertips felt like he'd grabbed a hot pan barehanded.

Faith turned and went to her first-aid kit. Rather than letting her hand the burn pack to him, he motioned for her to drop it on her camp table.

She paused, frowning. He watched her eyes change from blue to silver. She swept his figure once over, angling her head like a quizzical cat. Her mouth opened and snapped shut again.

Ian began to feel like an experiment. He was on the point of telling her to hurry up and figure out what was wrong with him when she reached out and grabbed his hand.

Nothing happened.

"The shock wasn't you." She handed him the burn pack.

"If it's not me, then what the hell is it? She looked like I was going to attack her."

"Is she okay?" asked Faith.

"Yeah, if you count scared as okay!"

Faith went to her trunk and rummaged through a pile of sweaters to get to a case at the bottom. She pulled it out and withdrew the handheld device within.

"Come on."

They returned to Sara's tent to find her trying to put the mess on her camp table back into order. Ian hung back in the doorway, shoving a hand in his pocket. He dug the fingernails of his other hand into the burn pack.

Faith went forward without hesitation. Sara retreated before the advance. "Relax," Faith said, and flipped open the thing in her hand.

Sara frowned at it. "What on earth do you need an electrometer for?"

"I'm finding out what's going on. The electrical readings around here have been bouncing all over the scale, and I think we've found out why."

"Me?" Sara spluttered. "Since when can I shock people?"

"Ian said it wasn't you." When Sara shot him a leery glance, Faith added, "It wasn't him, either. You can stop eyeing him like he's going to bite you."

Sara's gaze sought his at last. "I'm sorry."

He looked away with a hostile shrug. The mental picture of Flintrop touching her, brushing against her, and flaunting his nearness to her played over in his head. He itched to hit something, and crushed the burn pack in his fist. The plastic pack protested under the squeeze. He wished it were Flintrop's neck.

Faith moved closer to Sara. Ian turned his attention back to the matter at hand. Looking dissatisfied with the results from her electrical gadget, Faith studied her sister with those creepy silver eyes. She reached a hand out and passed it across the air between them.

He saw Faith jump in surprise, but she didn't seem hurt, and he didn't hear or smell the static fizz from before.

Faith's brows shot up. Shaking her head, she took her sister by the arm.

Ian tensed for her yelp of pain. Sara recoiled, but nothing seemed to happen. Faith pursed her lips and beckoned Ian forward. He obliged.

The air hissed, and he froze in place.

"Whoa, back off!" Faith dodged in front of him.

He took a careful step backward, and then another. The prickling sensation in his skin faded.

Faith flapped an impatient hand in the air. "All right, just hold it. It's neither one of you by yourselves. It's both of you together." She divided a brooding look between them. "Oh, holy shit."

"What?" echoed Ian and Sara.

"Sara, didn't you say Becky had burn marks on her cheek and arm? Finger marks?"

"Are you saying *I* did it?"

"Of course not!" Faith jerked her chin at Ian. "You're electrically charged—both of you—just enough so you can't touch each other. If what's going on here is what I think it is, we just bought ourselves a whole bunch more problems. This looks like electrokinesis."

Sara went ghastly white. Her legs buckled, and she collapsed onto her cot. "Flintrop."

The name sent a wave of ice roiling through Ian's veins. He flung the burn pack down. "What did he do to you? I'll fucking kill him!"

"Wait, just wait!" Faith snapped. "Sara, how do you know it's him?"

Sara touched a hand to her lips. She avoided his gaze. "He tried to kiss me. I'd be working at the dig, too, and he'd walk past and put a hand on my arm or something. He was building up a charge. Ian, did he touch you today?"

With his blood sizzling, Ian remembered Flintrop's conciliatory handshake. The friendly clap on Ian's shoulder when Flintrop offered him the canteen. "Son of a bitch."

Sara hunched her shoulders. "Who else would want us not to touch each other?"

"Ian, you'd better sit down. There's more to it," said Faith, looking grave.

Ian shook his head. "No. He's a goddamn walking dead man."

Faith rounded on him. "Don't you dare leave this tent," she ordered. "If he touches you, he could kill you!"

He drew up short with fury snarling through his body. "Would one of you please explain this?"

"Electrokinesis is the ability to throw an electrical charge. If you have it, you can touch something and put a charge on it." Faith gave them both a meaningful stare. "Or some*one*, apparently."

"His eyes don't change," Ian pointed out. "All day today, the bastard's eyes were still blue."

The girls looked up, dismay evident in their expressions. "He wears contacts," they said together.

Faith pitched the electrometer onto the table. "Damn it, how did I not see it? First, we think we're the only ones. Now Callander, and Becky, and Flintrop, too."

"Faith, he's trying to rebuild the druid order," Sara blurted. "He's bringing them together to help open the ley line."

Faith rubbed a hand across her face. "Ian, your dream about the ceremony. There were four of them. Four druids. That means there has to be at least four now, to reopen the ley line."

Sara frowned at him. "When did you dream the serpent ceremony?"

"Do you hear me?" Faith interrupted. "Four! Callander, Flintrop, and two others. There are more. Sara, we can't stop them all."

Ian turned toward the tent door. "I'll take care of one of them."

"Damn it, Ian!" Faith snapped, rushing out of the tent after him.

Chapter Eighteen

Shaking, Sara clawed at her shirt as if she could wrest the electrical charge out of her body. She still felt it, a singing power surge that raised the hairs all over her skin, the same charge that had been causing her sleeplessness and mad drive to be active. *Get out. Get out of me!*

She shuddered at the memory of Ian reaching for her arm and sending an electric shock through both of them. The feeling had only gotten worse, as if that near-touch had woken a sleeping demon inside her. Flintrop had used her, *used her*. The charge hummed along her skin. She sprang to her feet to pace her tent, feeling sick.

Violated.

They need me. They need help, she thought, panting.

Oh, God, he'll kill Ian. With her heart in her throat, she bolted from the tent.

The moon hung uncomfortably close to its zenith. She swept the deserted moor with a desperate look and started across it toward Faith's tent, hoping her sister and Ian would be there.

As she reached the stone wall of the ruin, someone grabbed a fistful of her shirt and hair. A hand clapped over her mouth. "Hello," Flintrop rumbled in her ear.

She gave a muffled shriek and kicked at him. He

clamped his other arm around her and pulled her close. "If you can't see me, you can't use your power against me, right? Powers, *plural*, sorry. Where's your sister and that son of a bitch nature boy? Noticed my little electrical trick, did he? I hope it hurt like hell."

She struggled again, but he held her harder. "I wouldn't do that. Unlike you and your sister, I don't have to see my victim...just *touch*." He pulled at the neck of her shirt. His hand slithered inside, over the curve of her breasts, making her squirm and cry out in revulsion. Static fizzled against her skin. He dug in with his fingertips, bruising her until she yelped.

She tried wrenching her head around to get an eye on him, but his hand gripped harder against her face. How did he know about her and Faith?

As if she'd spoken aloud, Flintrop wrestled with her one-handed. He reached into his back pocket, then threw something onto the ground before her.

Faith's missing journal.

"Your sister keeps impressive notes," he drawled. "Cameron thought it was just another book. He was going to give it back until Thomas got hold of it and called me."

He threaded his fingers through the leather lace hanging between her breasts, and drew the amulet out of her shirt. "Thanks for finding this for me. Looking for it had become something of a bother." He hauled her against him, keeping out of her range of vision. His breath was hot on her ear. "If you have anything to say, you'd better do it now, because the serpent rite starts in about ten minutes." He removed his hand from her mouth.

Frantically, Sara glanced to the sky. Was it her

imagination that the moon inched higher and higher as she watched? Could she stall him? "You can't do it," she said. "You need four. What do you have? You? Callander?"

"Michael's a pyrokinetic. Rivero's got nothing, but he's useful. I would have used Becky, but I see you've sent her off to the States. Stupid klutz actually thought I was beginning to see some value in her work, can you believe that? Since you've deprived me of her help, you're my fourth."

She wheezed. Struggling in his arms, she couldn't even find the concentration to shapeshift. "Is this worth *murder* to you?"

He crushed her to him. "I had hoped we could do this together. Don't you wonder what it would be like to have all that power in the palm of your hand?"

"The ley line's unstable. Alan, don't do this. It'll destroy everything!"

He tightened his grip still more. "It only needs stronger blood. Gifted blood," he whispered. "I'd rather not end it like this, Sara. I still want you." He ground his hips into her backside.

She drew breath to scream, but a warning crackle along her back made her cut it short. How dare he threaten her! "Let me guess," she spat. "Faith didn't have the amulet when you seduced her, so I was next on your *sick...little...list*!" She punctuated her words by thrashing in his grip.

He dug his fingers into her skin. "You are not going to ruin the work my family has done all their lives."

She looked wildly around for Ian and Faith, but the moor remained empty. Another glance at the moon confirmed it almost risen to its highest point. *Stall, stall, oh God, something, anything. Think!* "Your family?"

Flintrop laughed, low and chilling. "My father offered yours a share of the wealth twenty years ago. Robert wouldn't take it." He pulled her still closer. His lips brushed her ear, and he dropped his voice to a lover's whisper. "I was fifteen years old when I first used my power. This *is* worth murder."

White-hot rage seized her body. She shook from head to foot and split the air with a scream, kicking. *"You killed my father!"*

He tightened his arm around her throat. Swinging helplessly, she choked in his grip. "If I have to bleed you of every drop, I'll do it. You sure you don't want to be with me? No? All right, then." He began dragging her into the excavated ruin. Strangling, she clawed at his arms. He kicked her legs out from under her and picked her up so she couldn't use her feet for leverage. Once they reached the hearth, he set her back down.

Her spine fizzed. Electricity tingled in her nose. She held her breath, afraid to hope.

Flintrop grunted and went rigid. "Let go, or I pull the trigger, you bastard," Ian said from behind them.

Flintrop's grip slackened. Sara twisted away with her heart pounding. Ian stood with the point of a rifle barrel jammed in Flintrop's back.

Flintrop leered at her.

She sprang toward him. "No! Ian, get ba—"

Flintrop spun and shoved the barrel aside just as Ian fired. The shot went wild. Electricity fizzed from his grasp, and sparks raced down the length of the gun. Ian hissed, dropped the gun, and punched him. Flintrop staggered back.

Across the moor, Michael, Callander, and Luis ran from their tents.

Hell had officially broken loose. Sara called on her telekinesis. "Faith, where's Faith?"

Ian dodged an angry swing from Flintrop and tried to answer, but their adversaries surrounded him.

Glaring at the others, Flintrop snapped, "It's about time you showed up! Where's Dustin?"

"I don't know. His tent's empty," Michael said.

Flintrop waved a hand at Ian. "Take care of this annoyance." He turned on his heel and faced Sara with a malevolent smile. "Time for the show, sweetheart. Remember, you could have been on the other side of this."

She backed up a step, searching for her sister with no luck. She retreated farther into the rough circle of the hearth, hoping to draw Flintrop away and give Ian an escape route.

Luis snatched up Ian's gun. With a shrug at Ian, he cocked the rifle. "Sorry, *amigo*. Money talks." He put the rifle to his shoulder and aimed it.

Sara tensed. *No. NO!* She didn't even get the word out.

A brilliant flash appeared between them. Metal screeched.

Faith appeared between Ian and Luis, swinging Hakon's sword and knocking the rifle upward. The gun fired into the air.

Thomas sprang toward them. Faith tossed the sword to Ian and threw a hand out. A searing white arc of flame flew from her fingertips. Thomas screeched and whirled away, covering his face. "That's for Cameron!" Faith snarled.

Ian swung the sword at Michael, then rolled as the man threw a bolt of flame in his direction. "Damn it! Him, too?"

"I didn't know!" shouted Faith.

Behind them, Sara took another step backward. Seeing Flintrop reach into his shirt pocket, she held out a hand to blast him with telekinesis.

"Oh, no, you don't." He jerked her against his body so hard it knocked the wind out of her. She caught the glint of a knife in his hand. "A shame I have to damage this skin."

Wordless with wrath, she slapped her other hand on his chest and released her power. *Whoosh.* Flintrop flew backward. The knife sliced along her arm, and she cried out in pain.

Faith scrambled behind the pile of peat bricks they'd been stocking for fire fuel. She seized one and hurled it into the air. Flinging a hand out at it, she set it ablaze. "Sara! Throw it!"

Without hesitation, Sara swept her hand out and sent the peat brick racing through the air at their adversaries. The fiery missile exploded against the ruin's south wall, and a rain of sparks lit the night sky. Another gunshot split the air. She dropped to her belly as it zipped past over her head. Her heartbeat banged around inside her chest so hard, she thought it might punch holes in her ribcage. *Snap out of it!* she begged herself.

Faith tossed brick after brick, lighting them as they flew into the air. Sara recovered and sent them rocketing toward Flintrop and his men, forcing them to retreat out of range.

Flintrop barked something at Luis, and tossed his

knife. Luis caught it and disappeared into the darkness of the ruin. Sara sent another blazing peat brick toward Michael, who ducked behind the ruin wall and returned it with a volley of flame. *We can't keep this up,* she thought frantically.

Thomas lurched in Ian's direction. For a second, Sara caught the pale flash of Ian's T-shirt, then lost them both in the shadows. She pushed onto her hands and knees, wincing at the pain in her arm. The amulet swung close to the bleeding gash. With a gasp, she snatched it away.

"Sara!" Faith cried again.

She looked up in time to see three fiery peat bricks falling toward her sister. She flung out a hand, sending them away toward their adversaries an instant before they burst against the ground.

She wrestled upright. An arm snaked around her throat. Choking, she dragged at the ground, but her captor—Luis—hauled her backward.

"Now! Do it!" Flintrop screamed. She looked up, gasping for air around the viselike grip on her throat, and saw Flintrop, Michael, and Thomas stagger into three of the compass positions.

And her, the fourth. *No!*

Luis jerked the amulet from her throat. With his arms around her, he gripped her injured arm and slashed the knife across her palm. She screamed. Faith shouted something, and then Luis slapped the amulet against her bleeding hand.

The very air tore open. Every hair on her body stood on end. The amulet blazed against her palm. Mindless with pain, she battered herself against Luis's body. The earth roared open under her feet. Luis released her, and they plunged into the fissure.

The amulet fell from her nerveless fingers. She pounced at the torn edge of the crevasse. Peat and gravel spilled around her head as she clutched at the precipice. The sky overhead boiled with gathering storm clouds and echoed with thunder. Beside her, Luis clawed his way upward and scrambled out of the gap to disappear into the maelstrom.

"Sara!" Faith rushed toward her and threw herself down at the edge of the fissure.

"The amulet! I dropped it!" Sara clutched at her sister's hand. She squinted into the darkness of the rift, searching in desperation, but could find nothing among the shadows.

"Give me your other hand! Please!"

Sara looked back up. In a flash of lightning, she caught Flintrop's silhouette behind Faith, tall and confident and with a terrifying snarl on his face. His fingertips snapped with lightning of their own. Panicking, Sara lunged over her sister's shoulder and cast a bolt of telekinesis that sent him sprawling backward.

Faith seized her other hand and leapt upward, jerking Sara out of the fissure. The ground rumbled under their feet. A line of light exploded open along the crevasse, running the entire length of the island.

Dazed with exhaustion and blood loss, Sara heard thudding footsteps and turned in time to see Michael flying at her. He raised a hand to attack.

From the side came another gunshot. She and Faith ducked in unison. Michael grunted, spun backward, and crumpled to the ground.

Ian came running into the glow cast by the ley line

and skidded to a halt with his rifle, panting. A darkening bloodstain spread across the torn shoulder of his shirt. "The sword, where's the—"

A shining arc of metal swung at his head. Sara snatched his collar, wincing at the electric burn of touching him, and yanked him down as the sword swept over their heads.

Luis swung again. Sara threw another blast of telekinesis that knocked him back just out of range. *Tapped, I'm getting tapped.* She turned to look for Faith, and then something crashed against her head. Everything went black.

****

Ian lunged to stop Flintrop as the man dropped his stone and reached for Sara's body. Hardly pausing to think, Ian gripped his rifle in both hands and smashed it in Flintrop's face. Flintrop lurched back, swearing, his nose pouring blood.

Faith cringed beside him, and even Ian could feel the echo of the ley line's power running through his body. Gritting her teeth, Faith threw a burst of flame at Flintrop to keep him at bay. "Get the sword. I have to do the incantation." She whirled and dove into the fissure.

The ley line roared with voices. Pain scorched through him. Ian dropped his rifle and doubled over in agony. Several feet away, Flintrop seemed to be having the same trouble. At least that took *him* out for now.

But not Luis.

The man charged at Ian and swung the sword again. Gasping for air, Ian just managed to duck the blow and threw himself at Luis's midsection. They tumbled backward together. Luis struck his head on the edge of a mangled stone wall, and went slack.

Ian grabbed the sword from Luis's hand and raced toward the fissure.

Flintrop, recovered now, leaped to stop him. Too close to swing, Ian slammed the hilt of the sword into the other man's temple, and Flintrop collapsed.

Ian dropped at the edge of the fault and reached for Faith. "Get out of there!"

She hung on the edges of stone sticking out in the side of the crevasse, spewing a stream of unintelligible words as she reached one-handed down into the gloom. She stopped her incantation. "The amulet! I've almost got it!"

He cringed as the ley line screamed again. "Are you crazy?"

She stretched her fingers out with a look of desperation. The amulet dangled from a broken stone. A tremor shook the earth, and the necklace slipped farther. Her fingers swept by it, inches out of reach. She grasped again, fingers waving at empty air.

He threw the sword down and grabbed her arm in both hands. Another quake shook the ground under his feet.

The amulet plummeted from its ledge. Faith snatched it as it fell, then flung it upward. She grabbed the edge of the crevasse and braced her feet in its trench. "Smash it!" She went right back to her incantation.

He let go of her, grabbed the amulet from the air, and seized the sword from the ground. With the amulet in one hand and the sword in the other, he sprinted toward the nearest stone wall. The amulet hissed as if its engraved snake were real, and he nearly dropped it.

Ian slapped the necklace down on the flat stone, spun the sword in his hand, and brought it down on the amulet with a ringing crash.

The explosion knocked him off his feet and ripped the sword from his hand. The earth trembled again. Dirt and gravel rained down on his head. He rolled to escape a slide of stone as the wall collapsed, then grappled to his feet. His breath seared his throat.

The ground convulsed underneath him. Panting, fighting to keep his balance, he searched for Sara. She remained unconscious where she had fallen. Flintrop lay several feet away. Ian ran for the edge of the fault again. "Faith?"

A mass of earth and stone had piled into the fault. He couldn't see Sara's sister. "Jesus. Faith!" Ian vaulted into the fissure and began flinging stones away.

"Don't move it!" she shouted.

Ian froze, and then realized the stones had formed a perfect wedge in the fault. In a crack between two boulders, he saw Faith lying cramped at the bottom. "Hakon's protecting me. Don't worry about me. He'll get me out."

"Are you *serious*?"

She coughed as dirt spilled onto her. "Listen to me very carefully, Ian. You're gifted."

"I'm what?" The earth shuddered once more. He gripped the edge of the crevasse with his mind reeling. He had to get her out. *How* was he going to get her out?

"You have power," she said. "You carry it, but you don't use it. I need you to say the last part of the incantation. Luis opened the fault. You need to be touching him when you say it."

"This is crazy."

She coughed again. "You dream, yes? You know things, and you don't know how. Ian, we don't have time."

Ice raced throughout his body. All the cues, dismissed before now, flooded his mind. His inexplicable pull toward Sara. The dreams of her murdered father. The way his skin prickled when he met Flintrop. "What do I have to say?"

"Just grab him and say *terminatus*. And Ian—get Sara out of here. She's pregnant, and that makes her more powerful. They'll kill her to hold the ley line open if they can." Silver eyes blazed into his through the crack in the rubble. "Stop them."

Pregnant. They'll kill her.

Before he could react, the rift shook, spilling gravel onto both of them. Sizzling air stung in his nose. The atmosphere snapped and guttered. A charge burst along his spine, and the ley line flickered. He braced his feet against the sides of the trench and pitched upward with his heart thundering.

Clouds surged in the sky. The ground screeched again, and he stumbled. Pain spiked in his belly as it echoed the rending of the earth. His breath whooshed out, and he heaved for air that had gone blistering cold.

Sara struggled to her feet, close by the collapsing wall of the ruin. Swaying in the quake's aftershocks, she lurched away from the fault and dropped to her knees.

Luis stirred and shook his head. His attention landed on Hakon's sword, and he crawled to it. Picking it up, Luis battled to his feet and stumbled toward Sara.

Oh, Christ, no. I love her.

Ian sucked in a frigid breath, but it wasn't enough

to shout a warning. He forced himself upright and staggered toward them. Luis raised the sword to swing at her. Sara knelt gasping, unaware of the danger. Step, stagger, step...too damn slow! He forced his feet to move faster.

Racing footsteps sounded behind him. Ian glanced over his shoulder. Flintrop dove toward him, his face a livid, bloody mask of hatred.

Ian whirled to avoid his grasp, but not fast enough. Flintrop seized his right arm and unleashed his power.

Electricity fizzed though their point of contact and raced, snapping, up Ian's arm. His world exploded into agony. He screamed and toppled, reaching even as he fell. His left hand brushed Luis's arm. *"Terminatus,"* he gasped out with the last of his breath.

The shock flew, sizzling, from his fingers and into Luis, who gave an earsplitting shriek and crashed to the ground just short of Sara. The sword thumped to the earth.

Ian dropped like a stone.

****

The ground lurched. The screaming of a thousand voices rent the air in a wild surge, and then cut short. Stunned into incomprehension, Sara looked from Ian's prone form to Flintrop, standing above him. Flintrop's lips pulled back in a snarl of satisfaction, then he lumbered toward the collapsed wall. He hefted a stone the size of a cement block to his shoulder, then staggered back toward Ian with the gleam of bloodlust in his eyes.

Wrath swept through Sara and washed away her fog of confusion. Trembling, she thrashed to her feet, calling on everything she had left and pouring her fury into it. The shapeshift took hold in a brutal storm. Flintrop's figure blurred as her human vision gave way to animal sight. She smelled the blood-mad reek of his scent and heard breath whistling in his throat. She opened her mouth to scream, and out came the enraged roar of a grizzly bear. She charged.

Flintrop raised the stone over Ian's head, growling, and it began to fall.

She plowed into him and took the blow on one broad, flat shoulder, arcing over Ian's body. Her momentum carried Flintrop backward. Snarling in his face, she hooked an enormous paw around him and scooped upward. The stone tumbled from his grasp. Flintrop sailed into the air and landed ten feet away.

Ian's rifle lay nearby. Flintrop launched himself at it and turned it on her, then fired.

The shot missed her by inches. She galloped the few strides to him and bashed the rifle out of his hands.

He clapped a hand against the left side of her muzzle and released an electric charge. Lightning exploded inside her head. Bellowing in agony, she jerked backward and swung blindly at him with the last of her strength.

Her strike connected with a *thwack*, and she heard bones breaking. Flintrop's body went slack, and he tumbled into the fault. *He's bleeding. Gifted blood.*

No sooner had that thought entered her mind than the eerie voices screeched one last time. The ground rumbled, and then all was quiet.

It was over.

The scent of burnt fur stung her nostrils. A tremor ran through her body. She swayed and collapsed, losing hold of the shapeshift, then passed out.

****

When Sara came to, tearing pain settled in behind her eyes. She raised her head. Gooseflesh bloomed along her arms, and she trembled in the icy air. Her breath puffed out in steaming clouds, adding to the fog covering the ground. Her right shoulder throbbed. She didn't have the strength to cradle it.

A dark haze hovered somewhere to her left. She shook her head, but it didn't dissipate. She pushed herself up onto her hands and knees. Disoriented, she shuffled forward. Her hand landed on something sharp that sliced along her palm. She snatched it away with a hiss and saw fresh blood welling in a drying cut. Old blood crusted along a gash in her forearm.

A sword lay on the ground before her. She looked along its length without recognition, trying to rid her vision of the partial haze.

The mirror shine of the sword blade, edged with feathers of frost, revealed the reflection of her eyes. Her right eye showed hazel. Her left was green. She blinked, and it didn't change to brown. She knew it should have, but couldn't remember why. Confused, she waved a hand in front of her face from right to left. A little more than three-quarters of the way across, her hand disappeared from her line of vision, swallowed by the haze plaguing her.

She had lost part of the vision in her left eye.

Her head pounded. She shook it again, trying to come to terms with the blind spot in her vision.

Faith. Ian. Memory returned, and with it, awareness of her surroundings. Sitting back as if in a trance, she looked around.

The reddish glow of sunrise lanced through the fog,

gradually unshrouding the bodies strewn like wreckage across the moor. Michael lay twisted several feet away. Luis was sprawled at the edge of the ruin.

And Ian. He lay face down, eyes closed, limbs thrown askew in the way he had fallen. Dried blood stained the shoulder of his T-shirt. She saw blackened scorch marks on his right arm where Flintrop had touched him, and more on the fingers of his left hand where he had, in turn, passed the shock through his own body to Luis. His hair fluttered in the breeze. No other movement disturbed the silence.

Choking, Sara crawled toward him and clutched at the back of his T-shirt. "Ian." She nudged him. His body jerked with her push, then lay still again. Her throat tightened to a strangle. She shook him harder. "Ian. *Ian!*" He didn't respond. Dark blood collected, glistening and sluggish, in the torn flesh of his shoulder. She bit off a moan. With her hand shaking so hard she could barely steady it, she touched two fingers to the hollow in his throat.

No charge. No pulse. His skin felt cold.

No. No no no no no. "Nooooooo!" Sara balled her fists, nails digging into her palms, heedless of the stinging wound in her hand. She turned her face upward and screamed, long, incoherent, full of rage. Her power burned through her body, humming in her ears, sizzling along her skin...

...but it wouldn't bring him back.

She let the scream die off, its muffled echoes ringing across the foggy moor. When it faded, an awful emptiness replaced it. Tears surged up and began to flow down her cheeks. She gave a thin howl of misery and crumpled beside his body.

A hand descended on her shoulder. She flung out an arm to decimate her attacker.

Her blow never landed. "Sara, get up," Faith murmured.

Dazed, Sara raised her head. "Faith?"

Her sister gave her arm a gentle tug. "You've got to get up. The ley line isn't finished closing. Hakon says we have to go right now."

Weary, chilled, Sara laid her head back down.

"Sara." Faith's voice rang through her throbbing skull, and she winced. "Get up right now. You're pregnant."

Shock. The return of her senses blasted her back to reality. She whimpered and curled into a ball, folding nerveless fingers over her belly.

Pregnant. The word knifed through her, and she ached. She couldn't look at Ian's body. *He's dead, oh God oh God oh God...* She rolled and battled to her feet, groaning as her frozen muscles protested the movement. Faith wrapped a supporting arm around her, and a fresh onslaught of tears stung down Sara's cheeks. *Don't look. Don't look at him. Just walk.* As they staggered away, she caught a flash of white from Ian's T-shirt. Cutting off a mournful cry, she hugged her belly, and stumbled away with her sister into the fog.

She didn't know how far they'd staggered when she saw someone approaching through the haze. She swayed, wrestling with her blind spot. "I can't fight them, Faith. I have nothing left."

They lurched forward, step by step, to meet whatever came.

Dustin materialized first, sweeping out of the fog in

a long coat, with a knapsack and shotgun on his shoulder. He spotted Sara and her sister and shouted, "Lambertson!"

Lamb came out of the haze at a fast walk, which became a jog that overtook the younger man.

Sara turned her head to watch his approach with her good eye. *He's going to kill us,* she thought, remembering Ian's warning about Lamb's involvement. She halted, swaying on her feet. Faith stopped beside her.

With an oath, Dustin drew to a stop several strides from where she and Faith stood. The shotgun remained on his shoulder.

Lamb reached them in another four running steps. Sara braced and raised her fists. She began sliding into unconsciousness even as a feeble rumble of defiance bubbled from her throat. Her knees buckled.

The older man caught her and swept her off her feet into his arms. The dizzying movement shook the last of her strength out of her. "Sara. Bloody hell! Dustin, radio the helicopter and get it down here. Now! Sara, darling, hold on..."

The waters of oblivion closed over her head once more.

Chapter Nineteen

"How did this happen, Faith? *How did it happen?*"

Faith had never seen Lamb so upset. She turned in an uncertain circle in the otherwise empty hospital waiting room. How much to tell? "I..."

Lamb came forward, looking angry. "Three people have died on this project. With Cameron, that makes four. This is a disaster. And now your sister is injured, and—" He broke off and spun away to pace the polished floor.

She reached into her coat pocket for the two journals wedged there: the one Flintrop had stolen, and the new one that had replaced it. "I think— Lamb, can I trust you?"

He stiffened. She knew the question had stung him. She'd never had to ask before. "With your life. You know that."

She hated the doubt creeping through her skin. She called on her psychic power, and tears blurred his figure. A shiver skipped down her spine.

He stared. Stared some more. Nothing in his aura suggested deception. She didn't bother blinking to let her eyes change back to their normal blue, wanting him to get a good look at the silver. She handed her journals over. "There are some things you need to know about Sara and me."

With an unreadable face, he took the journals and

sat in a corner of the room. For the next hour, he neither spoke nor looked at her, absorbed in her written words.

Faith gazed out the waiting room window at a park across the street. A blond man in a red sweater was pushing a curly-haired child on the swings.

For no particular reason, she thought of Hakon. He'd protected her...as much as a ghost *could* protect her against a group of madmen bent on destruction. She'd never felt that safe before, even when the fault caved in on top of her and stopped just short of crushing her.

Now that their secret had been revealed, would she and Sara ever be safe again?

The door opened. Her mother rushed in. "Oh, Faith. Sweetheart, I came as fast as I could get here. Are you all right?" She pressed her hands to either side of Faith's face.

Faith hugged her mother. "I'm fine, Mom. Sara's still unconscious, but the doctors say all her vitals are good."

Lambertson closed the books, and stood. "Angela. It's good to see you. I only wish it were under better circumstances."

"Hello, James." Her mother kissed him on the cheek.

Faith tried not to look surprised at the affectionate gesture. Lamb's gaze flickered over her, still unreadable, and she looked away. In the park across the street, the red-sweatered man and the child had moved on to a slide.

"Angela, why don't you go and sit with Sara? I'd like to speak with Faith for a few minutes."

Faith tensed. She murmured a quick goodbye to her

mother. The door closed with a thump, and the waiting room went silent and sterile.

When Lamb spoke, she heard him force calm into his voice. "Robert told me once that if anything ever happened to him, I was to watch over you and Sara. He sounded so grave at the time that it worried me. Now I know what he was protecting. Not just his children, but their gifts. *Your* gifts."

She couldn't find anything to say at first. She cleared her throat, but no words came. She crossed the room to sit down. "Dad... He knew?"

Lamb sat beside her. "I think he must have. I never saw him so serious. He wrote a letter, sealed it, and made me swear to give it to your mother when you were older. I guess it's time." He studied her journals, still in his hands, then gave them back to her. "I spent a lot of years working with your father. Nothing ever made me question his judgment until now. I don't know if I'm the right person for this."

"I'm scared," she whispered.

A warm, rough hand slid into her own. "You don't have to be. I made a promise, and I intend to honor it."

Lamb reached up without hesitation, and pushed an errant lock of her long, blond hair behind her ear. "I've known you girls since you were children. You're as much mine as you ever were your father's. You are bright, talented, beautiful young women who make me proud. Whatever else you are, you're still that, Faith, darling."

They sat there for a long time, just holding hands.

Lamb cleared his throat, and sat back in the chair. Faith sat back, too, their hands still linked. "Do you know," he said, "I always thought it strange, but your father had an uncanny knack of knowing things before they happened." His mouth twisted into a rueful smile. "He was appallingly good at betting on sports."

Faith laughed, but it came out as a sob. She covered her mouth, and hot tears trickled down her cheeks.

He squeezed her hand. "As for what happened on Hvitmar, I had some of my contacts comb the site before the police arrived. They'll find nothing to endanger you or Sara. I've spoken to the inspector, and so far, it appears he's attributing your actions to self-defense."

She nodded and wiped away her tears.

"You should get some sleep," he said after a long silence. "I've rented a room at the bed-and-breakfast down the road. Take my keys, and go rest a while."

"No. Not until Sara wakes up."

"Your mother and I can stay with her."

"I want to be here, Lamb."

They fell into silence again. Faith heard the faint ticking of the clock on the waiting room wall, and counted the passing seconds.

Dustin entered the room. Lamb and Faith stood up. "Thomas is in a bad way," Dustin said. "The doctors don't think he'll ever see again. He's already confessed to Cameron's..." He trailed off and wiped his sweat-beaded forehead. "He's willing to testify."

"Thank you, Dustin," said Lamb. "Someone will need to call the Flintrop offices, and tell them what has happened to Michael, Luis, and Alan. If you'll excuse me."

When he had gone, Faith went back to staring out the window. By now, the red-sweatered man and the child had left. A pang seized her as she wondered if Hakon would ever contact her again. She hadn't heard so much as a whisper from him since the closing of the ley line. *I miss you,* she thought, only now understanding how much his ethereal presence had comforted her. During all that turmoil, all that uncertainty on the island, she had always felt he was watching out for her.

Warmth spread through her body. She'd find him again. Someone, somewhere cared about her, and for now that was enough.

Dustin came up behind her and laid a hand on her shoulder. "Are you all right?"

"Yes. Thank you," she murmured.

"And Sara?"

"Still not conscious," she said.

"Would you like me to stay?"

"No, thanks. My mother is here now."

His hand lifted from her shoulder. She heard him move toward the door, and turned around. "Dustin?"

He paused with his hand on the door handle.

"How did you know to go get Lamb before the— before it happened?" she asked.

"Lambertson asked me to keep an eye out for you." He sighed and rubbed the back of his neck. "I never trusted Flintrop, anyway." Before she could say anything further, he left.

Faith sighed, too. Her sister hadn't woken up since they'd brought her in.

Faith sat down and prepared for a long, restless wait.

****

Sound returned first.

307

The incessant drone of a television chattered away in Sara's ear. "...Authorities are still investigating last week's tragic events on Hvitmar, where geologists say an earthquake split the island almost entirely in two. Madeline Burgess has the story."

"Lawrence, I'm reporting from Unst. With me on satellite is Inspector Ritchie of the Unst police. Hvitmar is the northernmost point in Shetland, unpopulated, and until now fairly quiet. It has now been closed to the public due to last week's violent quake. Archaeologists had been excavating what was thought to be a Viking ruin on Hvitmar, and authorities say there were a number of deaths. Inspector Ritchie, what can you tell us?"

"We're continuing to investigate at this point, Madeline. We know of three fatalities, but we have no further information at this point due to the island's instability. We intend to keep working until we've fully completed the investigation."

"Thank you, Inspector. Back to you, Lawrence."

Lawrence buzzed on like a nagging mosquito. Sara woke fully, blinking in the glare of fluorescent lights. The hospital room came into focus, but the blind spot hadn't gone away. Her headache had dulled to a persistent heaviness behind her eyes.

She was alone in the room with her grief.

It choked her.

She angled her head, and saw the television mounted on the wall. A polished, suit-clad news anchor glanced down at his stack of papers. The view cut to a smiling photograph of Ian. She couldn't bear to look at the image, but neither could she wrest her eyes away. "...In related news, American biologist Ian Waverly is thought to have discovered a nesting pair of endangered Eurasian peregrine falcons on Hvitmar—"

"Thought, nothing."

Ian's voice. She stopped breathing for a long, suspended minute.

Ian balanced in the doorway, panting, on a pair of crutches, then adjusted a brace on his knee. She closed her eyes, unable to stand the hollow ache. *A dream,* she told herself, heartsick.

But when she looked again, he was still there. She gave a strangled cry and pushed into a sitting position.

When he saw her awake, the joyous expression that flooded his face left no room for doubt. He flung his crutches down with a clatter and staggered to the bed. His leg gave out and he dropped beside her, smothering her in a hug and pressing his face hard into her hair.

"You're alive," she said on a sob. "You're alive! Oh, God, Ian." Anything else she meant to say dissolved into tears. She hugged him close, willing it to be true, terrified to let go of him and find out otherwise.

He drew a shuddering breath against her ear. His hands came up to thread into her hair as though he, too, wanted to be sure he wasn't dreaming. "I love you, Sara. I always have, and always will. Marry me. Now, right now, before anything else happens."

Crying, she kissed him everywhere she could reach, then cupped his face in her hands to look at him to be certain it was really him.

"You didn't answer me," he said, then smiled. "Our baby needs a father, doesn't she? I want to be there for her...and you."

Sara's heartbeat did a quick flutter, and she raced to absorb the impact of his words. "She? You know?"

She didn't even know what it would be.

His smile twitched. Ian slid a hand between them to rest on her still-flat belly. He kissed her. "I don't want to lose either of my girls."

Sniffling, she hugged him close. "You never will. I love you, Ian Waverly, and I can't wait to be your wife."

****

Four weeks later, Sara stood in her office studying the newly hung wedding portrait on her office wall. She angled her head first one way, and then the other. She'd never get rid of the blind spot, but she didn't need to. Not with the range of senses her powers gave her. A tiny price to pay for what she had now.

The wedding hadn't been large on such short notice, but a simple ceremony in Central Park had been more than enough. "I think you look fine in a tuxedo."

Ian's arm came around her waist from behind. "We all know who the pretty one was, honey, and it wasn't me." He pushed aside a lock of her hair to nibble at her earlobe.

"That way lies trouble, mister." She giggled and batted at his roving hands.

He chuckled.

Someone knocked at the door. "Sara?" came Faith's voice through the heavy oak.

Her new husband gave a reluctant sigh.

"Come in," Sara called.

The door swung open and her sister ducked in. "Lamb's here to see you. Hi, Ian."

"Hey, Faith." Ian kissed Sara on the cheek. "I have to drop off some of these pictures to Mom. Want a sandwich for dinner tonight?"

"Stick around," Faith said. "This concerns you, too."

Ian shrugged and sat in one of the office's armchairs.

Sara watched him sink back into the plushy chair. Good grief, he looked cute, just sitting there. He wanted to honeymoon in Yellowstone when his knee healed.

She wanted to lock her door and honeymoon right there in her office.

Lambertson strode in with Becky and Holly in tow. Faith came in and closed the door behind them. Lamb maintained a businesslike air, but Sara caught the affectionate gleam in his eye and returned it in kind. She sat on the arm of Ian's chair. Ian took her hand, and she threaded her fingers through his.

"I'll get right to the point. Here is what we know," Lamb said, setting a briefcase on her desk. "Nicholas Flintrop, Alan's father, has been arrested for conspiracy to commit murder. Shetland and Scotland police have been tracking a series of cultlike murders for the past few years, and Nicholas and Alan finally left enough tracks for them to follow."

Sara nodded. Robert Markham had only been the first of a string of victims who couldn't be made to cooperate with the plan to rebuild the druid order. Ian's father, and at least two other men, had paid with their lives for standing against the Flintrop family.

Lamb sat on the desk, looking grim. "What these arrests mean to you all is that Flintrop, L.L.C. is back under direction of the grandfather, Elliott. He's lost a grandson, and now his son, and he's not getting any younger. He's going to be at odds with Gemini, and he'll be looking for an heir to run the business. I expect whoever replaces him to be equally hostile. Elliott was never known for his leniency, and he'll handpick the man to follow him. I suggest you watch yourselves."

Sara exchanged a concerned look with Ian, and then her sister.

"Now, on to the next point of my trip," Lamb added. "Alan Flintrop left an encrypted file at the Flintrop offices containing the names and whereabouts of two gifted individuals. We need to find these people. Becky has already located one in Kentucky, a young girl. Eurocon's contact at the Flintrop offices has found the other in Australia. Faith, you're on the Australia project. Sara, I know you and Ian have other things on your mind right now—"

Faith snorted. "When don't they?"

"—but," Lamb continued with a mock-stern glance at Faith, "I'd like you to go there, and contact the girl. She's living on the streets, and the sooner you find her, the better. These people need to know we're here to help them if they need us. I'd rather not find out if Elliott has plans for them before *we* get to them."

"We're on it," Ian said, squeezing Sara's hand. "I have the rest of my vacation before I start teaching in the fall."

Sara smiled down at him, and her heart swelled with pride. Once they'd discovered the truth behind his father's death, Ian had vowed to protect others from the same fate, if he could.

He'd become quite a celebrity in wildlife circles, too. His publication on the Eurasian peregrines had helped him toward his tenure, and several naturalist groups were now calling to turn Hvitmar into a wild bird sanctuary. Shetland bird enthusiasts had even reported Horus and Hathor's first chicks.

He'd gained his dream and given her so much more. He had turned her life upside-down and made her believe in the power of love and acceptance. He'd changed everything.

He must have seen the loving look on her face, because he hooked his arm around her waist and rubbed the barely-there swell of her abdomen. They'd already begun discussing names and baby furniture. Whatever happened next, she knew they had each other to see it through.

For once in her life, she truly felt a sense of belonging. People who cared about her knew what she was, and accepted her in spite of it. She and her sister weren't alone.

Now, she could pass that sense of sanctuary on to others who needed it every bit as much as she had. She looked across the office at Faith and grinned.

Gemini had a whole new sideline.

A word about the author...

Nicki Greenwood graduated SUNY Morrisville with a degree in Natural Resources. She found her passion in writing stories of romantic adventure, and combines that with her love of the environment. Her works have won several awards, including the Rebecca Eddy Memorial Contest. Her first book, EARTH, debuted in 2010 through The Wild Rose Press, Inc.

Nicki lives in upstate New York with her husband, son, and assorted pets. When she's not writing, she enjoys the arts, gardening, interior decorating, and trips to the local Renaissance Faire.

Visit Nicki at: http://www.nickigreenwood.com

Thank you for purchasing
this publication of The Wild Rose Press, Inc.
For other wonderful stories of romance,
please visit our on-line bookstore at
www.thewildrosepress.com.

For questions or more information
contact us at
info@thewildrosepress.com.

The Wild Rose Press, Inc.
www.thewildrosepress.com

To visit with authors of
The Wild Rose Press, Inc.
join our yahoo loop at
http://groups.yahoo.com/group/thewildrosepress/